DATE DUE

MARVELOUS WORLD

⇒ A.K.A. ⇐

The Marvelous World
of the Supposedly Soon to Be
Phenomenal Young Mr. Louis Proof

BOOK 1: THE MARVELOUS EFFECT

MARVELOUS WORLD

≫ A.K.A. ≪

The Marvelous World
of the Supposedly Soon to Be
Phenomenal Young Mr. Louis Proof

BOOK 1: THE MARVELOUS EFFECT

◆TROY CLE◆

SIMON & SCHUSTER BOOKS FOR YOUNG READERS
New York ◆ London ◆ Toronto ◆ Sydney

SIMON & SCHUSTER BOOKS FOR YOUNG READERS
An imprint of Simon & Schuster Children's Publishing Division
1230 Avenue of the Americas, New York, New York 10020

SIMON & SCHUSTER BOOKS FOR YOUNG READERS
is a trademark of Simon & Schuster, Inc.
Book design by Jessica Sonkin
The text for this book is set in Cochin.
Manufactured in the United States of America
2 4 6 8 10 9 7 5 3 1
Library of Congress Cataloging-in-Publication Data
Cle, Troy.
The marvelous effect / Troy Cle. — 1st ed.
p. cm. — (Marvelous world ; bk. 1)
Summary: Strange things are happening on Earth, and twelve-year-old
Louis Proof discovers that he is one of the few people able to see—and
combat—the responsible beings, who came from Midlandia, the planet at
the center of the universe, to continue a battle that rages there.
ISBN-13: 978-1-4169-3958-0 (hardcover)
ISBN-10: 1-4169-3958-X (hardcover)
[1. Heroes—Fiction. 2. Adventure and adventurers—Fiction. 3. African
Americans—Fiction. 4. Science fiction.] I. Title.
PZ7.C579185Mar 2007
[Fic]—dc22
2006039685

For Mom, Dad, and
my older younger brother, Bryan.
Thank you for affording me the
opportunity to be a dreamer.

⇒ SHOUT-OUTS ⇐

Mom, Dad, and my brother Bryan! My relatives the Tompkins, Ramsey, Hall, Pryor, Jones, Williams, Kemp, Ivy, Peters, Bostic, and Dash families. Aunt Betty, everyone needs an aunt like you. All my little cousins.

Tierra, Najah, and Cassandra, thank you for being my Lacey Proof. My super grandmother who sacrificed so much for me.

Mr. Harry Dawson, the best teacher I have ever had. Your class influenced the way I saw the entire world. This book would never have been written or if it was it would have sucked without what I learned in AP Seminar.

My publisher, Elizabeth Law, for being a champion of my novel. You showed up and believed when others did not. Your love of literature is immeasurable.

My editor, Rebecca Davis, for fleshing out the book *The Marvelous Effect* was always meant to be.

My entire Simon & Schuster family.

Daryl Mandryk The Official Marvelous World Artist and Joe D.

Super Fresh; Harrison Jr.; Jamal Kales; Pete Sidoriak; my neighbors the Thomas family for everything, including that important trip to Harlem; Trevor Baldwin, Greg "Mayhem" Taylor, Jamel Sweat, Yahaira, Skam, Ed, Ski, Sheri, Nida, Matt Batista, Billy "Bang" Orr, Rome, Rahk, Samad Davis, Kemol, and Joshua Horowitz. Rebecca Bullene for all of the help; James "The Glow" Goff, Pop, Isadore, Jude, Del, Audrey, the Lorquets, the Andrews, Joe G., Unit, Pal Moore, Michael Jackson, Larry Brown, Oliver Kennedy, Elf, Glenn, Chris Papa, Obi, Renee, and Kim. Marvelous Harlem World for giving me my start and making me an instant success. My publicists, Paul, Jody, Pam, Pamela,

Jen, and Mr. Alan Chase. Kiley for always being friendly. My lawyer, Lisa Davis. Amanda Funaro, Principal Watts, and the students and staff of Wadleigh Secondary School of Harlem. Seton Hall Prep. New York University. Bloomfield and Orange high schools, New Jersey. Locke, Professor Smith, Skyu, and Bookworm Girl for keeping my forum alive during its early stages. The Hue-Man bookstore for welcoming me with open arms. Nubian Heritage. Glenn and BJ of TekServe for stocking my book. Video Game World of Bloomfield, New Jersey.

David Finn, Susan Slack, and Bryan D'Orazio, and all of the Ruder Finn staff, who have given me so much help.

Kemberly Richardson for doing the news piece that set so much in motion for me.

Sum Patten, Kelechi Ubozoh, Carrie Stetter, and Corey Kilgannon.

Maurice Sendak for writing my favorite book of all time, *Where the Wild Things Are.* It taught me that if things do not go quite my way, it is cool to have another world to escape to every now and then.

Steven Spielberg, Joe Dante, Richard Donner, Penny Marshall, Mel Stuart, Terry Gilliam, and Wolfgang Petersen for bringing the movies *The Goonies, Gremlins, Big, Willy Wonka and the Chocolate Factory, The NeverEnding Story,* and *Time Bandits* to the screen. Those films were so important to me as a child.

Jay-Z, Nas, John Mayer, De La Soul, Fall Out Boy, Taku Iwasaki, P!ATD, 50 Cent, Coheed and Cambria, and Kanye West for providing some of the music I wrote to.

All of the video games that I play now and have been playing since I was much younger.

Foster's Home for Imaginary Friends, Dragon Ball Z, Fullmetal Alchemist, *South Park,* PPGs, *Samurai X (Rurouni Kenshin), FLCL.* Thanks for keeping my mind occupied in between writing.

PRONUNCIATION GUIDE

eNoli (e no LIE)

iLone (eye low NAY)

⇒ PROLOGUE ⇐

I am thankful that the apostrophes, commas, periods, and such are all in place. But those darn Crims have stolen the prologue right out of this book. I just don't know if Crims can be trusted. Be careful, because something of yours may be next!

Rumor has it that you can find the prologue online at www.marvelousworld.net. Please try to find it, because it contains very important information about Midlandia, the Midland Isle, the Alorian Treaty, and both the eNoli and iLone Celestial Entities (CE for short).

That is all I have to say and I have said it.

Thank you,

Troy CLE

Troy CLE

MARVELOUS WORLD

 A.K.A.

The Marvelous World
of the Supposedly Soon to Be
Phenomenal Young Mr. Louis Proof

BOOK 1: THE MARVELOUS EFFECT

✦LEVEL İ✦

➤ CHAPTER ONE ⇐

2 cups sun.
2 tablespoons heat.
1 pinch of breeze.

All part of a recipe for one thing: a hot day supreme.

Sweat poured down Louis Proof's face. He didn't know if this was from the weather or the extra pounds that made up his pudgy frame. Reminders of sunblock, dehydration, and other such "momly" warnings echoed through his head but meant nothing to him on this great day—his and Brandon Davis's first trip to the JunkYard JunkLot. On the outside, the lot looked like any other home for discarded cars, visionless television sets, retired refrigerators, and whatever else makes its way to a junkyard. But the truth is, it had a secret that only the most trusted kids would come to know about: The JunkYard JunkLot was a modern marvel of juvenile amusement, if only you could get past three grand obstacles.

Louis and Brandon had had no knowledge of this secret before they found the mysterious envelopes in their school desks at the end of yesterday's class. Each envelope contained a piece of paper with an introductory letter, a riddle, a silly rhyme, and a map, and also a book titled *Tha Rules*, which made no sense to either of the boys.

Louis's letter read as follows:

Dear Louis Proof,

This is indeed the luckiest day of your life. Due to your excellent standing with almost all who know you, you have been selected as a visitor to the most spectacular place on Earth. Forget about Disneyland and Universal Studios. You are invited to the JunkYard JunkLot. Yes, the JunkYard JunkLot.

This is your passport to this most special place on its opening day. The enclosed elements must be deciphered and followed to a T. Once you are alone in your room, a riddle, a rhyme, and a map needed to gain entry to this place will appear on the opposite side of this letter. You will have one hour to memorize this information, after which all of the words will disappear.

If you attempt to show anyone this letter, the words will vanish and you will be forbidden to enter—forever. If you try in any way to copy its contents, the words will vanish and you will be forbidden to enter—forever.

Be advised to take this seriously, as this is not a joke.

Signed,

The Magnificent ProfFnGlitcH

PS: Doors open immediately after your last class. Feel free to bring one of your best you-know-whats, because a special race begins promptly at four p.m.

PPS: We took the liberty of also inviting your friend Brandon Davis, because friends should stick together. We will invite Angela after she returns from her trip.

The boys had eagerly followed the directions, memorizing what they were supposed to, and now they stood before towers of dented, pounded, and banged-up cars. Brandon was empty-handed, but Louis carried a metallic black case with the initials L. P. etched in the side. It contained one of his you-know-whats. The cars created a labyrinth that appeared impossible to thread, and they were just the first of the three obstacles that had to be overcome. Louis and Brandon could tell from the map that was printed clearly in their minds that this was where they needed to begin their quest.

"Okay. Step one. Bang on the bumper of the brown Buick," Brandon said as he stepped up to the car that rested on the bottom first row. *Bang! Bang!* Nothing.

"No, Brandon. The map told us to bang on the *back* bumper of the brown Buick," Louis said. Brandon quickly moved to the back of the car and thwacked the rear bumper twice. It shifted a few inches down. Then, with a loud metallic churning sound, the entire pile of cars began to rumble and shake.

"Yo, man, this . . . these cars are going to fall on us!" Brandon yelled.

Dust. A huge cloud formed around Louis, not from the wobbly car stack, but from Brandon. He kicked it up as he ran out of sight behind a refrigerator about thirty feet back. Brandon tried to pull Louis with him, but Louis paid no attention to him other than to let out a cough. Even though it seemed as if the cars would collapse on Louis, he felt no desperation or fear. Instead he felt that this was the start of something big and worth sticking around for.

Soon the commotion was over. The entire side of the Buick swung open from its center on hidden hinges at the front and back of the car. Louis could now see that the cars were not really cars at all. They were hollow inside, stacked to create the outer shell of a hidden pathway that no one could have suspected.

Bright Christmas lights flickered, enticing travelers into the secret pathway.

"Brandon! Hey, Brandon, come check this out!" Louis yelled.

"You sure, man?" Brandon replied in a distant voice.

"Yeah. You really need to see it. This is the way," Louis assured him. Brandon ran back, but not as fast as he had run away.

"Yeah. You know, you can never be too careful. Being squashed by junked cars is not on my list of acceptable ways to go," Brandon said.

Louis let out a sarcastic "riiiiight," holding back a fit of the chuckles. Brandon was an excellent friend, but he put his self-preservation above all else, which was not such a bad thing for a twelve-year-old.

Brandon regained his confidence and decided to lead the way. Big deal! Leading is easy when there's only one way to go. But as they set off down the path, they heard the car doors swing closed. Now the decision to continue was final.

"I don't see anyone else. We're probably the last people to get here," said Louis, following the flashing lights as they blinked, highlighting everything in different colors.

"Hey, it's not my fault—oh wait, yeah, it is, but I couldn't get out of staying after school today," Brandon replied, thinking about the makeup tests he'd had to take.

After many turns and twists, the two found themselves standing in a large circular clearing surrounded by more cars stacked high and wide—with no exit. The door of the car they'd stepped out of had mechanically slammed shut. The only way forward was through seven wide green pipes planted in the ground straight up and down; each one rose about three and a half feet above the surface. Louis did not know why, but these pipes looked familiar. Before he could put his finger on it, Brandon said, "What is this, Super Mario Brothers? Let me guess. We have to slide down one of those things?"

"That's right, Super Mario Brothers! *That's* where I've seen these pipes before," Louis said. He felt silly he hadn't made the connection. That had to be one of his brother's favorite video games.

It was time to solve the riddle from the back of the letter.

"What the number of PPGs equals when multiplied by the prequels and then divided by *Friday* and its sequels. Figure this out and you will be more than halfway there. Mess it up and you will be sent home without a care."

Easy enough, Louis thought. "All right, there are three Powerpuff Girls. There could be many prequels, but the most well known are the three *Star Wars* prequels, so that's three times three. That makes nine. Now divide that number by two, since there are only two *Friday* movies. That makes four and a half. That can't be right. No pipe is numbered four and a half."

"Wrong, Louis, wrong! There are three *Friday* movies."

"No, there was only *Friday* and *Next Friday*," Louis said.

"What did I tell you? Wrong! There's one that takes place during Christmas. Right now there are three," Brandon said.

"Yeah, right. I forgot about that one." Three times three divided by three is three. The third pipe was the one. Louis stood in front of that pipe, looked at Brandon, then leaped into it without regard for the possibility he might be falling to his death. Brandon rushed to the pipe and stared apprehensively into the darkness.

"Louis, you sure that's safe? You okay? You sure this is something for *me* to do?" Brandon asked. No response. He almost got worried for a second; then he heard, "Come on, you punk." For the first time, a smile cracked Brandon's face, and he too slid down the pipe.

Brandon went feet first and was amazed that the pipe was no longer straight up and down but on an incline and extremely smooth. Soon he felt a spray on his face. Next a splash. Then he was drenched. The pipe became a waterslide, its sides covered in moss here and there. He found himself running up the sides of the pipe and sliding around in 360s. He lost track of how far he was sliding and even of how wet he was. He just put his arms in the air and screamed with elated enthusiasm.

Brandon knew the ride was almost over. He saw a

light ahead and Louis's new Air Max 90s. The slide spit him back onto his feet, dripping wet. He couldn't have cared less that he was soaked. In fact, he couldn't remember ever having had a better time. But in true Brandon fashion, he was not going to let Louis know that he was having so much fun.

"Now what?" he barked at Louis, trying to hide his exhilaration. Louis stood a few feet from him, bone dry. "How come you're—" Brandon could not finish his question, because as he walked toward Louis, hoses spat out of the wall and blasted him with air at every angle until he was completely dry.

"Oh, never mind."

Louis smiled, then pointed to a wooden door that looked tattered and worn but sturdy nonetheless. In its center was a glowing blue button marked RING ME in red letters. Brandon, still hiding his exuberance, did the honors. After a tense moment of silence, the sound of machinery suddenly exploded inside the chamber. A slot in the middle of the door opened, revealing a pair of eyes. Louis saw nothing odd about them, but to Brandon they somehow looked familiar. Very familiar.

"Okay," said a kid. Then there was a bang and a screech as if someone were trying to get something to work by hitting it. As the speaker continued to talk, his words turned into a menacing adult voice that made the boys cringe, not because it frightened them but because it was so excruciatingly loud. "You guys got this far and you know what to do!" said the unseen orator.

One thing Brandon hated was anything blatantly stupid. "Aw, man, we really have to do that? I thought that was a joke! That is just too stupid—that's not cool. Not cool at all, no way, nope!" Brandon said.

"Come on, we have to. Look what time it is. I am going to miss the race," Louis pleaded.

"I mean, can't we go through some more cars or slide down some more slides?" Brandon said.

"Jumpin' monkeys. Why did I have to be on the door?" the voice asked. It was still loud, but no longer menacing, just frustrated.

"Jumpin' monkeys? Jumpin' monkeys? Derrick. Derrick Carlton, is that you? That's you. I know it is," Brandon stepped up to the door and pushed his head into the slot, trying to see if it was indeed Derrick. "You better let us in without all of that nonsense."

Derrick Carlton sat in front of Brandon in school because of alphabetical seating. Brandon hated alphabetical seating. Derrick said "jumpin' monkeys" after everything good or bad, and only his tone changed.

He said it with despair after failing a test.

He said it with excitement after passing a test.

He said it with relief and a laugh when he let a silent one go right in front of someone.

Brandon said it when he was that someone.

"Okay, fine, it's him. Let it go. Come on, we got to get in here. I'm going to miss the race. Let's get it over with," Louis said, calm but firm.

Brandon said, "Just get ready. One, two, three—"

They glanced at each other and, skipping backward in a circle, began to sing:

"Ohhhh . . . the most specialest place in the world I'm
*   told*
isn't Fort Knox or filled with pirates' gold.
It's the best place where a kid can play;
xenon lamps keep it lit all night and day.
If you let me in, I promise not to tell or my breath
*   will smell*
because I'll have to eat stinky snails
wrapped in slimy fried kale.

"Sooooo . . . Keeper of the JunkYard JunkLot's
*   secret, let me in!*
Let me in. Please let me in.
Keeper of the JunkYard JunkLot's secret, let me in!
Let me in. Please let me in.
So my funnest days as a kid can begin."

They both tripped and landed clumsily on the ground. As they got up, about to start the second verse, the voice behind the door broke into a fit of laughter. It told them to stop because he couldn't take it anymore. The door split apart in four squares with the button still attached to the lower right corner of its upper left. Each square retracted into the wall. Derrick Carlton was there, exactly as Brandon expected. He had tears in his eyes as he rolled around on the floor of what appeared to be an elevator, holding his stomach and kicking his feet. Derrick somehow managed to stop, took a good look at the two, then laughed even harder.

"Aiiight, get up—take me and L. Proof to where we need to go. He can't miss this race," Brandon commanded.

Derrick got himself together and stood up. "The great Brandon Davis acting like a fool. That's a first. Come on, we're all the same down here . . . no one is better than anyone else. Sometimes we all need to humble ourselves. Maybe not as much as that, but no one told you to be so good at it."

The elevator was roomy, with a place to secure bikes on the right. "You have to put that briefcase in the slot," Derrick told Louis. Derrick banged on the left wall and a compartment opened. The case easily fit inside.

"Okay, guys, stand on this circle and you'll be fine. Don't get scared. This thing moves pretty fast." The three stepped into a blue circle in the elevator's center. The door closed with a clank, and Derrick pressed a button identical to the one Brandon had pressed on the other side. The elevator began to move quickly. In an instant they were suspended weightlessly in the elevator's center. They were safe there, never once wavering toward the top, bottom, or sides. The elevator went up, then down. Right, then left. It spun counterclockwise, then clockwise. It moved so freely and spontaneously no one could keep track of the crazy directions it traveled in. Brandon looked worried, but Louis was relaxed. He was at peace because he knew that for better or worse there was nothing he could do other than enjoy the journey. So he surrendered control and rode it out with an optimistic heart. The experience reminded him of one of his favorite activities: riding roller coasters.

The elevator began to slow down, making Brandon even more nervous, because they were not as stable in the center as before. He knew they were going to crash to the floor, but before they could, the elevator rose up with lightning speed, planting their feet soundly on its floor. Then, ever so slowly, the elevator lowered itself until it came to a stop. *Ding!* Everything was perfectly still, but boisterous children could be heard beyond the sealed door. Neither Louis nor Brandon had any idea where they were, or even if they were still in the JunkYard JunkLot.

Wherever they were, it was where they wanted to be, and they were finally there.

⇒ CHAPTER TWO ⇐

Of course what was outside the elevator's doors had to be utterly fantastic.

Of course this had to be the most spectacularly splendid place on the planet.

Of course whatever happened here would change Louis Proof's life forever.

Quite frankly, this would not be much of a story if that were not the case.

The elevator's last move was a half rotation counter-clockwise; then the doors opened. Louis, black case in hand, and Brandon stepped off. "Have fun, guys!" Derrick said through the elevator's closing doors. In a second he was gone.

Louis and Brandon were in the center of a super subterranean playtime palace the length of twenty football fields, with a ceiling so high it was able to house a roller coaster that rose to at least one hundred and eighty feet. This had to be the biggest playtime palace of any kind on any planet in any universe.

The colossal walls had live feeds of outdoor landscapes from all over the world projected on them. The different images blended together so they seemed connected and real enough to walk into. IMAX had nothing on this place. The rides were more imaginative than any they could have dreamed of, and so abundant that no one had to wait in line for more than a minute. The ground was firm but made to absorb any impact from any height, leaving the fallen completely unharmed.

Kids and teens were everywhere. Running. Laughing. Being launched from bungee-cord-like devices which flung them forward, then snapped them right back. Playing forty different video games on forty huge plasma screens. Being spun at lightning-fast speeds in contraptions that neither Louis nor Brandon had ever seen before. Eating pizza, hot dogs, hamburgers, Chinese food, candies, and cakes. Launching from huge half-pipes and ramps on bikes and skateboards with illuminated wheels to etch freestyle patterns in the air. Hooting and hollering and waving their arms on a roller coaster that could jump its tracks at random to land on one of three other tracks. So many activities it would take a whole book to describe them. Most importantly, this was a place where kids were being kids, to the tenth power.

Louis loved the look of the amazing roller coaster but was more excited about the elaborate racetrack for radio-controlled cars that wrapped around the entire underground palace. It dipped, looped twenty feet in the air, had huge gaps that had to be jumped, was twenty feet wide in some places, housed dangerous obstacles, and even had see-through tunnels.

One detail about this palace that really surprised them but should have been expected was that everything here, even the mighty roller coaster, was made out of junk. Not dirty, cruddy, or rusty junk, but junk recycled, polished, smoothed, and put together to create all of these glorious rides. If not for the soda-can logos and such, no one would have been the wiser. Here the old became new and better than it ever was.

What were they waiting for? "Let's have some fun!" they said enthusiastically while looking for the best way to get to the beginning of the racetrack. Louis noticed that everything was marked in some way with the words "The Magnificent ProliFnGlitcH." That was the name on the letter. *ProliFnGlitcH, that's quite an unusual word*, Louis thought. He tried to think what it could mean. But the Branch brothers—Stan and Dan—with their middle sister, Jan, rode up to him and Brandon on their BMX bikes.

"So you guys are finally here," Dan said to both Brandon and Louis.

"Yep, I can't believe this place," said Louis in amazement.

"It's great, isn't it? Glad you guys could make it. Everyone else has been here for at least an hour," Stan said.

"I can't believe the entrance to this place is in our

dad's junkyard. Oh, and remember the rules—don't break them," Dan said.

"Come on, man, how long have you known me?" Brandon asked.

"A long time—that's why I'm reminding you. You know your history. Hey, I'm only playin'," Dan said.

"Louis, I see you brought it," Jan said, looking at the case in his right hand.

A wily grin crept onto Louis's face as he thought about the contents of the case. "Of course I brought it. It's not my best, but for my first time here I'm sure it will be more than enough," Louis said.

"Well, follow the green lights to get to where you want to be. You better hurry up," Jan said.

"No doubt! I'm on my way!"

"Great. Have fun. Do anything you want—just remember the rules," Stan said.

"We know! We know!" Louis and Brandon both said as they reached into their pockets and pulled out the white glossy pamphlets stamped in red with the words THA RULES. Now that they had reached this place and seen its wonder, *Tha Rules* made perfect sense.

"Right," Stan said as he and his siblings rode off.

Louis remembered his question and yelled, "What's the Magnificent ProliFnGlitcH?"

Stan quickly turned to look at Louis. A smile crossed his face before he shouted, "Like I said, this entrance just happens to be in our dad's junkyard. So we don't know everything about this place. When you find out, you can tell me. Forget about that for now or you'll be late."

"ProliFnGlitcH? What the heck is that? Where do you see that?" Brandon asked.

"That's how our letters were signed, and it's on everything. See?" Louis pointed to a huge emblem on the support beams of the highest loop of the roller coaster.

"You and the questions! Always with the questions. Come on, let's see what that case is talking about," Brandon said as they headed to the beginning of the racetrack.

The DJ was playing the best new and old hip-hop, rock, and pop hits. Everything just seemed to flow together here. "We got Louis Proof and Brandon Davis in the house. Give it up for the newest members of the club," the DJ said as he turned down a new song by Jay-Z. The DJ was Alex Tacashi. He was high up in a booth in the center of the palace. Louis and Brandon knew him from the neighborhood. All who could stopped what they were doing to look at the two new members. There was an inquisitive silence, then an uproarious cheer. A wireless microphone from the DJ booth sped toward Louis and Brandon. Brandon's eyes lit up as he grabbed it, not at all amazed that the microphone was flying. He was only mesmerized by the possibility of hearing his voice echo in such a huge place. Louis knew this was probably going to be trouble.

"Thank you! Thank you! I know you had to make do in here without my commentary. Henry, don't think I didn't see you fall off that bike and almost bust your—" Louis clamped his hand over Brandon's mouth. Most times that was the only way to stop the verbal avalanche.

Still covering Brandon's mouth, Louis grabbed the mic and said, "Thanks, everybody. We're glad to be here." He let go and the mic sped back up to the booth. Alex turned up the music again. The party was back on.

The two boys arrived at a silver shuttle marked with the words "The Magnificent ProliFnGlitcH Raceway Transport." The shuttle doors opened as they neared it. Louis and Brandon got in, and the shuttle whisked them high above the kids and the rides. The doors opened into an executive skybox designed exclusively for kids. Here there were wild-colored leather seats, TV screens, arcade-style video games, and a robot-manned bar that only served kid-approved beverages.

The center of this particular skybox was large and wide open. To Louis's surprise it was the beginning of the ten-lane racetrack and marked with the word START. The opposite side of the skybox was the end of the racetrack. Pretty cool, Louis thought. That's exactly how he would have built it.

The race was about to begin. Louis's name was on the board of ten contestants, and he'd made it in time.

Unknown to Louis, word had spread of the arrival of a formidable new opponent, and he was that person.

Louis opened his black case to reveal a sleek radio-controlled car: a metallic blue, pearl-painted Bugatti Veyron—one eighth the size of the original. This car also had a small action figure in the driver's seat, clutching the steering wheel, ready to drive. Louis pulled one other thing from the case—a black visor with silver and neon blue highlights. It looked high-tech and similar to the ones held by the other RC drivers. Brandon, reclining lazily in one of the seats, ordered a soda from the robot bartender.

Everyone in the skybox looked at Louis's car in awe—all except Grant Hoffson. He was two years older than Louis and in his second year of high school. Grant was from the other side of the country and well known in the world of radio-controlled racing.

"How the heck did *he* get over here?" Louis wondered aloud. He had no time to find out because the digital display board above the racetrack now read 4:00. It was race time.

Louis and nine other kids stood eagerly with their cars in hand. The anticipation that the contestants and the audience felt for such a grand race in such a grand place was one hundred times more than what was felt on the release day of the newest PlayStation or Nintendo. Those were just games; this was real and just might prove to be way more exciting than anything found in any video game.

The children put on their visors, covering their eyes with plasma screens. As soon as these were in place, the mechanical drivers in the cars came to life. Their head, body, and arm movements mirrored those of their controllers. The children were able to see the racetrack from the perspective of their mechanical race-car drivers. Except for the crystal-blue electric static that distorted the screen of the visors every now and then, they were in extremely clear resolution.

The third contestant immediately gave the finger to all of the other players. His tiny driver gave a corresponding finger to his fellow mechanical drivers. Louis saw this and let out a chuckle. The race board revealed that this kid's name was Sammy James.

"Place your cars on the track and prepare your ignite sticks." Alex Tacashi's voice echoed. Louis set his car down, then took the ignite stick from its case. He flipped a switch on the stick, and the others did the same. Each stick began to pulse with light. The kids pounded the bottoms of the sticks on the track, making them flash feverishly. That is, everyone's stick flashed except for the one belonging to Doug Everly, who was in lane seven. His let out a bang and exploded, leaving him unharmed but dust-covered and surrounded by smoke. The others slipped the glowing portion of their rods into the matching ports on their cars. The cars hummed and vibrated. The kids stood behind the line and waited for the countdown.

3 . . . He was about to partake in the greatest race of his life.

2 . . . Today was the day to see how good he really was.

1 . . . No time to think! Go!

The cars sped off lightning-quick as the glowing sticks disappeared inside them.

The start of the race was clear and straight, but soon came the first turn. Louis took the outside track. Cars passed him by. He was in eighth place. The track became much narrower. A glass tunnel was coming up with only enough room for cars to enter in single file. Sixty-four mph and rising. Depending on the length of the tunnel, Louis would be in eighth place for a while. That was unacceptable. He had to use this tunnel to his advantage. Of course! He was stuck here only if he thought in a straight line. Louis flipped a safety guard on his controller and pressed a button. Nitro boost. Seventy. Eighty. Ninety mph. He turned left and rode up the side of the tunnel. Breakneck acceleration allowed him to pass the seventh car and return to the lane. Seventh place. His boost was still in effect. In a split second, he jolted to the right side of the tunnel and with a huge sweep shot up above the cars to ride on the tunnel ceiling. As the miniature drivers looked up, Louis imagined the facial expressions of his competition. He came down on the left side, passing four cars for third place. The crowd cheered. Louis had come to race, and these kids were witnessing him at his best.

Out of the tunnel.
Accelerate to clear five consecutive loops.
The track banks left, then right.
Maneuver through seven hairpin turns.
Seventy mph.
Halfway finished, half energy left.
Hip-hop beats blazing in the background.

Coming up were ten separate tunnels, each wide enough for one car. Louis could see that when a car went into a tunnel, it closed, preventing another from entering. One tunnel seemed just as good as another. "Take two! Take two!" Brandon yelled. Why not?

Louis picked the second tunnel. It was pitch black inside. He flipped on his headlights.

Drive! Drive! Drive! The tunnel soon became transparent, and Louis could see the other racers all over the track. Louis had no way of telling what place he was in because the positions listed in his visor were replaced by question marks. *This must be leading up to something,* Louis thought. Suddenly, he had two ways to go: left or right. He chose left, accelerating to 80 mph. The tunnel spit him out and he was flying through the air. Cars passed above, below, to the right, and to the left of him. He landed in a huge opening, another glass tunnel that spiraled and made sharp downward turns, releasing him onto the main track. *What the hell!?!* He was in last place. *How'd that happen?* No time to think about it. He had to make up ground.

Straight ahead were the three huge gaps that Louis had seen earlier. He was sure these would be the biggest obstacles. Each gap was big, but none as big as the first. The cars had to use magnetic grappling beams to cross the chasm. At precisely the right moment, the cars had to target the beams at floating metal hooks in order to swing to the other side. But Louis noticed another hook, high above the rest. None of the other drivers were going for it. He would. He had nothing to lose.

When he reached the gap, Louis targeted the first hook, locked onto it, and released the magnetic beam, swinging to the other side, past the point where he should have released it. "What are you doing? Aw, man, you messed up!" Brandon yelled.

Louis didn't care. He had to get to that other hook. He swung his car until it was almost vertical. Then he hit his second nitro boost and deactivated the beam, thrusting his car high up into the air, five, ten, fifteen feet above the first hook. Once again he used his visor's targeting system to shoot out the beam, to latch onto the second hook. He had done it!

The entire track began to flash, and the words HEAVEN'S WAY WARP—ACCESS GRANTED illuminated

Louis's visor and all of the big screens. Kids began to yell, "L. Proof! L. Proof!" while making *L*s with their index fingers and thumbs.

The silver hook carried him high above the track, then released his car. The car plummeted toward the ground, but Louis had no fear. The entire track below started to shake, making it hard for the other drivers to race on. Pieces began to rip from the track and fly under Louis's car, fitting together like a jigsaw puzzle and creating more track, high above the other contestants. The faster he drove, the faster the pieces came together. His car skipped over the other two gaps, descending onto the main racetrack as the Heaven's Way Warp ended. He was in first place.

On a straightaway now, Louis noticed HELL'S BOULDER DASH—OPEN flashing on the screens and two crafts hovering overhead. They flew over the track and dropped two metallic spheres, missing him by only a few centimeters. The spheres landed hard behind his car and left cracks in the track. The crowd would have been on the edge of their seats if they had had them.

"Louis, look behind you!" Brandon yelled. Before Louis could look he saw a car being thrown overhead, sparking violently. It started to smoke and landed on its roof with a crash a few yards in front of Louis's car.

Karen Maci threw her controller down and yelled, "Now I have to build a new car. But that was ridiculously fun!" She gave her friend a high five and began to cheer for Louis.

"What the heck?" Louis said as he looked back, then forward. He had to get out of there. The spheres had cracked open and released two mean-looking, spiked, mechanical cheetahlike devices. They had taken out Karen's car, and Louis figured they and Hell's Boulder Dash were the result of opening the Heaven's Way Warp. Louis swerved to the left as one cheetah came up on his right. He went into a turn and one came up on his left, matching his speed.

Suddenly they stopped and moved to opposite sides of the track, communicating with each other. This couldn't be good. The ridges of their metallic bodies began to shine, and simultaneously they charged toward Louis's car at 85 mph. This was a speedy attempt to crash his car on both sides. No amount of acceleration and no maneuver could shake them. He would be smashed.

"Stop, Louis! Stop right now!" Brandon screamed. He was right. Louis slammed on the brakes. The cheetahs could not stop fast enough and crashed into each other. The kids went crazy.

"We came to play no games! Recognize the skills!" Brandon yelled, and the kids screamed louder.

The cheetahs lay on the track, smoking and twitching. In all of the excitement Louis forgot he was at a dead stop. It wasn't long before Grant and Sammy caught up and rushed right by him. "Catch 'em! Catch 'em! You can do it!" Brandon shouted. Zero to 70 mph in five seconds. His tires smoked in hot pursuit. Still behind in third place.

They went into a turn. Louis caught Sammy and fought him for the inside track. Sparks flew as they bumped hubcaps and doors, but Louis won. The inside track gave Louis the advantage and soon he was three car lengths in front of Sammy. Sammy had no boost left and was done for. His driver gave Louis the finger, but Louis was too far ahead to see it. Grant was still in the lead.

In a loud, funny voice Brandon said, "Louis, use your last boost! Use your boost! Use it now and you will win!"

Louis knew that it was too early to use the last one. Why would Brandon say that? Then Louis understood. Would Grant be that stupid? Yep. He used his last nitro boost in anticipation of Louis using his. Louis could see Grant's exhaust pipes spit out blue flames as he took off like Iverson going to the hoop. Big mistake.

"Now catch him and make him eat nitro!" Brandon yelled. Grant realized his dumb move would probably lose him the race. All Louis had to do was get close enough to fire his last boost and win. It would be easy. So easy that Louis began to think about what he was going to do next. He would ride the roller coaster twenty times and eat two of everything served here. He loved to eat, especially after a win.

"Take him down! Take him down!" Brandon implored. The lights of the finish line appeared. Yeah! Grant held the lead by only a few feet. He tried desperately to block Louis from being able to pass. Louis waited for his opportunity. There was still time. The lights of the finish line began to flash faster and brighter: ninety . . . eighty yards left. Time for Louis to hit the nitro boost and claim victory! Ready, set . . . Then it happened.

A gust of wind rushed toward Louis. He felt as if he were caught in a tornado, but he was not moved. He felt extreme heat blow past him, but he was not burned. Louis forgot about the race and ripped the visor off in fright. Everything seemed to move in slow motion: the kids cheering, Grant crossing the finish line, Brandon looking confused.

Then Louis saw waterless waves displace and distort everything in their path. Within these waves were two objects that sped toward him in a blur. He glimpsed two sets of blue-gray eyes as true as his own. Before he could react, they passed right through him. He turned to follow in their path, but they were gone.

The kids cheered and rushed to congratulate Grant on his win. Apparently they hadn't seen what Louis had. Down below, though, he saw a boy and girl rush out of the tower in the center of the palace and look around with fright. There was also a crash. A kid had toppled one of the food stands over. He had an expression of fright not only on his face but tattooed over his entire body. He could not reach the elevator fast enough. He was gone. He and the other two must have also seen it, Louis thought.

"Hey, Proof, what happened? I thought you had it in the smash. How could you lose?"

Louis looked at Brandon like he was crazy. How could he have not seen and felt that? And what of the others? He turned and searched for the boy and girl, but they were gone.

Grant came over and extended his hand. "You almost had me. I thought for sure you were going to go nitro and blow right past me," Grant said. He saw the desperate look on Louis's face.

"Hey, it's no big deal. It's only a race," Grant said.

"Yeah, you got me. I'll beat you next time." Louis quickly let go of Grant's hand, then collected his car, case, and visor.

"I'm out of here," Louis said to Brandon.

"What? What? What do you mean? Aw, man, I didn't even get to play any games. And we won't be back tomorrow—you have work! I know you want to ride the roller coaster!"

"Sorry, man, I'm out of here."

"All right, let's bounce," Brandon said reluctantly, thinking that Louis must be pissed off by the loss.

Louis looked around one more time, packed, then rode the silver shuttle to the ground level with Brandon.

On the way to the elevator, he suddenly noticed that there was more than one—and that the frightened kid had used one of the others. Each elevator was marked with a different location from all over the world. After finding the one labeled "JunkYard JunkLot—East Orange, NJ, USA," Louis pressed the blue button. Every time Brandon tried to say something, Louis waved him off. Derrick arrived and they got onto the elevator.

Nothing would ever be the same again.

CHAPTER THREE

Louis's quickly placed footsteps could not get him away from the JunkYard JunkLot fast enough. He'd been so happy to be there and now he couldn't wait to leave it behind. It's funny how things can turn out.

"I still don't know why we had to leave so soon. Come on, man, just because you lost doesn't mean party over. I mean, I didn't get to play any games. Plus I saw like three girls that I'm pretty sure were smiling at the kid," pestered Brandon.

"Brandon, I don't care that I lost! That isn't the reason why we left."

"Stop lying—then why did we?" asked Brandon.

"Nothing funny happened down there? You didn't see anything?"

"Sure I did."

"So you did see it?" Louis asked with inquisitive enthusiasm.

"Yeah. I saw you cross the finish line second and lose. I don't know what you saw, but that's what I saw. It was on the big screens. The little screens. The screens in the front. The screens in the back. It was kind of hard to miss," joked Brandon.

"Never mind, forget it. I have homework, and you know how I am about homework," said Louis.

"Now I know you've lost it. We're in the same class, remember? If I don't have any, you don't have any. Why would we have homework before the last day of class? Wait, my bad, you do have homework — not to be late for the last day before summer vacation. You're always late. Even when you're on time you still manage to be late," Brandon said with a laugh.

Louis was not joking. Brandon could tell that something was up.

"Look, Louis, if you say you saw something that wasn't right, I believe you. No big deal. When you move out, I move out. But can we go back soon? Like tomorrow?"

It meant a lot to Louis that Brandon said this and Brandon had left with him — even though the new Gears of War was being played down there.

"I have to work at my uncle's tomorrow. But the day after that we can go. We'll celebrate the first day of summer vacation."

He had to go back — not because of Brandon, but to find those kids who looked as if they had seen something.

"Well, I'll see you tomorrow in school. We're going to have a great party!" said Brandon.

The boys had reached Brandon's street, and he made the turn for home as Louis continued on his own. Before he was too far away, Brandon called to him.

"What are you going to do about Ali Brocli tomorrow? You know he must have something planned. He hasn't tried anything in a while."

Ali Brocli had been a pain in Louis's side for as long as he could remember. He was a fifteen-year-old seventh-grade derelict prone to deviant behavior which included, but was not limited to, wedgies, lunch-box-content extortion, in-class beat-downs when the teacher wasn't looking, wet willies, and other horrible behavior that would get the entire class detention. On top of that, he was not called Ali Brocli because his teeth were green—that was actually his name. He was so mean that no one used that as an opportunity to make fun of him. Well, at least not to his face. What made him dangerous to Louis was that Ali knew that since Louis was well liked, messing with him might cause a back-lash, ending Ali's tyrannical reign. So Ali always tried to beat on Louis when he least expected it and when no one was around to help. In short, Ali Brocli was no friend of Louis Proof or of anyone else for that matter.

"I don't even want to focus on that now," Louis said.

"Well, you know if anything does go down, I have your back," Brandon told him. Brandon was all about preserving his own well-being, but was no one going to beat up his best friend. No way! No how!

"I know," Louis said.

Louis did not have a long walk home, but it seemed

even shorter because he was preoccupied. The secret of the JunkYard JunkLot was one thing, but the phantom-like spectacle was something entirely different. He needed to find those kids when he returned to the JunkYard JunkLot to ask them a few questions. Even if they couldn't explain it, at the very least they could confirm that he was not alone.

Suddenly he was at his doorstep. The door was locked and he had forgotten his key, but this door was never closed to him. He didn't need a key because someone was always here. Neither he nor anyone in his family ever had to come home to an empty house unless they all left and returned together. They didn't plan for someone always to be home; it just somehow worked out that way.

Louis knocked once. No answer. He knocked again and heard footsteps. When the door opened, his mommy was revealed. She was lovely, in her very early forties but looking much younger, as though she had stopped aging—or at least she had in Louis's adoring eyes. She was not overweight, but her face looked a little chubby, as if her cheeks were made out of fluffy pillows.

"What's the deal, Mom?"

"What's the deal, Louis?"

They both smiled and gave each other big hugs as they did every day after school. Louis's chubby fingers and arms wrapped around his mom and his face pressed against the circular medallion that hung from a chain on her neck. It was composed of a flat, round, marvelously blue precious stone set in etched platinum. It was always there when he hugged his mom, and always warm like a slice of summer as it touched his face. A hug would not be a hug without it.

His mom was great. His mom was a real mom. Even though she was into many of the things that Louis was into and felt young herself, she knew the sacred boundary between parent and friend. Brandon and Angela were his friends, and she was his mom. She kept him in line. She did not let him step out of bounds in the effort to seem cool. She was Mrs. Proof—phenomenal mom of Young Mr. Louis Proof. No one would have it any other way.

"Why home so late? Besides that, what's on your mind?" his mother asked. As always, she knew when her youngest was deep in thought or something was wrong.

"Well, first I had to wait for Brandon to take some makeup tests, and then I had an RC car race and I didn't win. I guess I'm a little pissed off about it. I'll be okay." Louis trudged upstairs as part of his performance.

This was not a lie. Louis rarely lied to his mom. It was just not the entire story. He had found that if he was smart enough, he'd never have to lie. He'd just selectively decide which parts of the truth were enough to satisfy what someone wanted to hear while keeping troublesome details from slipping out. He could not tell her about the JunkYard JunkLot; she would never believe him, and of course it would be against *Tha Rules*.

"You'll win the next time. I can tell from the case you're holding that you didn't use your best car. You didn't want to hurt them too much this time. You were being nice," Mrs. Proof said.

A smile graced Louis's face, and from the sixteenth step, which was the top step, Louis said, "Aw, Mom, stop playing. I'll be in my room." There were five doors upstairs, and the one marked by a Fullmetal Alchemist poster was Louis's. Before he entered his room, he looked at the closed door across from his own—his brother's room. Camron was five years older than Louis. Louis turned the crystal doorknob, bejeweled with his brother's initials, and gently pushed the door open. What he saw in the room puzzled and bewildered him. For the past few weeks his brother, by some strange means, had acquired various pieces of recording equipment such as keyboards, samplers, and a brand-new souped-up computer with tons of the latest music software—all of this without a job. Louis knew his parents were not buying it for him. Whenever Louis asked about it, his brother would either close the door or tell Louis not to worry.

This time the new items were much less expensive, but they still didn't belong in his brother's room. He had five Xbox games, which was odd, because Louis owned an Xbox but his brother didn't. Besides, Louis already had those games. Then he noticed a pair of female Prada shoes. Louis didn't know much about shoes, but he knew Prada was expensive. That was odd, since his brother never spent a lot of money on his girlfriends unless he really, really, really had to. That was one of his most steadfast "player principles." Finally, Louis saw a stack of unopened CDs, bubblegum-pop, which he knew his brother would never casually listen to. The CDs seemed out of place in his brother's room, which was filled with official hip-hop artifacts.

Weird, but no big deal, Louis thought. Then he saw something that sent a chill down his spine. On his brother's computer screen was a picture of their aunt — in a funeral program documenting her death. Now, as far as he knew, she was alive — he had just spoken to her yesterday. His mother would have mentioned if her sister had died. Why on earth would his brother have such a thing on his computer? How could he make something like that? What kind of sick game was his brother playing?

Louis quickly closed Camron's door to force the computer screen out of his sight. He should have told his mother, but he was not supposed to be in his brother's room. Louis had a way of winding up in places he should not be and looking through things he had no business looking through. Brandon called it rambling.

Louis crossed the hall and entered his own room. It was the only place that was totally Louis Proof. The blue walls were covered with everything from hip-hop stars to comic book characters such as Spawn, Spider-Man, and Wolverine. Most of his friends considered it odd that he had posters of Dale Earnhardt Sr. and Jr. on his wall. They didn't understand why he cared about NASCAR. Louis believed that NASCAR was one of the fastest and most dangerous sports. Each driver risked his life with every lap. Even greats like Dale Sr. could die. It had happened some time ago, but that was a sad day. *Major respect to those brave NASCAR drivers,* Louis always thought. LeBron, Shaq, Allen I—not even Jordan had ever run the risk of literally crashing and burning, even while trying to make the most elaborate slam dunk.

This is what had sparked Louis's interest in the radio-controlled super cars that were parked in their own special cases on the shelves that hung over his desk. He had five different cars. He had made each one, and he knew that on his worst day he could not be beaten with his best car. On his best day he could not be beaten with his worst car. Today was a fluke. Something crazy had happened to throw his game off.

Louis could not race those cars in the house, so he had much smaller ones that he raced on a grand track that hung from his ceiling and looped around his entire room. He'd built all of this, including the bigger cars, during the many times he'd been sent to his room for bad behavior. Specifically, it was all built during his eleventh year of bad behavior. Almost every night he would turn the cars' lights on and race them around the track until he fell asleep.

Louis walked to his Mac computer to check his e-mail. Two messages. One was from an online video-game store confirming a shipment. The other was from Angela, who along with Brandon was his best friend. The message was a reminder that she would be leaving the day after tomorrow. She had been cast in a movie called *Cause and Effect* that would be filming on the other side of the country. It was a big part, and she was going to be a star, playing Denzel Washington's daughter. Angela was official.

Louis replied:

Angela,

When you're a big star, we'll still talk every day so your already uncommonly large head does not get any bigger with a crazy ego!

Your number one fan,
LP

Louis began to play some video games, but he soon began to feel dizzy. Moving toward his bed, he stepped on one of his game controllers and was sure that he had broken it. Normally, he would have had an unruly fit, but the feeling overtaking him was so severe that he didn't care. For a second he was in that earlier odd moment. Even stranger, he saw something else, something he had never seen before. It was a place, but it was not a place where anything was familiar. There were people, but they were not like any people he had ever known. Louis could have sworn they were calling him and motioning him to come to them.

Louis could not understand any of it. There were too many new images and sounds. He felt as if he were going to collapse. He sprawled across his bed, and pain invaded his body. Then it quickly went away, leaving him exhausted.

Sleep. He had to get some sleep.

Everything was eerily silent in Louis's room except for the low whirr of his computer. But as it went into its own silent sleep mode, it seemed as if the life had been sucked out of the room.

Sleep, Louis, sleep.
We only hope that you may wake.

CHAPTER FOUR

Dimensional thought. Breath. Consciousness. Movement. Galonious and Trife had reached their destination, and it was about to be on, or so they thought.

"Galonious!" called Trife. But Galonious was too busy feeling proud of the fact that he had escaped Midlandia. He walked around the underground palace, eager to begin his mission. Once again Trife tried to have a word with Galonious, and once again Galonious ignored him. Trife had assessed the situation and realized a very important bit of information. Galonious would soon notice that something was very wrong. Then he would get a chance to explain the problem.

Galonious saw children running around, and to his amazement they didn't react to his presence. He yelled and they still didn't respond. He took a swipe at one of the many rides of the underground palace and had no effect on it.

"Trife! Situation assessment. Where exactly are we? We are here, but we are not really here, because I cannot touch anything. Why is everything fading away?"

"That is what I wanted to tell you. It seems that we have made it to Earth. We are here—but not in the same dimension. Everyone you see is in the third dimension, and we are in the sixth."

"The sixth? That is the thought dimension! It must have been that blast that Vivionya and that stooge sent at us when we escaped. I knew something was not right," Galonious said. "Well, let us see if we cannot do something about getting out of here."

He focused for a moment and with vicious vigor pushed his arm forward. It took almost every ounce of his strength, but Galonious forced his arm into the third dimension. Kids near his hand stood wide-eyed and openmouthed. One of them, unafraid, grabbed the arm as if it were some kind of ride.

"What the heck? Get off of me! How dare you!" Galonious shouted as he shook the kid off of his hand. The rest of the kids looked at each other, then tried to grab the arm and were shaken off like their friend. Though they were inside, they felt a gust of wind, and the lights began to flicker. Strange.

Galonious could not push any farther, and his arm was sucked back into the sixth dimension. He tried again, but it would not work.

"Galonious, dimensional travel is going to be extremely hard. We have shifted improperly into this dimension; we cannot just freely enter the third dimension. There is a simple law of physics that says that two things cannot occupy the same space at the same time. We have no proper space there.

"Vivionya got us good. You have got to respect that—she didn't stop us, but she got us. Not for long, of course," Trife said. He knew this was nothing but a puzzle for him to solve.

Galonious had realized that the contingency plan against the arrival of CE on any planet would be a true obstacle—but he had not expected to be stuck in the wrong dimension. That was not on his list of possible things to look out for. As he paced back and forth, images flew past him.

Battles on Midlandia . . .

The eNoli and iLone fought this eternal war with magnificent technology and armor. Nothing seemed more boring to Galonious as he pushed those thoughts to the side. He was tired with war and wanted no more of it.

Their escape from the Midland Isle . . .

Galonious liked this thought! The events that had led to their forbidden exit from Midlandia had not taken place entirely on Midlandia. Surprisingly, many had taken place on Earth . . .

But what he really stopped to ponder was a conversation with Arminion . . .

He and Arminion were in a grand Midlandian room some time before the escape. Arminion had outlined every point of his tremendous plan. He explained to Galonious that it was simply time for such events to happen and that they would indeed be able to exit Midlandia.

As each image flew in front of Galonious's eyes, he marveled at what he was looking at. Anything that he thought about became a vivid, visual reality. Each thought stayed in his sight, but as soon as he thought of something else, it flew off to be replaced with a new image. Something dawned on Galonious.

"The thought dimension! That can work to our advantage," he said, beginning to laugh. Then, with a single intricate thought, he created an empire of grand technology. Just that quickly, in that instant.

It was all Horribly Marvelous. An entire city with white-hot lights and awesome technology partly rose out of the ground, partly fell from the sky, and partly built itself from nowhere. There were tall, clean buildings elaborately detailed. At the center of it all was a towering throne, and Galonious rose to it.

He refused to let being stuck in this dimension hinder him. He had done the forbidden by leaving Midlandia to come here. That was supposed to be the hard part. He was so close to his ultimate goal that he was sure this would only prove to be a minor —

It was shocking! It gave no warning! It happened out of nowhere! Galonious was suddenly paralyzed and stood silent and still. Trife called to Galonious but got no response. Trife crept closer and poked Galonious— still nothing. As quickly as it had come on, it was over, and Galonious was shouting.

"That bastard! I was just contacted by Arminion. I did not know he could overtake me like that from afar. He better not do that again. He is greatly gaining in power. He has reached his destination and is moving forward with gathering support," Galonious said to Trife.

"Is that all? When will he come here? Will it be soon?" Trife asked.

"He is far from this planet and uncertain how long it will take him to complete this phase of his plan. But there is more. I can tell that he is hiding something. I do not know what it is, but he is trying to do more than escape our endless war and eradicate the iLone's influence here. Everyone will have so much fun when our influence spreads. Nonetheless, we must be ready for his arrival. Trife, devise a plan so that we can leave here and continue pursuing our objectives as intended. Leave me to enjoy all of this. Do not return until you have worked everything out."

Trife walked away, eager to return successfully. Galonious sat back and marveled at the ideas floating by. He grabbed one that caught his eye: a shiny platinum ring with glowing lights circling furiously around its perimeter. Clueless, he let it go. Wait. What was that? It was floating. It was long and slender. Galonious clutched it. It was a sword. A flawless sword that had to have been a thought of the most legendary sword maker. A sword that was beyond anything he could have created. Galonious pulled it from its sheath, and it was perfectly balanced. On the side of the sheath was a set of throwing knives, nearly as exquisite as the sword. Galonious would surely keep this with him, as it just might come in handy in his quest to liberate each and every person on this marvelous planet.

All that Galonious, Trife, the missing Arminion, and the rest of the eNoli CE want is for Earth to be free.

Doesn't everyone want to be free?

Seriously, don't you?

CHAPTER FIVE

"Louis. Get up! School, Louis, school!" Louis's mother yelled from the living room. No answer.

"Louis, this is the last day before summer vacation. Get up! Be on time for once!" Still no answer. Mrs. Proof hiked up the stairs to see why her son had not come down yet. To her surprise, he was lying on top of his bed fully dressed in yesterday's clothes—sneakers and all. Mrs. Proof shook her head as she entered his room and saw the crushed XBox controller on the floor. She picked it up and tossed it into his metal Dragon Ball Z trash can, where it landed with a loud crash. Louis woke abruptly and asked if it was time for dinner. As one would expect from his chubby size, he hated to miss a meal.

"No, Louis. It's time for school. You've been asleep since you came home. I checked on you and you were hugging the bed. I was sure you'd have at least changed your clothes during the night, but I guess you didn't even wake up."

School, Louis thought. *School*. He was going to be late, and if he was late again this week, he would have to stay after school on the last day and help teachers clean out their desks and the classrooms in this crazy heat. No way! Not today!

He jumped into the shower while his mother went into his dresser drawers and closet to get his clothes. "If you give me a ride in your new car, I won't be late!" he yelled from the shower.

"Okay, Louis, I can do that. Just hurry up," she answered.

Mom had many things to do, and she hadn't planned on giving Louis a ride. So he had to be quick.

Open the door to the passenger seat.

    Seat belt on.

    Whiff of new-car smell.

    Ignition started.

    Exit upon immediate arrival at Parker Street School. But not before . . .

    Kiss on the cheek.

    "Aww, Mom! Not when people can see!"

    Once again, Mom is great. Sometimes affectionately embarrassing, but still great!

Mrs. Engia's seventh-grade class. A terrific class indeed. Four rows of five chairs. Twenty bright, young, and sometimes rambunctious students. It was early, but they were already preparing for the Last Day party. All were being promoted to the eighth grade. That was reason enough, but it was also a party to wish Angela success and to wish Nicole Raymond farewell (she was going overseas with her father). Nicole and Louis had always gotten along great and had promised to stay in touch.

As everyone was setting out the food, cakes, and cookies, Angela pulled Louis aside.

"Louis, you're coming to my house before I leave tomorrow, right? You have to be there at, like, seven a.m.," Angela said.

Seven a.m. That was really early, especially for the first day of summer vacation, but that didn't faze Louis. If Angela needed him there, he would be there on time.

"Yeah, I'll be there, and I'll be on time. I'll ride with you to the airport and wave good-bye to you and your mother as you take off. No doubt," Louis said.

"You promise?" Angela asked with a smile.

"I promise. I'll be there."

Angela put her hand in the air and Louis grabbed it, crossing their fingers. That was something they always did when they made a promise or important plans. They had yet to break one, and Louis was not going to let an early wake-up time ruin his perfect record. The truth was that neither Louis nor Angela would make promises they could not keep. Their promises were saved for important things and worth the effort used to utter them.

Coldness. Darkness. Unrest. All of this wrapped itself around Louis and snatched his attention. He couldn't focus on what Angela was saying. He looked out the window. Somehow he was sure the cause of his uneasiness lay there.

On the school playground Louis saw the unimaginable. What was it? Spider? Snake? Man? Millipede? Eel? Evil? A mix of all of the above. Louis did not know it, but it was Trife. He flickered between visibility and invisibility, but not all at once. Louis could never see Trife's entire body, only random parts of it. Louis let go of Angela's hand and walked to the window. He watched as Trife moved. Trife's head, arms, and torso stretched ahead of his lower body. He had twelve legs that were like those that would be found if a spider and crab were involved in a horrific genetic experiment. His upper body could stretch a very long distance, but when he walked it would usually only stretch out about six feet. When his upper half got to where he wanted to go, his lower body would catch up, and his torso would become shorter and shorter.

The third and fourth graders were outside playing like they always did, so Louis was sure that they did not see Trife. Some of the children even ran through him. *Why am I the only one who can see this thing?* Louis thought. He had seen enough movies to know that if he asked any one of his friends if they had seen anything funny outside, he would not get the answer he wanted. Brandon had proved that yesterday.

No, it couldn't be. Trife slowly tilted his head and looked at Louis. This creature could see him, and that made his entire body run cold and twitch. Would he come after Louis? Louis stepped back from the window and bumped into Angela. She was talking to him, but he could not hear anything except a weird scratching sound and words he could only partially understand. The words were something about seeing and finding. *See . . . found you . . . I can see . . . contingency. . . . I can see . . . earthbound CE* was all he could decipher.

Louis, still disoriented, tried to pull himself together. *What* is *that?* He wanted to scream and run home—or at least to the sports supply closet to get a bat to beat the snot out of that thing—but instead he told himself:

Don't freak out. Don't freak out. Don't freak out.

This can't be real.

Don't embarrass yourself.

Did I wet my pants? No, I did not wet my pants. That's a good thing.

Talk to Angela. Talk to Angela. What was she talking about?

"I don't know," Louis said out loud.

"What do you mean you don't know?" Angela asked with deep concern.

"I'm only playing around . . . seven a.m., I'll be there," Louis said randomly, hoping it would be the response she was looking for.

"I know that. I want to know when I should call you. The time zone is different where I'm going, and I don't know when I'll be shooting," Angela said.

Time zones? Shooting? Oh yeah, the movie. Louis

looked out the window and whatever he had seen was gone. Thank goodness. Louis tried to pretend that he hadn't seen anything and attempted to return to his normal life by speaking to Angela. Good luck with that!

Louis and Angela decided how they would coordinate things by e-mail and text messages. They would talk to each other as much as possible, if not every day. Angela could not stress enough to Louis how important this was to her. Louis was so happy for Angela, he could not help but give her a hug and a kiss on her cheek. He was still a bit on edge, but being with Angela did much to ease that feeling. And what was that? All of the food was laid out on the back table. Food could make Louis forget about anything. He and Angela made their way to the table and grabbed cake, cookies, and soda. All of it was good, plus free. That couldn't be beat.

Brandon was being Brandon, which meant talking loudly and being the center of attention. Louis and Angela chuckled over his antics. Angela had been Louis's friend since preschool, the first child to speak to him during the first day of his academic career. They had some real history together. How could he go a whole summer without her? With a sigh he glanced out the window. The warm feeling he felt while thinking about his friend was not enough to stop the air escaping from his lungs. His heart began to race, and his eyes widened. Whatever that thing was, it was outside again, staring straight at Louis. Two stories up, right through the easily breakable glass.

He would have collapsed in fright, but a nearby desk prevented him from falling. It took every ounce of his energy to stop from screaming. This time he pointed to the window. Everyone looked, but no one saw it. Without warning, without being excused, he left the classroom. A major no-no and grounds for detention!

He walked down the hallway to the bathroom as he tried to understand what was going on. The only place he could think to hide was the bathroom. Bad decision. He opened the door and within two steps found himself pinned against the wall.

Ali Brocli had caught him. He had not been waiting, but today he'd gotten lucky.

"Proof, you punk! Where're your friends now? What you gonna do now, huh?" Ali began punching Louis in the side.

Ali had never gotten the drop on him like this before. Louis struggled to break free, bumping into walls and stalls, but it was no use. The sounds echoed and reverberated in the bathroom, but no one would come in to help. The bathroom's teal and white color turned into a blur as Louis writhed. He stepped on Ali's feet as hard as he could with his heel, to no effect. Ali was a mammoth mass of misery.

"Get off me! What do you want? You want money, huh? I know your heinous mom has a hard time walking these streets, and your father is a jobless, shirtless bum. Ali, why doesn't your dad have a shirt? Please, I beg you, take the few dollars I have in my pocket and buy that potbellied retard a shirt!" Even in this situation Louis would not cower. If he couldn't strike physically, he'd command a verbal assault.

Ali wanted nothing but to clobber Louis, which he continued to do. Then something happened that made this ordeal seem like nothing. The coldness and darkness Louis had felt in the classroom came back. Time froze. Louis could see the drops from the faucets suspended above the sinks. Ali's words no longer made sounds in Louis's ears. Ali's punch was stuck in the air and his face locked into a dumb expression. The scratching sound echoed through the bathroom, joined by a whistle so unsettling that it made Louis want to vomit and cry. Both sounds got louder and louder. Louis could see one of the bathroom walls change. It stretched and bent as if it were made of rubber, and something was trying to poke through. It was here! Trife's upper body slithered and worked its way through the wall. The whistling stopped and Trife again began to speak words that Louis could barely make out. *Found. Earthbound CE.*

Trife paused, and an evil smile graced his face. "Found you!" he said with unmistakable clarity. Trife then reached through the frozen Ali Brocli in an effort to grab Louis. That was it. No way was Louis going to stick around for any of this. Time reset itself, and everything once again moved at life's normal speed.

With strength Louis had never known before, he

broke free from Ali and pushed him toward the toilets. Ali fell backwards, landing in a toilet that was, well, a toilet, filled with what one would expect to find in an unflushed, smelly toilet. Ali screamed with disgust as he wiped feces off his face.

Louis was out! Past Trife. Away from the bathroom. This time he could not control it. He screamed at the top of his lungs. No words, just screams. He ran past about seven classrooms, alarming the teachers so much that they rushed out of their classes to see what was going on. Louis was not stopping to tell anyone anything.

School was still in session for another hour.

Louis did not care.

This would be his last chance to say good-bye to some friends before vacation.

Louis did not care.

His book bag was still in the classroom.

Louis did not care.

He would not get to eat any more cake or cookies.

Louis still did not care.

Now that's how serious this situation was . . .

He was out the front door of the school and down the main steps. Right now, he could think of only one place to go.

Got to get to Uncle Albert's as quick as I can! Louis thought to himself.

Albert was Louis's favorite uncle. He was a young man in his thirties and as smart as a supercomputer. Louis was positive his uncle would be able to rain sanity on this situation.

Louis ran and ran at top speed until he reached the store. Young Proof was out of breath and heavily panting when he grabbed the store's door. He frantically looked in every direction to make sure he had escaped whatever it was he was fleeing. No sight of it. Thank God!

Pause.
Back away from the door.
Wait a few moments.
Get yourself together if you can.
Think about something else . . .
My uncle's store.

In a split second Louis remembered that the store was here all because Louis had said he wanted *Where the Wild Things Are* knobs for his drawers. That gave his uncle an idea that everyone except Louis thought was crazy. That idea was to abandon a successful law practice to make customized knobs and handles. That's right, knobs and handles. These knobs and handles were officially licensed and extremely special. They featured basketball teams, cartoon characters, movie stars, TV shows, top athletes, singers, rappers, etc.

This ingenious yet simple idea had caused such a stir that Albert Proof was even featured on *Oprah* and *Martha Stewart*. After that everyone wanted personalized knobs, especially all of the stars in Hollywood. Albert Proof went from successful lawyer to crazy dreamer to bona fide genius.

Nearly no time at all had passed while Louis thought of this, but he had caught his breath and wiped his face with a hand towel that he usually carried with him. He was still shaken but no longer stirred. He could enter the store without seeming like a raving lunatic.

Albert was behind the counter, and as always he was happy to see his nephew.

"Hey, Louis, you're early. Last day of school? You don't have summer school? Of course you don't. Put this next to the door so FedEx can pick it up," Uncle Albert said. Louis was anxious to talk to his uncle, but did as he was told. He noticed the package was going to someone in Cali named Cyndi Victoria Chase. It made no difference to him.

"Louis, where do you want to go on vacation this summer?"

Vacation? This was the furthest thing from Louis's mind. Without thinking, Louis blurted out, "Atlantis."

"Atlantis? The Atlantis resort in the Bahamas? Didn't expect that. No Disney or Universal Studios? Fine, Atlantis it is."

"Uhh . . . cool. Hey, Uncle Albert . . ." Louis looked around to see who was in the store. Two elderly women were browsing through *Foster's Home for Imaginary Friends* knobs. Probably shopping for grandchildren. They were paying no attention to him. Still, he wished there were no one in the store so he could be more direct.

"Have you ever seen something that you knew couldn't be real? But you knew it was real?" Louis blurted out.

Uncle Albert thought for a minute. "Wasn't real? What does that mean? The world is a big place, where just about anything can happen, good or bad. I know that for a fact—and man oh man, can I tell you some stories. So maybe what you saw was real, but you just don't have a reason to believe it, or don't want to. What did you see? Is someone in trouble?"

Louis thought for a second. His uncle was right. The secret of the JunkYard JunkLot proved that anything was possible. In the instant he realized the truth, his body began to feel as though it was being eaten up from the inside out. He hunched over. He thought he was going to vomit up all his internal organs. He wished that he could. Then maybe this pain would end. The sound and vibration of his heart filled his ears and shook his body. He had to get outside. If he was about to die, he wanted to experience the warm sunlight one last time. The sun was shining so brightly. Just maybe it would make him feel better during his last minutes. As he walked through the door he could hear his uncle, along with strange voices, calling him. Outside in the fresh air and sunlight, Louis felt no better. He did not really think he would. The pain was not even comparable to what he'd felt yesterday.

This time there was a pain no child should ever have to feel.
This time his life was quickly slipping away.
This time he was close to death.
This time . . . why on Earth, why was Trife here?

It made no difference that Trife had finally found Louis again. Louis had made it five yards from the front of the store, then collapsed, motionless on the sidewalk. No one, not the best doctor, his friends, nor his parents who loved him would be able to wake him.

Good-bye, Louis Proof.
They miss you already.

MARVELOUS WORLD

A.K.A.

The Marvelous World
of the Supposedly Soon to Be
Phenomenal Young Mr. Louis Proof

BOOK 1.5: OLIVION'S FAVORITES

◆LEVEL ÏΪ◆

MISSING

MARVELOUS WORLD

≫ A.K.A. ≪

The Marvelous World
of the Supposedly Soon to Be
Phenomenal Young Mr. Louis Proof

BOOK 1.5: OLIVION'S FAVORITES

✦ LEVEL ÏÏÏ ✦

MARVELOUS WORLD

 A.K.A.

The Marvelous World
of the Supposedly Soon to Be
Phenomenal Young Mr. Louis Proof

BOOK 1.5: OLIVION'S FAVORITES

LEVEL IV

MISSING

MARVELOUS WORLD

 A.K.A.

The Marvelous World
of the Supposedly Soon to Be
Phenomenal Young Mr. Louis Proof

BOOK 1: THE MARVELOUS EFFECT

✦LEVEL V✦

⇒ CHAPTER SIX ⇐

Sunrise is the epitome of ease. Sunrise is graceful. Sunrise is flowing. Sunrise is beautiful. Sunrise is tremendously unlike the way Louis woke up. He woke abruptly with a bewildered look on his face.

He did not notice the metallic device around his wrist. It was sleek and slightly reflective and looked like a bracelet. It also had a circular meter with glowing lights that went dim as Louis woke up, as if they had reached the end of a countdown. When Louis opened his eyes, the device disappeared but left a small metal pin in his arm. He didn't see this either because he had one thought on his mind—getting to Angela's on time.

Things he had to do to accomplish the goal:
Take a shower.
Get dressed.
Eat four waffles with butter and raspberry syrup.

He was already out of bed when a quick glance at his clock told him it was 6:04 a.m. He assumed the time was right, but the date was all wrong: September 29. No big deal. He would adjust it later. He had to get to Angela's by 7:00 a.m. Barefoot footsteps carried him toward his door. On the way out of his bedroom, he noticed that balloons were floating in his room. Some were marked GET WELL SOON, others HAPPY BIRTHDAY. They were pressing against the ceiling or suspended in midair, lacking enough helium to reach the ceiling. They hadn't been there last night, Louis thought. No time to think about that now.

Louis entered the bathroom and turned on the water while looking into the sink. He closed the medicine cabinet over the sink and looked into its mirror very quickly while still half-asleep. What did he just see? He looked again. That could not be right. He opened the medicine cabinet to look behind the mirror. Someone had to be playing a joke on him. He shut it after finding nothing special. Louis was overcome by a goofy smile as he shook his head in disbelief. He looked down into the sink, put some water on his face, rubbed his eyes, then looked up again. It was still there. Now it was no longer funny. He stepped back, turned around, and quickly stood beside the mirror with his back to the wall as if he were hiding from it. He then mustered up the courage to look again.

An unfamiliar familiar person stared back at Louis. It was indeed Louis Proof, but a thinner, leaner version. He stood back and looked at the rest of himself. Louis was Louis, but not Louis. He was no longer a pudgy little guy. What had happened? His pajamas were baggy. His stomach was no longer puffy, and his arms were toned. He was still a kid, but in about the best shape a twelve-year-old could be in. *How could I lose this much weight overnight? Oh, no! Oh, no! I must have contracted some disease in my sleep! I'm going to melt away within hours,* he thought.

He went to find his mother. He was sure his dad would not be home, since he left for work around five o'clock every morning. Louis still wanted to get to Angela's and wish her off.

Wait a minute. I should get a second opinion before I worry Mom with this, he thought. He headed to his brother's room to see what Camron had to say. He noticed that the special initialed doorknob had been replaced with a regular one. Weird. The door was open. What the heck? His brother's room was there, but not there. It was now a room for a little girl. And guess what? A little girl was sleeping, with her back facing the door. He could not see who she was. He didn't care. Nothing was right. He backed out of the room and ran to the top of the steps.

"Mom! Mom! Mommy! Mom!"

His mother sped from the kitchen. She rushed up the stairs with a quickness Louis had never seen before. Tears rolled from her eyes. She hugged him harder than she ever had before. She kissed his cheeks more times than she'd ever kissed them before.

What was this all about? Louis wondered.

When his mother released him from the biggest

mommy hug *ever*, he noticed the metal pin in his arm. It was like a large splinter, only smooth. Louis had trouble getting a grip on it. His fingers kept slipping as he pulled. With a grand effort he was able to yank it out. It was deep in his arm, but he felt no pain as it slid out. He stood dumbfounded as he saw a dark electric substance flow out of the wound, then back into his arm, leaving no sign of injury behind. The pin shimmered and flashed, then simply disappeared. Louis's mom saw this but was not alarmed.

"What the heck was that? Mom! What's going on? What happened to me? Where's Camron? Who's that girl in his room? What just happened to my arm? What the heck was that in my arm?"

By this time, the little girl in Camron's room had been woken by the shouting. She ran up to Louis, hugging him from behind. It was his favorite little cousin, Lacey.

"Lacey, what are you doing here?"

"You're awake! I live here now!" she replied with a huge seven-year-old grin.

"You live here now?" Louis looked at his mother in confusion. Mrs. Proof kissed Lacey on the top of her head, then told her to get dressed.

"After I do, can I play with Louis? It's been a long time," Lacey said.

"Yes. That will be good. Good for you and good for Louis," Mrs. Proof said.

"But, Mom, I have to get to Angela's. I can't play

right now," Louis protested, as if getting to Angela's would undo all of the crazy things that had just happened.

Mrs. Proof took Louis by the hand, leading him downstairs to a seat at the dinning room table while Lacey got dressed.

His mother told him many things, including the fact that he had missed his thirteenth birthday, but what was most important were words that Louis could not believe: "Louis, you've been in a coma for three months."

"Three months? Three months? What the—"

"Hey! Watch your mouth. Did that coma make you lose your mind?" Louis's mom said jokingly.

"No, but come on! What type of thing is that to find out! If I was in a coma, how come I'm home and not in the hospital? Were the bills too much? I thought you and dad had good insurance. You know, benefits. What happened?"

Mrs. Proof marveled that Louis was so in tune with the details. He was indeed back. Thank goodness the waiting, the doubts, and the helplessness were finally over. She couldn't stop herself from scooping Louis up into her arms again.

Everything had been so crazy in the past three months. Events of epic proportion had happened involving Louis, his brother, and the entire town. The strange Dr. Schwartz had told her that she had to get

Louis out of the hospital. He had made it possible for her to do so and believed he had destroyed all of the evidence that Louis had ever been there. He then checked in on Louis to monitor the special device on Louis's wrist. Her heart told her the doctor was good and Louis would be fine.

"Louis Proof, if you were supposed to be in a hospital, you would have been in one. You're fine now without the help of a hospital, right?" She said this with a smile, but with the authority only a mom can command. Louis knew he couldn't argue, and he took his mom's word for it.

"Mom, I've missed so much. Everything's different. I just woke up, my brother's gone, and Lacey is here. How did that happen?"

"Your brother has taken a sort of leave of absence to find himself. I think that's the best way to put it. I promised he'd be able to tell you about it himself when he returned. Lacey, well . . . let's just say her mother is up to her old ways, and of course we were more than happy to step in."

Louis understood. Camron was always getting into something. Never anything too bad, but Louis guessed that this time it had really caught up to him. A funny feeling told Louis that even if Camron were in some sort of trouble, he would surely return home. But knowing he was gone created a hole inside of Louis.

Lacey's mom was always on the verge of falling off the edge, so no more needed to be said about that.

"Louis, I think you may need some time to yourself to take all of this in. Why don't you go ahead up to your room and I'll come see you after I call everyone and tell them you're okay?"

She was right. He did need to take this all in. Before Louis went upstairs, he asked, "What about Angela? Did she do well? Is she back yet?"

"She's not back yet, but she is worried about you. Her whole family is," his mom said.

Louis sauntered upstairs, sat quietly on his bed, and thought. Three whole months he had been asleep. His brother was gone. Not to mention he had broken his promise to Angela. He was a boy of his word and never broke a promise to a friend. He couldn't even pick up the phone to call her. She wasn't back yet, and he did not have her number. She probably had new famous friends and had forgotten about him since he hadn't kept his word. No way, he thought. That was just silly. But what if?

Instead of grabbing the phone to call Angela, he grabbed one of the controllers for a car on his racetrack and squeezed the trigger. Nothing. No action. Nothing was working. Nothing was right. Louis had missed the summer. He had missed three months of candy-coated memories that no child, good or bad, should ever go without. No late days at sunset when the streets are lit with a magnificent orange tint. No summer racing in the biggest RC tournaments around. No trip to Atlantis with Uncle Albert. No hot days just doing nothing. He had also missed his birthday. Did he get any gifts? If so, where were they? If not, could he request them now?

Louis sighed and began to fight a battle against tears. His eyes got red and his face felt a bit warmer, but he won. It was just horrible—not even Horribly Marvelous—but he held it together.

He looked on his shelf and saw an opened game that he had never played, the one he had been waiting for. His reward for good behavior. He had no idea who had opened it. No matter. He popped it into one of his game consoles.

Better late than never.

The way video games came out so frequently, it would be considered old. Well, it was new to him. He was about to play it when his cousin Lacey came in. She jumped on his bed behind him, wrapped her arms around his neck, kissed his cheek, and rested her head on his shoulder.

"Hey, Louis, what's up? We can play all day now that you're no longer in that boring coma. I knew that you'd be okay. Did your mom tell you that I wasn't fibbing and that I do live here now? I wish Camron were here. That way I could live with two big cousins, but he had to leave. Did your mom tell you that? I don't know what he did, but I heard your mom and dad talking. What he did was really bad. He had to leave." Lacey's marvelously childish tone lessened the stinging reality.

Lacey always spoke to Louis with abundance and speed. She said everything on her mind at once. She considered people who could answer all of her questions in the order she asked them extremely smart. Louis was on point when it came to this.

"Yes, Lacey. She told me a lot, but she didn't tell me what my brother did or where he is. She said she'd promised Camron he could tell me himself when he came back."

"Okay. A lot of weird stuff has been going on. I've been talking to this boy named Timothy. He's strange but still really cool. He said you were going to fix it. He told me he's not the same as you, but someone like you. He said you're really important. Yep, my cousin Louis Proof—a very important person," Lacey said.

"What weird stuff are you talking about, Lacey? And who is this Timothy? I can't fix anything. I don't know anything. I've been asleep for three months."

"There are so many weird things that happened while you were sleeping. Too many to even talk about. Some good and some bad. Did you know that dangerous things called Crims walk around here? You should have seen me on the playground when they came after me. I don't know how I did it, but I took care of them. Timothy is a kid but he seems to know what's going on."

Weird things? Crims? That thing in the bathroom! Louis remembered what had happened the last day of school, and it sent him into a frenzy.

"Lacey, you saw him? You saw that thing with all of the legs and the stretching body? There's more than one and they're called Crims? Is that what you're talking about?"

"Whoa! Whoa! Whoa! Nooooooo! That's not what I saw. What I saw were these things. They were weird but they had no stretching bodies or crazy number of legs. It's a good thing I know how to fight. 'Cause when they came after me, I beat them all up," Lacey said.

"I know you don't lie to me, but I swear after all that has happened . . . I just . . . I just . . . What the heck? When did you see them? When did this happen? Lacey, you fought these things? How? For real? That just sounds . . . I don't know, Lacey. I really don't know. And how do you know they're called Crims?"

"This happened at the playground when I was with my friends Harrison, Rayne, and Imoni. We were playing, and then they came out of nowhere looking all short and mean and just terrible. Louis, I was scared at first. I called for you but you couldn't come. Then something happened and I was able to fight for real. I was on fire kicking some serious assets all over the place! You hear me, Louis? Some serious assets! But hey, why are you surprised? You remember how I used to smack you up?" she said, jumping off the bed and throwing punches in the air.

Louis put his fists up to play fight and Lacey showed him she was ready to stop him in his tracks. They both laughed, but Louis was amazed at how confident she was.

"Timothy told me they're called Crims and said my fighting spirit reminds him of someone named Vivionya. I don't know who that is, do you?" Lacey said.

The name Vivionya had a unique effect on Louis. He could remember something, but he had no idea what it was. And there was another hole inside of him. He was missing something or someone, but he had no idea what.

"I think I should know that name, but I don't. Sorry, Lacey. I'm confused now. I don't know what to think."

"That's okay, Louis. I mean, come on, you've been in a coma. Hey! Look at this—my own special ready-to-fight stance," Lacey said, taking a few steps back. She crouched, then slowly began to rise and move forward while swaying from side to side with a slight stagger. Soon she raised her arms up and out toward Louis and came to a complete stop. Awkward yet graceful. Even though she was little, she looked as if she could let out something fierce. He felt that just as she always had with him, she was telling the truth. It seemed far-fetched, but well, if he told anyone what he'd seen on the last day of school, no one would believe him.

"This is my Short Moon Rising stance. Do you like it? I'm sure you can come up with your own; then you can name it. Next, I want to invent my own fighting style and name that. That would be really, really cool. I can help you take care of those Crims! Timothy told me that's what you'll do, but don't worry, I have your back. I don't know where Timothy is now. You'll have to ask him about all of this stuff when you meet him. He's the best person to ask, and he said he would tell you everything. Just wait, I'm sure he will be along sooner or later."

"Lacey, I know you don't make things up, but you know most of this sounds ridiculous. You have to tell me more—I don't know this Timothy person."

"Made up? No way. You're right I don't make stuff up. Never have! Well, unless it's for a story or something. I told you Timothy said he would tell you everything. I don't know enough. You'd better just wait for him to show up," Lacey said.

"I have to wait for Timothy?" Louis asked.

"Yeah, Louis, that's what I said. That's the only way. But hey, Brandon was around when most of the crazy stuff was going on. He can back up just about everything I'm telling you," Lacey answered.

"Brandon? Do you know how Brandon has been? Have you seen him?" Louis said, at the moment realizing that he needed to know about his best friend.

"Brandon? Yeah, he didn't forget you! Brandon came here like three times a week. He told you about everything happening in the neighborhood. He played you all of the new music. That's not all—he told you how some guy named Dale Jr. was doing in the standings. He even brought new video games over and played them. He'd tell you that if you were playing, he'd be whipping you. He played your games for you too. He said as soon as you got better, you guys had to go back to some place and have fun. He said something about how things were not working and he couldn't get in anymore. What place is this? Can I go? I want to go with you guys," Lacey said.

Louis could not tell her about the JunkYard JunkLot, but he could not lie. He needed an elusive half-truth.

"You know the junkyard?" Louis asked.

Lacey pulled her head back and frowned.

"The junkyard? That place is no fun. It's full of junk. Rusty, dirty junk, too big to carry around or play with. I don't want to go there. I'd rather go to the basketball court. You know that I'm real good at basketball, right? Really good! Brandon has seen me play," she said.

Lacey again wrapped her arms around Louis's neck from behind. Louis began to stand up, but Lacey did not let go and dangled. As Louis turned, she was whipped left and right. She laughed and laughed, then finally let go, landing on both feet.

"Lacey, you're too much. I knew that you were trying to play ball, but I didn't know that you were really good. I want to see you play," Louis said.

"Hey, what do you mean trying to play? I don't try— I do. And I do very well, thank you. I want to show you my skills with the rock." Lacey gave Louis another big, semitoothless smile.

Family comes in handy in times like this.
Family is important.

"Lacey, what about the way I look? Do I look funny to you? I lost weight."

"Oh, yeah. No, you don't look funny. I'm used to it. You've looked like that for a while. You're in shape! You can probably play basketball with me and not sweat all over the place like you used to." Lacey grabbed her stomach and laughed and laughed. "Yeah, you look different, but you're the same Louis. I can see it in your eyes. Timothy told me to look in your eyes to see if you were the same. He told me that you would look different. Not too different—but different. But I could look in your eyes and tell if you were the same. He was right. I can see it in your eyes!" Lacey said.

"Timothy seems to know a lot," Louis said.

"Yeah, you're going to have to talk to him for the whole story. I don't know everything. I know you can't help but think that I do, but I don't," Lacey said, then giggled.

Louis went to his desk and looked into the mirror. He could have sworn he was a little taller. His dark hair was as it always was when he went without a haircut for a while. Curly, with a nice shine, but not wild and out of place. His skin was still flawlessly smooth, without any sign of breaking out. All of that was cool, but why was he in such good shape? How could that be? But hey, being in shape was not something to get upset over. After trying really hard, he was able to see his old chubby self. That put a smile on his face. One of the things he was going to do was get chubby again.

They heard footsteps on the stairs. Louis's mom entered his room with a smile. "Everyone is of course coming to see you tomorrow. I told them that today would be too much too soon. It will be short notice, but I'm sure I can throw together a family party. Your dad is on his way. I've been working from home so I could watch you," Mrs. Proof explained.

Mrs. Proof gave Louis another huge mommy hug. Lacey gave him a huge little cousin hug.

"Awwwww, guys," Louis said, hugging them too.

Louis Proof was back in business.
There was no need for him to fix his clock.

CHAPTER SEVEN

Quite often the mischievous, magical mystery of night hangs heavy in the air, yet goes unnoticed. Two Crims stood behind the dimensional barrier watching two parents who had fallen asleep on their living room couch. The couple would have been easy targets if it had not been for a minor setback—four bear-sized dogs that lay around the first floor.

One of the Crims tore through the dimensional fabric and snatched a convection oven and espresso maker into the thought dimension. The Crim replaced these items with two slabs of grade A meat that it threw onto the kitchen floor. It did not take long for the dogs to realize the meat was there and go to work on it, forgetting about their loyal masters. The Crims nodded to each other with delight. Back to the couple.

It was time to make the move to cross over. They tore through the dimensional fabric again and stepped into our world. Two objects cannot occupy the same space at the same time, and our world would fight against the Crims' presence. Lights flickered. The TV changed channels rapidly. The fan sparked. The Crims could feel a vigorous pull on their bodies. They were being sucked back into the thought dimension. They had to act fast, because in order for them to stay two people had to be snatched away.

One Crim = One Person

The couple awoke, but it was too late. Before they could realize what was going on, they were tossed into the thought dimension. Calm once again returned to the house. Now for the next step, which would leave no one the wiser of what they had done. What would they take?

The man's cell phone lay on the coffee table alongside the woman's PDA. Perfect for the exchange. The Crims quickly snatched them up, threw them into the thought dimension, and replaced them with two shiny metallic devices with flashing red buttons.

Buttons pressed. The devices floated in the air and projected people identical in appearance to the ones just stolen.

One Compact Electronic Device = One
3-D Holographic Projector

The Crims smiled at each other and let themselves out the front door. The new parents sat down, cuddled together, and watched TV.

Mission accomplished.

For the entire next day, Louis was surrounded by family. Mr. Proof, a hardworking, handsome, professional, and generous man, greeted everyone at the door and pointed them in Louis's direction. Family members told him how worried they had been. Now that time was over and spirits were very high. Louis wanted nothing more than to partake in the fun and start his quest to get chubby again, since there was so much exquisitely prepared, home-cooked food. Eggplant parmesan. Barbecue chicken wings. Macaroni and cheese. Pasta. Sweet potatoes. Louis had cooked some of the food himself and it all tasted great, but for some strange reason no matter how much he ate, he never felt full. It was as if he could eat and eat and eat and nothing would happen. Come to think of it, he was eating for the sake of eating, because he was not even hungry. He was not able to dwell on this fact because everyone wanted his or her time with Louis.

Having a good family is great, yet not one of the people who came to the Proof house that day even came close to being Louis's most important visitor. This special visitor came on the other side of midnight and showed up both uninvited and unnoticed.

He came when darkness had fallen over the Proof house and all were asleep. The doors were locked, but this visitor had no use for doors. The security system was on, but this visitor could not be detected by any type of security system. He was none other than Galonious, who had renamed himself the Galonious Imperial Evil.

Galonious and Trife were able to remain in the thought dimension and still see this one if they needed to. Trife had become quite familiar with the Proof house during Louis's coma, a time that had come to be known as the Karmayic Interlude because of Trife's exploits with Louis's brother. During that Karmayic Interlude, Galonious had watched this house from afar, but he had never come for a visit — until now. It was time to pay much more attention to the boy who had fallen silent on the sidewalk three months earlier. Louis was important to everything good and all things otherwise — namely Galonious.

Once inside the Proof house, Galonious knew precisely what turns would lead him to the room that contained the boy who was so essential to the success of every one of his plans. Since the stairs were not in his dimension, under each foot a solid beam of luminous metal appeared, spinning and flipping into position as he climbed. When he reached the second floor, a solid path appeared for him to step on.

Galonious passed right through Louis's closed door. Louis was asleep, unaware of the entity that had entered his room. Galonious stood silently over Louis's bed and saw him as few could. He knew why Louis had remained unconscious for so long.

He knew that for a time roughly equivalent to three months here, Louis had been to the very place that he was from. Galonious was sure that Louis must have had the experience of a billion unique lives each more extraordinary than the last.

Galonious could see that the boy's raw, newborn power could soon rival his own. Louis was well into the change, but it was not complete. His organs had been engulfed with the same combination of Dark Matter and Dark Energy that composed Galonious's being. But Louis was not CE and never would be. At least not while he was here. He was something else. Galonious knew all of this because he understood the rules of the broken Alorion Treaty and the effects of the virus. Also, it did not hurt that he could see directly inside Louis. Yes, Louis soon would be so powerful that Galonious could swap spaces with him and properly enter this dimension without everything going crazy.

One Developed Louis Proof = One Galonious

Sure, there would be others like Louis, but none on the iLone side would quite equal his power. The power of the first earthbound iLone CE to return victorious from Midlandia could be immeasurable, just like the power of the first earthbound eNoli CE to do the same.

"Louis Proof. Young Mr. Proof. So *you* are the one who has been chosen . . . a sad choice if you ask me. Actually, no. I must respect you, because you did indeed return from my home. There is much to be said because of that. Bravo, Louis. Bravo! What secrets did you learn while you visited Midlandia? What did they teach you? Do they think you're ready for this? Most importantly, did you meet the Olivion? Of course you did. You completed your quest and are one of Olivion's Favorites. I know you do not remember, and by the time you do I believe it will be so very late," Galonious said to a sleeping audience of one. A mini throne built itself right underneath him with the quickness of thought; his dimension did have its advantages. He settled down and continued his one-sided conversation with Louis.

"You sure are young. Yet so powerful. You have just become, what is it? A teenager. What was the Olivion thinking to place such responsibility on you? Why children? You will probably receive an Alonis. I hope so; that will only speed things up. Nonetheless, you are still all alone, and I have an army whose numbers increase as we speak. They are taking up positions all over this town. And not to forget—I have this," Galonious said, holding a vial filled with a red liquid labeled L. PROOF, O POSITIVE. He then quickly made it disappear.

"You will not be able to understand your power in time—I move too quickly for the likes of you. Get stronger! Get as powerful as you like! I am truly in support of that, because power does not equal knowledge."

Nightmare! Louis woke from it as if waking were the only thing that could save his life.

Excited that his audience was now awake, Galonious wished that Louis could see him so that he could scare the breath out of him.

Unnoticed, Trife looked in from outside the window. Louis grabbed the covers, breathed deeply, looked around, and saw nothing. But Louis knew something was wrong. He could sense something in the room. Galonious moved close to Louis's face and looked him right in the eyes.

"Get as strong as you possibly can, as quickly as you possibly can. Good-bye, Louie P."

Had Louis heard this he would have undoubtedly been irate. He hated being called Louie.

Galonious left. He was about to walk down the steps in the hallway when something caught his attention. A smile twisted up his face as he sensed the presence of an Alonis very, very close by. He could feel its vibrations through the dimensions. He was sure it would soon be in Louis's possession; who else could it possibly be for?

Trife's upper body crept from the side of the house to meet Galonious as he appeared on the front steps.

"Yes, he will be the final part of the plan to help me properly cross over. Very clever how you found him. He is one of them—well, one of us," Galonious said to Trife.

"I have yet to be wrong," Trife replied as the rest of his body caught up.

"If you were not on point, you would not be here," Galonious barked at Trife.

They walked at a regal pace, but the streets flew past, and their locations shifted as if they were being switched like images in a View-Master. They were on Louis's street, then downtown in the business district, then in a flash surrounded by what looked to be the JunkYard JunkLot.

"Where are we with everything?" Galonious demanded. Trife thought for a second, and twenty or so compact, translucent, ultrathin plasma screens appeared and circled around the upper half of his body.

"The parental projectors are in perfect working order. Most of the children are happy with the change. Those who are not . . . well they have no one to complain to who could do anything. Regardless, none of them have a clue as to what is actually going on. We have claimed one hundred and twenty-four dimensional spaces thus far, so one hundred and seventeen of your Crims have crossed over. The other spaces are of course occupied by your generals. They have been hiding in various places since the Karmayic Interlude. We are claiming more and more spaces every day," Trife reported.

"Show me my Crims now!"

Trife ordered the screens to encircle Galonious.

Some of the Crims were in the darkest, most downtrodden parts of town, knocking over garbage cans and running amok, but most were in what seemed to be a bar, having an uproarious time. The bar was dimly lit. Some of the Crims were on a stage performing. Some were pulling boogers out of their noses. Some were drinking beer and other alcoholic beverages. Some were smoking. Some were watching TV. Some were throwing food. One pulled out a gun and pointed it at another who was cheating at cards. All were having fun. Among these rowdy patrons was a group of seven sitting quietly at a table nestled in a far corner. They were larger than the Crims and more humanlike in appearance. In fact they were fully dressed and quite stylish. They did not speak, but they had a sense of superiority about them. These generals did not participate in any of the festivities. They were too cool for such things.

They were not Crims.

They were diminished incarnations of Galonious's spirit.

They had a purpose far more important than any Crim.

They were generals.

They were ready.

Galonious looked at multiple screens and could see all of this and more. He rejoiced in the Crims' activities, but something was wrong.

"Trife, lower right-hand corner! What is that on the screen?" Galonious questioned.

"Oh . . . that is the *Late Show with David Letterman.* How did that get way down there?" Trife said as he floated the screen over so he could watch it.

"You and those TV shows, those marvelous TV shows," Galonious said as he swatted a few frivolous ideas out of the way.

"Yes, on TV I can see how well some of the thoughts that once floated here made it into that dimension. I can get so many channels, especially in this dimension. Next I am going to see if I can get the ultra-super-high-speed wireless Web in here." Trife was joking, because if he could think about it, he already had it.

"I want to speak to the entire army at once," Galonious demanded. "Open a channel."

Trife pressed a button on his control console.

"Listen, all . . ." Galonious paused and turned to Trife.

"Only *they* can hear me, right?"

"Of course."

"This is the Galonious Imperial Evil," he announced, with relish.

Who else would it be? Trife thought.

Every Crim in the city stopped to listen to the CE who had liberated them from the thought dimension.

"Soon I will be among you. The entire city will be emancipated, and we will continue to spread until everyone—CE, human, and all beings otherwise—is free. The dimensional barrier issue will soon be a thing of the past."

All the listeners cheered for Galonious—all but Trife. He had heard this speech many times over. It seemed to him that Galonious liked to hear himself talk. Trife was loyal, but he knew that Galonious had better complete his objectives soon. If Arminion—the most powerful—arrived before Galonious had accomplished his goal, Galonious would be in serious trouble. Trife decided to listen to the rest of Galonious's speech.

". . . some of you disappointed me. A few of you engaged in a conflict and were beaten by a child—a little girl, no less. Terrible, just terrible, and extremely unfortunate."

Some of the Crims in the street looked disturbed. Galonious closed the channel and gave a nod to Trife. With a thought, a new console appeared in front of Trife with one hundred twenty-four small red buttons. Three buttons flashed, and he pressed them. Three Crims were forced from the thought dimension onto a street with extreme force, their bodies stretching and snapping like rubber bands until they stood firm under the night sky. They were replacements. Trife pressed three more buttons, and three other Crims hiding on the same dark street began to scream. Their piercing cries echoed throughout the city, sending chills through anyone awake to hear them, including Louis. The screams were suddenly silenced as the

Crims exploded, their pieces sucked back into the sixth dimension—the thought dimension.

All of the Crims, including the new arrivals, went back to their festivities or into hiding.

Galonious's empire had grown immensely in three months—and its heart was still located at the JunkYard JunkLot. Though it existed in an alternate dimension, its concentrated energy seeped into this world, causing all sorts of accidents to happen. The JunkYard JunkLot had become unsafe. Whoever ran the JunkYard JunkLot had shut it down. That was a sad, sad day.

"Trife, where did you put the humans?" Galonious asked.

"Scattered all around. They pose no threat. Soon everyone specified will be replaced."

"Excellent. We will just wait. Put on the TV," Galonious said.

While watching TV, their window into every corner of the world, Galonious and Trife made plans on top of plans until it was morning. They did not have to sleep, so they kept making more plans.

Will L. Proof really be able to put a stop to all this? Do you want him to stop it?

CHAPTER EIGHT

Dear Board of Education,

This letter is verification that Louis Proof is no longer sick and never was looney tunes.

Timothy let out a laugh. *No, no, no. Now what was that principal's name? Skinner, Principal Skinner.*
Okay, no, no—Principal Hanks, he said to himself as he began to retype the letter on his laptop.

Dear Principal Hanks,

This letter is formal verification that Louis Proof has been found both physically and mentally fit to return to school. If there are any questions, you may contact me or a member of my staff at 973-555-9873.

Thank you,

That should do it, Timothy thought as he printed the letter on official Dr. Phillip Schwartz letterhead and signed the name Dr. Phillip Schwartz in indecipherable handwriting. The number was his cell phone, but he doubted the principal would check.

No way could Louis get back into school after what had happened without a letter from a doctor. Dr. Phillip Schwartz had been Timothy's name when he played that role during Louis's unconscious days and nights. He had had such fun playing a doctor. He wondered what other jobs he could try. He was about to take one on right now—the role of mailman. No, not exactly a mailman, since he had only one letter to deliver. More like a courier.

The letter was addressed to Mrs. Proof and tucked neatly in his back pocket. He could have easily put it in the mail. Better yet, he could have FedExed it for next-day delivery since it was so important. But Timothy did not know how long he would be here, so he turned everything he possibly could into an adventure.

Five a.m. Time for a special delivery. Proof house, target and destination. The world was beautiful from the rooftop sixty houses away. No, that was not enough. He leaped backward. Eighty houses away. He could barely see the house from here.

Timothy planted his feet. The sun was coming up, and no one was out. No cars. No trucks. He was alone.

Mission commence. Run five steps. Take a deep breath. The letter has to be delivered. Important. For Louis Proof, so jump off the first roof. Gentle landing.

Running again. Jump! Forward-flipping, the world spinning. Perfect landing. Timothy the outstanding.

Lightning speed. Twenty houses cleared. Sixty houses away again. Feeling the moment, leaping over three houses. Landing harder than before. He'd been heard inside that house; he felt sure of it. He was having so much fun that he didn't care. No one from Midlandia had told him to go unnoticed.

He could see the Proof house as he leaped high above the rooftops. Not far at all. He should have started miles away. He zigzagged across the street, from house to house, jumping as soon as he landed.

Arrival at the Proof house. Such a short mission. Time to put the letter in the mailbox. In one quick motion, he caught on to the support pillar of the porch, swung toward the box, kicked the lid open, and delivered the letter. Well done.

Mrs. Proof had been expecting the doctor's letter. She wasn't surprised when she found it in the mailbox early that morning. She knew she'd need it to get Louis back into school, especially after the problems Camron had caused there before he'd had to leave. She wondered if it would be hard for Louis to catch up. More importantly, she worried about how he would be treated. He'd missed only three weeks, but he had been sick for the entire summer. Brandon had told her what the kids were saying, and it pained her that people thought her son was crazy and diseased. But Louis had to continue his education as a normal child as best he could. She had set everything up for Louis to return to school today.

"Is Louis ready? Where's he at? I can't wait to see him," Brandon said after Mrs. Proof answered the front door. This would be the first time Brandon would see Louis awake since he'd stormed out of school. Brandon's mother had concocted some ridiculous reason to put him under house arrest, making him miss the party. When Brandon received the early call from Louis saying he was going to be able to return to school today, Brandon's face was attacked by a gigantic grin. One thing Brandon's mother couldn't really do was stop him from going to school.

"Sorry, Mrs. Proof. I mean, hello, how are you? Is Louis ready to leave?" Brandon said, rephrasing.

Mrs. Proof laughed at Brandon's excitement, which had made him forget his salutatory protocol. "Yes—and on time, for once," she said.

Brandon never came to Louis's house before school, but today it was a must. This was Louis's first day back, and Brandon did not want his friend to go to school alone, especially with all the rumors floating around that he had lost his mind and was dying.

Louis came up behind his mom. She smooched him on the right side of his face as he walked to the door.

"Aww, Mom, not in front of Brandon," Louis said.

Brandon would give anything to be embarrassed like that. He never understood how Louis could take it for granted. The way Brandon saw it, Louis had the greatest mom and dad. Actually, Brandon wished that he and Louis could swap mothers, though that would be a horrible thing to wish upon Louis.

But enough thinking about his terrible mother. Here was Louis awake after the entire summer and a small portion of the school year. Brandon was not an affectionate person, but he couldn't help hugging Louis and lifting him off the ground. He'd never done that before.

"Brandon, what the hell? Put me down!" Louis said with a surprised laugh that was cut short by the nudge his mother gave him for using unacceptable language. Brandon returned to his senses and quickly dropped Louis.

"Uh, yeah . . . welcome back," Brandon said, punching Louis in the shoulder.

Mrs. Proof began to laugh at the two of them.

"Remember to give that letter to the principal. I don't know what has gotten into her lately. And don't forget your cousin. Lacey, get down here! It's time to go to school. If you do not get down here, Louis and Brandon will leave you!" Mrs. Proof shouted to her niece, who quickly appeared at the front door.

"Wait a minute, come get these umbrellas. It's drizzling and it's supposed to pour." Mrs. Proof grabbed three umbrellas and handed them to the children. Louis, Lacey, and Brandon eagerly took the compact rain shields and promised not to lose them.

The day was dreary and overcast, with a murky, depressing morning fog. Last night's rain had left puddles everywhere in the streets and in the sunken sidewalk slabs. Right now there was a fine mist in the air, and the few drops of rain that hit Louis let him know that at any minute it could indeed start to pour. *Gee, what a great day to go back to school,* Louis thought.

Even though it was a lackluster day, this was no big deal, because as far as Louis was concerned, he had just been at school last week. At least that's how he felt.

"Louis, I have to tell you something. Oh, man, it's wild. Everyone thinks that you're sick and crazy," Brandon said.

"What? Why? I guess I was sick, but crazy—no way," Louis said defensively.

"Don't you remember running out of school screaming your head off? That was the last day before summer. What made you do that? Did you get nerby at age twelve?" Brandon asked.

"'Nerby'? What's that? Did you make that up? It sounds whack. You made that up."

"I didn't make it up. It means a nervous breakdown. Come on, L., think. Everyone is saying that you went nerby. Why'd you run out of school screaming?" Brandon asked while trying to avoid stepping into a puddle.

Louis recalled that horrible stretching thing, pushing Ali Brocli, running to his uncle's store, and the sickness that caused him to fall to the ground. Everything from that time was strange, but it wasn't all bad. There was also the JunkYard JunkLot. That was fun and real; Brandon could testify to that.

Once again Louis came to the conclusion that if the JunkYard JunkLot was real, then so was everything else. He wasn't crazy.

"I'm still trying to put it all together. A lot of stuff happened that I haven't had time to think about. When I know what's up, I'll tell you," Louis told Brandon. While he spoke, Lacey followed closely, thinking, *Timothy can answer everything.*

"Cool. I understand. But check this. You would have been the talk of the whole summer if not for all the weird stuff that started happening right after you got sick," Brandon said.

"What weird stuff?"

As if on cue, before Brandon could answer, a sturdy, perfectly built man dressed in flowing blue and white garments stepped into sight. He possessed a divine authority, carried an umbrella, and just happened to bump into Louis as he walked past. At that moment a barrage of vivid images developed in Louis's head.

Louis hovered. He floated. He traveled far, far away. He saw himself standing in a place unlike any other. The sounds of this place resonated in a mellifluous fidelity. The wind carried a symphony. It was something like eavesdropping on an angel's soliloquy.

It was raining, but Louis was not getting wet. The man who'd just bumped into him was here too. Without warning the man smacked Louis in an upward motion, then just as quickly punched him in a downward motion. Louis fell. But he got up with confidence to rush at the man. Louis attacked him with fighting skills he could not believe he commanded. Who would win?

Gone. Louis stood back in the street, wide awake yet dazed, longing to return to that place.

He immediately spun, expecting the man to be nowhere in sight. But he stood only a few feet behind Louis with his head down. He slowly turned to look Louis in the eyes.

"You always wondered. You always asked," the man said. Louis did not wonder about anything other than the answer to the question. He did not know the question, but something inside of him wanted to know the answer. Brandon and Lacey had no clue what was going on but didn't dare interrupt.

"Well, Louis . . . the answer is both of you. You both must win. Until next time, Louis Proof. Until next time." The man then zipped away without walking. Yes, he just moved out of sight as if he had wheels on his shoes.

"Who was that, Louis?"

"Where do you know him from?"

"He knew your name."

"What was the question?"

"I don't know. How *did* he know my name? I see these crazy things . . . everything is so weird right now," Louis said in confusion.

"Weird—you think that was weird? That dude moving away like that was nothing. Oh, man, where do I start? You know Mr. Brinkley from Eighth Street? You remember how sometimes he gets confused and starts fishing in the middle of the street, right? His dog, Mickey, got killed in a crazy car accident. He was super upset. Two days later he said, 'I'm going fishing. I'm going to catch some fish for Mickey.' And Louis, I swear he caught twelve fish right in the middle of the street. The paved and waterless street. That's not all. You know Willy Beans from Dodd Street? I saw this one for myself with my own eyes. He was crossing the street and fell into a hole that wasn't there. As soon as he fell in, he came down on the other side of the street from ten feet in the air. He was wearing his pajamas and for the next three days could only walk backward. And get this—you know all of those Japanese import games that he gets and needs special game guides for so that he can understand what he's doing? Well, he no longer needs them, 'cause he can read and speak Japanese. He can even watch bootleg, import anime without subtitles or dubs. What's up with that?

"This next one is even crazier. About a month ago it

was like the hottest day ever, so the firemen said it was okay to open one of the hydrants. Guess what came out?"

Louis thought for a minute. "Cookies-and-cream ice cream."

"How did you know? I guess your mom told you? It was incredible! It made no sense, but it happened. When the newspeople showed up, I got in the reporter's face and she interviewed me about it—I was on TV. I gave you a get-well-soon shout-out. I asked your mom to tape it. Did she show you the tape? Oh, and then there's your cousin—"

"Lacey?" Louis interjected.

"What about me?" Lacey inquired as she began to spin her umbrella.

"Yeah, you. Did she tell you she can play ball? I mean, really play. It's as if she's been genetically spliced with Michael Jordan and Allen Iverson. That one you will have to see for yourself. She is out of control on the courts. Out of control!"

"I told him, Brandon. See, Louis, I was *not* making it up!"

Ever since his trip to the JunkYard JunkLot, Louis's understanding of what was possible and what was not possible had changed. Still, he had a question about something.

"They all really think I'm crazy?"

"I told you. I stuck up for you, but there is only so much I can do. I told your mom that. Don't worry though. You know what else? People claim they have seen some weird stuff. I mean *really* weird," Brandon said with fear in his voice.

"Like what?" Louis asked.

Before Brandon could answer, Lacey cut in. "I told you, Louis. I told you. Dangerous things—the Crims."

"Yeah, and some people are acting different. Some people have—," Brandon began before being interrupted by Louis, who did not know what to make of any of this and wanted to change the subject.

"Okay, I get it. Other than all of that stuff, did I miss anything else?" Louis asked.

"Tell him about that girl. The one who went missing," Lacey suggested.

"Oh, yeah, how could I forget? A ridiculously rich girl in Cali named Cyndi. Her pops is like a billionaire, so when she disappeared, it was huge. What happened to you was local; she was national. She disappeared the day after you fell and went to the hospital. Yeah, and I'm sure that her brother found her the day after you woke up. Nobody knows what happened to her, and everyone wants to know. She's going to make her first TV appearance and do an interview on *Oprah*. Matter of fact, that's her right there." Brandon pointed to a display of magazines at a newsstand they were passing:

CYNDI VICTORIA FOUND, read *Newsweek*.
TRUE ORDEAL OR HOAX? read *Time*.

AMERICA'S LOST CHILD RETURNS HOME!
read *People*.

Every newspaper had a front-page story about her. Each pictured an attractive girl who Louis guessed was fifteen or sixteen years old. *Oh, man.* Louis grabbed his head. It was that same feeling he had had when he heard the name Vivionya. He knew this girl, but he didn't know her. How could he know a girl from the other end of the country?

Louis knew Cyndi's face; he even knew what her voice sounded like.

Louis saw himself falling through the sky at a tremendous speed. Where was he falling from? Where was he? More importantly, what would happen when he broke the surface of the water that he was speeding toward? The crash would have killed anyone else on impact, but he survived the splash. He was sinking. He tried to get back to the surface, but he was being pulled down. They were horrific. They were not mermen but merbeasts. They were aquatic eNoli CE, to be exact, but as far as Louis was concerned they were demons. They all seemed to have humanoid but gray-blue scaled torsos, with oversize arms and extended fingers. Their fingers had to be over ten inches long. The lower portions were webbed, and the upper portions were like claws that were fully functional as fingers and not hindered by the webbing. Some of them had lower bodies similar to squids. Some had lower bodies similar to dolphins or whales. Others had lower bodies like eels. They were varied but all equally terrifying. They surrounded Louis, laughing and taking swipes at him. One jerked him, using all of its force to throw Louis through the water to get hit by one of its cohorts. Another grabbed Louis by the shoulders, rushed him to the surface, and leaped sixty yards out of the water. It screamed in Louis's face and shook him from side to side. At least Louis was able to breathe. At the apex of its jump it threw Louis down violently.

Louis's vision, or whatever it was, sped up. He was underwater again. Suddenly patterns of light shone from below, and his captors started fleeing. Louis floated among the lights until once again he was snatched from behind and swiftly carried to the surface.

"Climb into the boat. I can't get you up there. You hear me? Climb into the boat!" his captor shouted.

Louis did as he was told and lay on his back in a boat that sure as heck hadn't been there when he'd been taken under. He coughed and spat out water. He opened his eyes. There was only one person standing over him. It was Cyndi Victoria.

She had saved him . . .
She would betray him . . .

"Louis, you paying attention to me? Huh?" Brandon asked.

"Huh?" Louis said, returning to the world right here, right now.

"Seems like you're a million miles away. Listen, man! Listen to what I am telling you about that girl. This is the crazy part—they have what happened to her on tape, and they still don't know what happened to her. She was in her brother's house and fell over like she was sick. They have it all on surveillance footage—rich people with crazy security, they tape everything. Her brother leaves the room to get help, and I swear, something really fast comes into the room—ghost, spirit, whatever—and picks her up and carries her away. It was freaky and spooky; no one believed it was real. But no one saw her, not her moms, pops, or brother, until the day after you woke up. People talk about her like she is the second coming or something—everyone wants to know what happened. All she did was go missing and now she's crazy famous. That's the trend, rich girls famous for nothing."

That's some story, Louis thought. But he still didn't know what to make of the visions he was having. He would keep them to himself. He didn't need an extra reason for anyone to look at him as if he were—what was that stupid word?—nerby.

"Yeah, Louis, crazy stuff was going on over here and in Cali—" Brandon was interrupted by a young girl's voice dancing in the air. "Hello, Brandon!"

Louis could see Brimley, Chim-Chim, Huntley, and Olivia—four nearly bear-size Rottweilers—led by one little girl wearing full-blown rain gear. She had on a powder-blue rain coat with matching rain hat, and powder-blue rain boots with white soles.

The girl was nine-year-old Jolee Jenkins, and she had a big crush on Brandon. When she got within a few feet of them, she raised her left hand and barked a command: "Stop, guys! Stop!" Her stern words brought the huge dogs to a complete halt. One might think this was odd, but the truth is that there was nothing unusual about it. As far as the dogs were concerned, Jolee was their older, upright-walking sister whom they loved.

"Hey, Louis, they let you back on the streets? Looking good—lost some weight, huh? But Brandon is still my favorite. Helllooooo, Brandon. What's going on, Brandon?" Jolee said.

Before Brandon could answer, Louis realized that one thing was strange. "Jolee, why are you walking the dogs instead of going to school?" he asked.

"School? My mom said that I don't have to go anymore if I don't want to," Jolee answered.

"Why not? What did your dad say?" Louis asked.

"He and my mom agree, so no more school for Jolee. All of a sudden they are so cool. They used to always fuss; now they just sit on the couch, watch TV, and let me do what I want," Jolee said with true happiness.

Louis looked around the streets. Kids were riding

brand-new bikes through puddles and walking in the opposite direction of school. Louis caught a glimpse of a kid driving a brand-new Hummer H3, blasting 50 Cent while his parents sat in the backseat, smiling.

"What's going on? How come no one's making these kids go to school? Was that a kid driving that car?" Louis asked.

"See? Really weird stuff is going on. That dude we just saw, Jolee, those kids. Weird is the new norm, and no one cares to do anything about it. You don't know the half," Brandon said as he, Lacey, and Louis opened their umbrellas.

The storm had just begun.

⇒ CHAPTER NINE ⇐

Everyone thinks you're crazy. Brandon's words bounced around in Louis's head as he stood outside his new eighth-grade classroom. After receiving the official Dr. Schwartz letter, Principal Hanks had told Louis to wait at his classroom door so that she could reintroduce him to his class. Louis waited, angling himself so he could see into the room but remain unseen.

Three things struck Louis as new. First, there was Mrs. Grant. She would now be his teacher, and she was great. Her husband taught music at the school, and they were among the most loved teachers here. Second, there were many new kids; where had they come from? Louis had never been in a class this large before. New names to learn, and maybe even new friends—but not if they thought he was crazy and sick. Finally, a snake sat coiled in a big sealed aquarium. Louis liked snakes and hoped that he would be able to feed it. Cool!

"Okay, Louis, are you ready? You have a lot of new classmates. One of the neighboring schools closed, and many of those students came here. Your new teacher will bring you up to speed. You've always been a good student, so you shouldn't have any problems. You don't know how good it is that you're back," said Principal Hanks with a hint of disdain in her voice—almost as if she meant the exact opposite of what she was saying. Her tone made Louis feel that something was wrong.

Principal Hanks opened the door and introduced him to the class.

He now stood at the front of the room, feeling like a new kid, waiting for his moment of introductory display to be over. Mrs. Grant greeted him with real enthusiasm. Brandon, of course, cheered, but others were quite a different story. Mostly he was met with funny looks and suspicious glances. He even saw some kids whispering to one another. Not at all the welcome he'd expected. What had happened to the kids who'd cheered him when he raced his cars? To the ones who used to run to him for help? To the kids who used to like him? Didn't they know he was still the same chubby L. Proof, but in new packaging? It was going to be a long first day back.

Lunchtime. The rain had begun to clear up, so Louis grabbed his lunch and went outside with Brandon. The playground hadn't changed much. The jungle gym was still the main attraction. Third graders swung effortlessly back and forth on the monkey bars, jiggling any raindrops to the ground. Kids on the swings tried to see who could touch the sky with their feet first; others stood in line to go down the three multicolored wavy slides; the younger ones ran on the rope bridge that connected the two separate parts of the jungle gym. All of the children looked happy. Louis was not.

Louis was finding it hard to shake the weird looks being thrown his way. He could hear his name whispered around the playground. Even the kids on the jungle gym, who seemed oblivious to the world, looked up when word spread that he was around. He was on everyone's lips. He noticed one girl, though, on the other side of the playground, who smiled at him. He smiled back. *Cool,* he thought. Then one of her friends whispered in her ear. She gave Louis a funny look and turned away.

Louis was startled by a sound that seemed to smack him in the back of his head—a mix of roaring buses and the cheering of children who were boarding them.

"Brandon, where are those kids off to?" Louis asked.

"Ever since school started this year, they've been going on lunchtime field trips to McDonald's every day. What's even funnier is that their teachers suggested it, and the food is free. The manager said so. Those kids are going to get fat. Maybe you should start going," Brandon said with a laugh.

"That's ridiculous."

"What's even bigger than that is that the fifth-grade class is on a trip to Disneyland with their parents and teachers. The kids came up with the idea, and the parents made it happen in like two days. They've been gone ever since. They had to find a substitute teacher for the ones who couldn't go. The second grade goes on daily trips to toy stores," Brandon said.

"Stop playing! They call me crazy? If I were, I'd fit right in," Louis said, noticing some first graders running around in Halloween costumes.

"See, I told you things are nuts around here, but only in certain classes and with certain kids. It's as if there are some parents and teachers who don't care anymore. I heard that the principal called some parents about the stuff their kids were doing. The parents said if that's what my kid wants to do, let him. The principal couldn't stand up to all of those parents. You should have heard the arguments. Then all of a sudden Principal Hanks didn't care anymore either. Now she agrees to whatever those kids want. I wish my mother would let me do what I wanted."

"How long has this been going on?" Louis asked.

"Like I said, since school started—but things have been weird for a while now. Wait a minute, Louis." A new girl was calling Brandon over.

As Brandon walked away, Louis overheard some kids talking. They were bragging about their parents buying them everything they wanted. One kid said he didn't even have to ask anymore. His mom had given him a platinum Visa with his name on it. He then pulled it out to show everyone. Another pulled out an American Express blue and said it didn't have a limit. Then they began to talk about all the video games they were going to buy.

No kid should have that amount of see-through-plastic purchasing power, Louis thought. One kid said he couldn't understand what was up with his parents. After he saw how all of his friends' parents were acting, he'd told his mom to buy him a new bike and some video games. He also told her that he was calling the shots from now on. To his surprise, unlike his friends' parents, his mother did not succumb to his demands. All he got was a smack and a month's worth of punishment. Apparently not all of the adults had lost their minds. Louis thought of his family. No way was his mother acting any differently. The fact that she'd popped him when he'd sworn this morning was proof of that. If his dad were different, he would not be working so much.

One by one these kids went silent when they noticed Louis. The kid whose mom had smacked him said he didn't know Louis but didn't have a problem with him. The others gave him a dirty look. Then they all walked away. Weird, Louis thought, but what wasn't nowadays?

Brandon was returning, looking at something in his hand.

"She's having a party in a couple of days and of course invited me. You need to do something about the way people are thinking about you so that you can get invited to these things. You used to be the first person invited, back in the day," Brandon said, holding out the invitation.

"Back in the day? It was three months ago. It's like

yesterday to me. I don't want to go to some new girl's party anyway. Who is she? I don't know her," Louis said, trying to sound as though he didn't care.

"Well, everyone is going. I stood up for you—I asked if you could come—but she said something odd," Brandon said.

"What did she say?" Louis asked.

"She said that her parents told her not to invite you. What's really funny is that this is only your first day back. How did they know you'd be back? I guess word just spread around somehow; like I said, you were once the talk of the town. Don't worry, it's no big deal. I'm sure all of this will blow over and you'll be on top again. I hope."

Louis had no rebuttal. He felt horrible inside and out. Eating lunch did not even soothe him. He still had no appetite, but the food tasted good, so he ate it anyway. He felt nothing. No satisfaction. All the baleful looks and under-the-breath comments made him angry. How could everyone flip-flop on him?

So what if I look different? he thought. He was thin and in shape. Wasn't life supposed to be better for thin and attractive people?

Why is life so messed up now?

Then he knew what he could do. He would show them.

The bell rang, and Louis returned to class. School was no longer fun; it was something he had to get through.

The only thing good about the day was that there was no Ali Brocli. But Louis was positive he would pop up sooner or later. That would just be great — Ali Brocli on top of all of this.

At last the school day was over and he was walking home with Brandon and Lacey. Lacey could tell that her cousin hadn't had a good day. He wasn't speaking, and he was no fun. Fun was Louis's trademark, and Lacey missed it. She wished there were something she could do to make him feel better.

"The sun's out! Louis, can we stop by the basketball courts before we go home? They should be clear now. I want to show you something that will cheer you up!" Lacey asked.

"Oh yeah, let's go to the basketball courts," Brandon said before Louis could answer.

Louis was not in the mood. He wanted to talk to his uncle Albert about the plan he'd come up with at lunch. But Brandon and Lacey both insisted, so he agreed.

Big steel topless cage more than ten feet high; three full basketball courts housed inside. Late September and they were all filled. A lot of kids were there with their parents, as if it were a weekend.

These parents should be at work, Louis thought.

"Look, Dad! Watch me take this shot," one kid said to his dad.

"That's great, Danny. Take some more," the dad said.

"Thanks for taking me here instead of school. No more

school for me and no more work for you," a different kid said to his mom.

"Of course, Kenny. We're going to spend so much time together—me, you, and your dad. No one is going to school or work again," the mother said.

This is weird—in both a good and bad way, Louis thought. His attention was diverted by loud cheering as Lacey entered the courts. Lacey waved her right hand and smiled.

"What's up, Short Moon Rising?" some people yelled.

"Just come to play—I got next!" Lacey answered as she instructed Louis and Brandon to take seats. She sat on the ground in her school clothes and began to do stretches. After a few minutes, she was able to go in.

"Check," Lacey said as she grabbed the ball.

Lacey ran the point. The point was run by Lacey. Lacey ran the other team into the ground. This was no "oh, it's a cute little girl who thinks she can play; let's let her win." She did the other team dirty. Crossovers. No-look passes. Three-point shots. Fadeaways. Alley-oops. This was "sorry about breaking your ankles—I am going to climb up your back so I can dunk." The beating that she served the other team was simply horrific. And the crowd loved it. Louis could say nothing. He couldn't help but feel good when Lacey dunked on a kid who had given him a funny look.

"Your cousin is going to get a Nike contract," Brandon said with excitement.

Once again the impossible was possible—it was happening nonstop every day, it seemed. Lacey told no lies. She really could play ball. Little Lacey Proof, Lordess of the Courts. Nothing was the same. It was definitely time to see Uncle Albert.

I've never walked with a superstar before, Louis thought jokingly as they strolled toward the bus stop. It felt no different. She was still Lacey and he was still Louis. She was a new Lacey like he was a new Louis, but the same. Maybe he should be different. That's what he was thinking. That's what he wanted to talk to his uncle about.

Uncle Albert's store was in the same location, but his uncle was not there anymore. He worked in an office downtown, and Louis and the crew had to get there by bus. Three once-empty seats were now occupied by three kids without guardians.

"You know that your uncle has become really successful, right?" Brandon began.

"Yeah, I know," Louis said.

"You know how he got that way?"

"He chased a dream?" Louis answered.

"Yes and no. Really, he's successful because he followed the John Tesh Method of Success," Brandon said.

"The what?" Louis asked.

"The John Tesh Method of Success!"

"Who's John Tesh?"

By this time everyone on the bus was looking at them. Those who knew who John Tesh was wondered why these kids would be talking about him.

"Way back in the day, John Tesh used to host *Entertainment Tonight*, and he left to start a music career. When he released his first album, he was nominated for a Grammy. Guess who won in his category?" Brandon asked.

Louis had no idea. This was all new to him.

"He did. You know why? I know you don't know why, so I'll tell you. He was the only person nominated in his category 'cause he created a new form of music," Brandon said as if it was the wisest thing anyone had ever blurted out.

"So what does that mean?" Louis questioned.

"It's simple. If you're the first to do something, even if you're whack, you can still win, 'cause you are the first and in a category all by yourself. Someone may come after you and be better, but you were the first. The John Tesh Method of Success! I made that up all by myself."

Louis did not know what that had to do with anything. Maybe Brandon was referring to the fact that his uncle had been the first to make his special kind of unique merchandise, but Louis still had one more question. "Is his music any good?" Louis inquired.

"I don't know. I've never heard it. You know my life's soundtrack is hip-hop. Still, he has a Grammy. You don't. I don't either, so don't feel bad."

Louis didn't know about the credibility of that story, but at least Brandon was always fun to be around. You never knew what he would do or say. He followed his own rules of logic.

Lacey was falling asleep on Louis's arm. He leaned back and noticed their reflection in the window, the three of them. What interested Louis was that he was sitting next to the person who seemed to be his only friend in the entire world. Everyone seemed to have turned their backs on him, but Brandon had not. Sure, Lacey was his friend and he loved her, but she was his cousin. She was like his little sister. In many ways she had no choice but to support him. Brandon could have been like everyone else. But Brandon was ride or die.

Friends. If you have them, love them. Don't be a dunce and take them for granted.

They soon reached their destination: a gleaming mirrored skyscraper that reflected all things big and small. On the opposite side of the building you could see a distorted reflection of the elaborate skyline of the even bigger city that lay just across the water. Uncle Albert had a whole floor in this beautiful building.

What a move up, Louis thought. In the past three

months, Uncle Albert's company had gone public and expanded. Uncle Albert was in the process of building fifteen new stores in different states. The Internet and mail orders were seriously booming. And that was only the beginning. He was going to diversify.

Elevator open. Button pressed. Twenty-fourth floor. Enter Unlimited Dream LLC. Louis, Brandon, and Lacey marveled at the large glass doors that led into the reception area. Every unique knob and handle his uncle had designed, from the X-Men to the Miami Heat, was artfully framed and displayed on the wall. The expensive bling-bling sets were in the star position behind the receptionist's desk in an exquisite—but bulletproof—case.

The receptionist was on a wireless headset, taking calls and directing them to the proper recipients. Louis could tell she was skilled at her job; she was quite cordial. The marvelous office, the receptionist . . . this all looked big-time and expensive. It was a lot to take in. It had only really been him and his uncle before. He had never had to wait for someone to tell him if he could see his uncle.

"Are you young ones trying to get some free samples?" the receptionist asked, digging through her top desk drawer.

"Young ones? I will have you know I am a bona fide teenager. You need to realize who you are in the presence of and show me some more love than that," Brandon said.

"Chill, Brandon. We're here to see Albert Proof," Louis said to the receptionist.

"Do you have an appointment?" she asked, trying to hold back a laugh.

"Babe, you're the receptionist. You tell us if we have an appointment. You should know," Brandon said. Brandon was right—that appointment question was a way to blow off people.

"No. Do I need one?" Louis pushed Brandon to the side.

"Everyone needs an appointment to see the CEO," the receptionist said. "But you're Louis, aren't you? I thought you were bigger. Mr. Proof says none of us would have jobs if it weren't for you. He says that something you said gave him the idea for all of this. So thank you, Louis." The receptionist rose to shake Louis's hand, then led them to Uncle Albert's office. "Your uncle makes you out to be a truly special child."

At least someone was enthusiastic about his arrival—and a gorgeous woman at that.

"Louis, Lacey, Brandon! How did you get here? I wish I'd known you were coming. I would have made plans, but this is as much your office as it is mine. Louis, how was your first day of school?" Uncle Albert asked.

Louis looked around, dumbfounded. Huge HDTV, super THX sound system, ultra-advanced smartphone, and the newest Mac laptop. And under the Mac? That was no regular desk. Italian marble—three iced-out sets housed in its hollow face and covered by glass. That had to be worth $150,000, easily. When did all of this happen? Uncle Albert had said that Louis was the most important part of his business. That had to be a lie. Miss three months and his uncle Albert becomes a mogul.

Truly, nothing was as Louis remembered it. All at once Louis voiced everything that was bothering him. "Uncle Albert, nothing is the same . . . everyone has lost their minds . . . no one knows me. I never used to know it, but I was the man. Now I have to wonder what people are saying about me. Forget them! I want to go shopping. I am going to get some new clothes and some ice. I am going to shine all over the place. I will be the man again and then diss all the people who fronted on me. Let's see how they like it!"

Lacey and Albert looked at Louis as though he were crazy. Brandon's expression and head nods, however, made it look as if he felt it was a possible plan.

"That's what I said—if you get some serious ice I want to floss too. You have to let me hold it sometime," Brandon said.

Disapprovingly, Lacey nudged Brandon in the side.

"Louis, you must be out of your mind. I've never heard you talk like that. Don't you ever let the way someone treats you take you off your game. You're going to allow one day of school and something that you had no control over change you? People depend on you because of who you are. Where would I be without your help? Did you forget that it was you who had a huge part in starting all of this, that you were the only one who supported me from the beginning? Who was the only one to stick up for the kids against that bully at your school? When your brother used to get into jams, who helped him out?" said Uncle Albert.

"Yeah," Lacey and Brandon agreed in unison.

Uncle Albert paused. He was about to take a small, thin, rectangular book with Louis's full name stamped in platinum on it out of his top desk drawer, but he decided not to. This was not the time. Maybe later.

He continued. "I won't go into it, but your brother can tell you—what goes around comes around. You start acting funny, being underhanded, dissing people and trying to be someone you're not, and you will suffer consequences. Stick to your original blueprint and you will be fine. People didn't like you because you had money or because of your clothes—they liked you because you were you. You still are you. Kids and adults get confused. If they cannot see you for who you are, just consider yourself lucky to be able to find out who's real in your life and who's not."

As always, his uncle put things into perspective.

Some things can change and still stay the same.

⇛ CHAPTER TEN ⇚

Saturday. It was the day of the big party that Brandon had mentioned. Today everyone from school would be there—everyone except Louis. Actually, Louis had learned that a lot of students were having parties. He was not invited to a single one. He would have asked his parents if he could have a party, but who would he give invitations to? For the first time, he knew what it meant to be left out. It felt:

Something like a vacant sensation.
Something like they put his face in the dirt.
Something like a feeling that can only be summed up by a song only John Mayer could write.
Were they having fun?
Were they dancing?
Were they laughing?
Were they playing games?
Oh, just forget it . . .

As Louis stretched out on his bed, he heard the phone ring. He didn't think twice about it until his mother walked in and handed the phone to him.

"Hello?" he said.

"Louis! Louis!" said an excited voice from the other end of the country.

"Angela! It's you! I'm sorry that I broke my promise. Where are you? I miss you. Are you back? Please tell me you're back. Are we still friends?"

"What, are you crazy? Of course we are. I've been so busy I haven't had a chance to call—have you checked your e-mails at all? I sent you one almost every day. Some were real short, but I was always thinking about you. I was upset when you didn't show up, but then I found out why. I knew something really had to be up for you to break a promise. It wasn't your fault. I mean, you were in a coma!" Angela said.

Great! Louis's other best friend was still in his corner.

"My bad. I have not even turned on my computer. So many things have been going on. I just woke up during the middle of this week, and I've already been back to school. I'll check them now. No, forget that. I have you on the phone now. Tell me everything!"

Angela told him about her new life as a young actress, new roles, and most importantly how much she missed her friend.

Why should Louis feel bad about being left out of the parties? He was talking to his girl Angela—young Ms. Angela Azay Conner—soon-to-be-superstar.

✦ ✦ ✦

Monday marked the top of a new school week when the teacher said, "Class, we have a new student. This is . . . well, why don't I let him introduce himself?"

The kid seemed to look through all of the students until he found Louis. He stared directly at him.

"My name is Timothy . . . Timothy Collins, and I just moved here from, ah . . . Brooklyn," Timothy said.

Timothy? Wait! Was this the Timothy Lacey had mentioned? Louis could tell immediately that there was something unearthly about him. Brandon noticed nothing of the sort—to him he was just another regular kid with blond hair and fair skin, dressed a bit oddly.

Collins . . . Collins is after Carlton, Brandon thought before he shouted, "Yes! Yes! You have to sit in front of me. Derrick, you're cool, but I don't have to smell your horrible flatulent discharges anymore." Brandon grabbed an extra desk from the back of the class. He then instructed everyone in his row to move their desks back one space. He put the new desk in the empty place where his used to be and told Timothy to have a seat. He did all of this while describing specific times when one of Derrick's silent bombers had made Brandon want to run out of the classroom to buy a new nose. It would not happen again. His prayers had been answered.

"Thank you, Brandon," Mrs. Grant said half seriously and half jokingly. Brandon gave her a nod and the biggest smile of the school year so far. Timothy thought about what he was supposed to do. He thanked Brandon.

"No, Collins, thank you!" Brandon said patting him on the back. Timothy quickly turned to Louis. Louis looked away, wondering if this was Lacey's Timothy or just another person to think Louis was sick and crazy. How far had the rumors spread?

Class resumed as they began studying algebra.

"Algebra—that's with all of the letters. Why do we need letters in math? It makes no sense," a student blurted out.

"Yeah, why do we need to know math with letters?" another questioned in support.

Louis felt like he was in an after-school special.

"Great! We are going to do algebra. Nothing could be better," Timothy said with deep interest.

"Glad to see you're enthusiastic about math, Timothy," Mrs. Grant said.

"Of course I am. Algebra is your most used form of math. It is imbedded in your informational decoding process," Timothy said.

Everyone but Louis looked at Timothy as though he were crazy. Louis was thrown off by what he said, but he knew what it felt like to be thought of as crazy. He would never look at anyone that way—even if they were.

"What I mean to say is that you use algebra more than any other kind of math," Timothy said.

"What are you talking about, new kid? Are you crazy, like Proof over there?" Tyler Reynolds said as all the others laughed.

Louis, enraged, stood up. Tyler Reynolds used to be cool with Louis, and Louis's mother even gave him rides home from school from time to time. There was no loyalty. Tyler had finally said out loud what everyone was whispering. Before Louis could utter a word in his defense, Timothy spoke.

"Joke. Was that a joke? You have jokes. I am supposed to laugh, right? Ha ha." Timothy looked deeply into Tyler's eyes.

It was as if Tyler and Timothy were the only ones in the classroom. Tyler couldn't explain why, but he felt he had to apologize. "Sorry, Louis. I know that you're not crazy. That was wrong. I take it back," Tyler said genuinely.

"Thanks," Louis said, surprised but not feeling much better.

Timothy nodded at Louis, then turned his attention to the teacher.

"Mrs. Grant, may I continue? I want to explain algebra," Timothy said.

"Please do, but there will be no talk of anyone being crazy, even if you do plan to apologize after you say it. Go ahead, Timothy. Take the front of the class, if you like."

Timothy was elated to be taking on the role of teacher. This had not been on his list of things to do, but he was happy to give it a whirl. As Timothy stood in front of the class, everyone could sense that he was not a typical kid. He was a new type of strange. Not bad strange, but strange nonetheless. His clothes fit him perfectly, as if tailored for his thirteen-year-old body. He was regal—a young prince secretly on leave from his royal duties to have a breath of fun. Or maybe some kind of genius. Either way, his entire demeanor demanded that the class pay attention. Even the class pet, Hank the snake, raised his head, shook his tail, and took notice of Timothy. There would be no more jokes.

"Well, class," Timothy said, smiling. He really *had* become the teacher. "How many of you play video games?"

The entire class, male and female, raised their hands with enthusiasm.

"That, my friends, is algebra. Well, a form of it anyway. How many of you have to come up with plans to get your parents to agree with what you want?"

"Well, it's a lot easier now!" one kid said. Everyone laughed, but they still listened closely to Timothy.

"With every decision that you make to get out of a jam when you play video games, you use algebra. Every time you have to figure out what will work to get your parents to do what you want, you are using algebra. Often you will have one or two parts of the equation. Most times you will have the answer, which may be that you want a new video-game system. One of the variables may be that you have sixty dollars saved up.

$$x + \$60 \text{ of your saved money} = \text{the newest PlayStation system}$$

Now you have to figure out what x is. X is what you must do to convince your parents to give you the rest of the money to buy the system. X may be straight As. I truly hope not, but x may be begging. X may be promising to do chores for three months. X may not even deal with your parents at all. X may be finding a job or asking another family member for money. Algebra is your ability to take everything you know about yourself, your parents, other relatives, the gaming market, and maybe even recent studies in support of video games that will aid you in solving for x. Studying algebra will sharpen your skills to do this. You have to take the info that you have and use it to figure out what the missing bits of information equal. On a grander scale, algebra is not really about numbers at all. It is about thinking. The better you get at algebra, the better you will become at figuring out how to get what you want. It is quite simple, actually," Timothy explained with utter confidence.

No one said anything at first, but soon a voice chimed in. "So you're saying that algebra will help me figure out how I can get my mom to get a pool?"

"Yes. You may have to be an algebra whiz, but yes, it will help," Timothy said.

"So algebra will help me beat everyone in Halo when I play online?" another kid asked.

"Oh, yes, in a big way. The algebraic process is used whenever strategy and tactics are involved. Like in sports or even war—for real or in video games. It is all problem solving and deductive reasoning. Algebra. Geometry. Trigonometry. Part of the higher thought processes. Use them well, wisely, and responsibly!"

Any other kid who tried this might have been picked on, but Timothy was different. He commanded respect.

"Thank you, Timothy. That was wonderful, and I can tell that your classmates enjoyed the lesson," Mrs. Grant said.

"Well, I am here to help," Timothy said to the entire class, yet speaking directly to Louis.

Timothy took his seat. Everyone was into algebra for the rest of the class, using real-life situations for problems. It was the first time math had ever been fun.

The bell rang, and all the kids went out to lunch. Louis did his best not to think about his situation, but he couldn't help it. Even though Tyler had apologized to him and class had been fun, everyone was avoiding him. Even the new kid was having a way better experience in school than he was. On top of all that . . . still no joy from eating lunch.

Louis sat under a tree and began to think. It really *was* an algebraic equation: He needed to figure out what plus his new self would equal his old life, or maybe even a better one. He had not been thinking for long before he heard a familiar voice.

"Louis, Louis Proof."

Louis turned his head around and saw nothing.

Then, from the opposite side of the tree, Timothy rolled into sight.

"Timothy? Do you know a girl named Lacey Proof?"

"Yes. Your cousin Lacey, she is a smart girl. I did tell her to tell you about me. I am very pleased to meet you. A pleasure indeed. I trust you are feeling better. Of course you are. How do you like your new self? Cool, huh?" Timothy asked.

"Cool? Hell no! When I was chubby, I had a lot of friends and no problems. Now look at me—I'm skinny and wondering how I can get my friends back. But I don't care. I'm still the same. It'll be fine. My uncle said so. He always knows what's up."

Everything that Louis's cousin had told him swam to the forefront of his thoughts—the Crims, the work he had to do, and his being sick. Most importantly, the visions he'd been having. "Forget about me. What have you been telling my cousin? Who are you?" Louis asked.

"Nothing but the truth. She is close to you. Have you ever known her to lie?"

Louis didn't respond. "Louis, we have to get started. No time for beating around the bush. Louis, you are special. You know it. But before I continue, there is something you must do. Something simple you must say to your mother."

Timothy spoke almost silently to him. Louis heard and remembered every word, as if his mind had a special place for what he was hearing.

"Do this, then find me. We will talk more about important things, but not until you complete this task," Timothy said to Louis in a normal voice. "Louis, wait — one more thing."

"What is it?"

"Louis, you made it back. You returned from Midlandia without failing. You have no idea what that means or what you have been through. After that, I know you are ready for whatever may lie in front of you. You just need a bit of help. That is why I am here."

"Timothy, I want to know —," Louis said before being cut off.

"No, Louis. I told you. Do what I said, and then we will talk," Timothy said.

Timothy looked like a kid. He moved like a kid. His voice sounded like a kid's. But just as before, he spoke with a directness and wisdom beyond his years. Louis believed every word as he got up to head for class.

Timothy was one to be taken seriously.

CHAPTER ELEVEN

Lacey raced upstairs and left Louis behind. She had matters to tend to that involved dolls and an imaginary championship WNBA game. Louis, scared and excited, walked toward the kitchen to find his mother. As Louis paced through the living room he could hear Oprah's voice say, "Cyndi Victoria Chase on today's *Oprah*." Louis stopped because he recognized that name. Hearing it had the same effect pulling on his ear might to get his attention. He wouldn't be able to watch Cyndi, because once again Louis was gone.

They were in a boat floating atop the bluest water imaginable. It glistened as if it had diamonds floating on its surface.

"Do you have any idea where we should be going?" Louis asked Cyndi. She didn't but wouldn't look unknowledgeable because she would be robbed of the chance to answer. The perfectly tranquil water became turbulent as a huge blue metallic structure pierced its surface. This behemoth object spat out glowing spheres that circled it like satellites or, better yet, moons.

Cyndi, Louis, and the boat they were in were on top of

the huge object, but not for long. It was not flat, and the boat began to slide down the side until it was in the water once again. This object was bigger than a skyscraper and towered over them. It was a floating city. It was made of what seemed to be lustrous metals that were engraved with patterns of brilliant light. This light was so stunning that it could turn the darkest, most horrific patch of hell into a celebration of heaven's wonder. Whatever this object was, it was bigger than anything Louis or Cyndi had ever seen, here or where they were from. It was a true phenomenon, and it had become nearly motionless after it completed its ascension from the depths of the water.

So small. So miniscule. Louis and Cyndi were the equivalent of the buttons on a video-game controller in comparison to this marvel. They looked at it, then at each other. One of the lights left its orbit and transformed into an elegant airship that zipped down to the two kids. Without hesitation Louis and Cyndi got in and were flown high in the sky to a large docking bay that had not been open before now.

The panels of a colossal door parted ways. A man walked out with his hands behind his back and greeted them.

"Hello, Cyndi. Hello, Louis. I did not expect you both to get here at the same time. I'm DiVarion Alonis, which of course would make me the Alonis Maker . . ."

+ + +

Louis abruptly returned to the present as his mom called out: "Hey, Louis. How was school and where's your cousin?" This vision had been unlike the others because it was more vivid and complete. This time he hadn't been watching himself; he'd been himself. He'd been with Cyndi and he knew her. But what did it all mean? Louis forgot all about the TV show. He had to have his questions answered. He had to do what Timothy had told him to in order to get more information.

"Lacey's upstairs. Uh . . . Mom, I met this kid. He's kind of strange but real smart. He's new at school. Oh, and by the way, school still sucks. Anyway, he told me to tell you something. It's kind of crazy," Louis said apprehensively.

Mrs. Proof grew very serious.

"What did he say, Louis? What did he say?"

"Calm down, Mom. I don't think it's that important. All he told me to tell you was, 'I believe you are holding something for Olivion's Favorite.'"

Mrs. Proof looked as if she had seen a ghost walk across her kitchen to have a drink of water. She dropped the pot she had been holding, but even its loud metallic thud did not draw her attention. She had had no idea when, but she had always been certain that she would hear these words from her youngest son. That was what had made her trust the doctor when he had told her that she had to take Louis home . . . a moment that had been written a little more than thirteen years ago, before Louis was born.

It was late, and the last time anyone would see Louis's grandmother. Mrs. Proof was sleeping and Mr. Proof was working. Louis's mom was gently awakened by a caring visitor, her mother. "Carol, wake up. I have to give you this," she said. She held a lovely piece of jewelry that sparkled and refracted the light, a blue stone set in a circular platinum base.

Still half asleep, with Louis unborn but listening in his mother's tummy, Mrs. Proof sat up. "Oh my goodness, that is so beautiful. I couldn't — "

"Shush. No words. This is for you. I will not hear anything else about it," Louis's grandmother said as she placed it around her daughter's neck. Mrs. Proof felt as if life's weight had been removed from her shoulders as soon as the jewelry touched her skin. Before she could take in the entire feeling, she heard her mother speak.

"Listen carefully. This is very important. One of your children will come to you and say . . ."

Today was the day Mrs. Proof had been told about.

"I knew it was you. When you were sick and everything started going crazy, I knew it was you! I always knew it was you! We love your brother, but he never was responsible. He is darn near a genius, but we let him be a dreamer, and that is what he is, a marvelous dreamer—and that's what got him into trouble. You were always helping someone, and you were always generous." She had tears in her eyes. Louis did not know how to react.

"I don't know what this will do, but I'm supposed to give it to you." She removed the medallion that Louis had always noticed from around her neck and gave it to her son.

As soon at it touched his hand, it began to shake and cast a brilliant blue light. The entire room lit up as if it were a planetarium doing a show on the most marvelous shades of blue. Royal blue. Ice blue. Silhouette blue. Marvelous blue. Any kind of blue you could think of sparkled and shimmered in the kitchen. The light grew with intensity until the kitchen no longer seemed to exist. It was as if they were being bathed in a multi-blue-colored ocean. Marvelous—the Marvelous Effect.

The medallion floated in the center of the kitchen. Soon it began to circle Louis's body like a flying dog, sniffing him out. Louis was the right one. Glimmering and glistening radiantly, the medallion rose slowly to Louis's face as if to say hello. After a few silent hellos and what's-ups, this pure, powerful light backed up sharply, then flew into Louis's body.

Nothing. All of that, then nothing. The kitchen looked the way it did on any other afternoon. The light show had been great, but Louis felt no different. Now, however, the medallion that had once elegantly graced his mom's neck hung majestically around his, as if it had always been meant to rest there—only it was larger, without any hint that it had ever been worn by a woman.

Louis admired his new hardware. Really, really cool. In a small way, he had managed to get iced-out, just as he'd wanted to after his first day of school. The only difference was that this was in a good way and for a good reason—out of necessity, not to ego-trip or flaunt.

Louis's eyes rose from the medallion to look at his mother for some sort of clue about what had just happened. He would not find the mother that he had known so long, because she had changed. Her almond skin was no longer perfect and tight; it had started to loosen and sag. The area under her eyes had darkened noticeably. She was the same mom, but different: She had lost her youth.

"Well, it was good while it lasted," Mrs. Proof said, without a trace of regret or disappointment. She had always seemed ageless, and now he knew why. Whatever was in the medallion had kept her young. Louis had taken her youth. Louis wondered if his mother would have stayed young and beautiful forever if he had not claimed the medallion.

"Mom, are you okay?"

"Yes. Are you?"

"Yeah, fine. I don't feel any different. Who gave you that?"

"Your grandmother told me to give it to the person

who asked about Olivion's Favorite. That person is going to be important in a huge battle. She also told me that I would never have to worry about that person's well-being. Louis, that person is you."

"Mom, I have to find the guy who told me what to say to you. He said he would give me important information. I have to find him."

"Well, I guess you'd better get going," Mrs. Proof said. But Louis had one more question. "Mom, what's Olivion's Favorite?"

"I don't know. I think you need to ask the person you're going to see."

Louis looked at his aged mother. She, like him, had changed but remained the same. He kissed her cheek, gave her a hug, then hurried out the door.

Louis did not know where to look for Timothy, but he figured he would start at school. Never one to go to school after hours, he nevertheless made his way toward the building that he had left not too long ago. The light, his mom's aging, and the medallion that swung carelessly around his neck — he thought about it all. Had he not had so much on his mind, he might have noticed how fast he was running.

Timothy was near the school, standing in the middle of the street, looking up in wonder at a magnificent cloud formation.

"I did what you said!" Louis yelled.

"No need to shout," Timothy said, appearing next to Louis instantly. Such feats no longer amazed Louis.

"I did what you said and my mom gave me her medallion and she—"

"And a light flew into you," Timothy said.

"Yeah! Then the worst thing happened: She aged. What was that light?"

"That light and the object hanging around your neck are one and the same and are an Alonis. Can you believe it? You are the owner of an amazing Alonis right here on Earth!"

"Alonis? The Alonises are made by DiVarion on that huge floating whatever it is. Cyndi and I . . . ," Louis said, straining to remember.

"Yes, Louis. It is coming back. You are remembering your time on Midlandia. It will all come back, and when it does, everything will be clear. Get ready, because those memories will be beyond anything you can imagine. I am sure you are beginning to understand that.

"If you remember DiVarion, you may recognize that the Alonis you hold now is the mirror of the one you must have been given while on Midlandia. You do not remember how special it is to have one. I have always wanted one. I hope that after all of this is done I will be worthy to have my own. The Alonis will be whatever you want it to be—as a matter of fact *you* will define *it*—but its primary purpose is to serve as your protection and perfect form of attack," Timothy said.

"Protection? Form of attack? Sorry, Tim, I have no idea what you're talking about."

"The Alonis is a piece of Midlandia, which is where I come from. It is a piece of its technology and energy. The Alonis makes you nearly impervious to attack. In its current form, it can never be taken from you. You have to decide if you want to release it. And even if that happens, you will still be powerful. The Alonis aids you; it does not make you."

"Well, what does it do?" Louis asked.

"I told you, it is your protection and form of attack. Louis, you are very important—you are a true first. Not the only, but the first and most important, for us iLone anyway," Timothy said. This made no sense to Louis. He was the second child of Mr. and Mrs. Proof, and the only thing he was ever first in was car racing, and the last time he'd tried that he'd lost.

"There is a war, and you have seen it," Timothy said.

"I haven't seen any war. I was sick for three months," Louis said.

"No, Louis, you were never sick. You were actually better than you have ever been. Nor were you ever in a coma. Your earthborn body only appeared to be in one while you were on Midlandia. I will explain it to you like this: If you were to take an X-ray of your body, you would not see anything normal. That is why I could not let you stay in a hospital. You would have caused a panic. Everything in your body has been either replaced with or fused with Dark Matter and Dark Energy. This is the effect of an ancient virus, which is a dormant part of your and every other human's genetic code. It is like no other virus and is undetectable," Timothy explained.

"So I *am* sick. No virus is good," Louis said, genuinely scared.

"No, Louis, I said you are physically *better than you have ever been*. Physically better than anyone else. The virus that I told you about is Celestial and the only one of its kind. What it does is the exact opposite of what you would expect. Instead of damaging and breaking down your body, it builds it up: Your heart and liver will never fail; your vision will be forever perfect. The virus has destroyed every impurity and toxin that you have allowed to enter your body by eating harmful foods, drinking impure liquids, and breathing tainted air. Physically, you are nearly pure and as close to perfection as a human can come. In fact, you are much like me and those from where this virus originated."

"I'm like you? What does that mean? What the heck are you? You say these things like I should know all this. What am I now?"

Timothy paused and thought hard for a moment. Louis was one of Olivion's Favorites, but he was not exactly a Celestial Entity. What should he be called?

"Louis, I am from Midlandia, a place at the center of all there is. As far as what I am, this may serve as the best definition . . ."

Timothy looked once to the left and to the right, then up and down. He was sure no one was around or watching—not in this dimension at least. Timioosiyon was his true name, and he now assumed his true form: a fierce, angelic, glowing darkness highlighted with magnificent bolts of bluish electricity. His form was almost beyond comprehension. It was the equivalent of meeting infinity in person. This blackness that was Timioosiyon continued forever and ever. Louis felt as if he were looking at a never-ending night sky during a Celestial storm. He had no idea that darkness could be so marvelously stunning.

The darkness drew itself into a brilliant point about the size of a pebble and began to shine and expand into one of Timothy's human forms.

"Louis—," Timothy began.

"Timothy. You made a mistake—you're not yourself," Louis informed him. Timothy had become a sixteen- or seventeen-year-old version of himself, taller with longer blond hair.

"I have got to get a handle on that. Sometimes it is hard to keep track of who I am supposed to be," Timothy said with a laugh, as he grew younger and shorter.

He continued. "The truth. No lies. No gimmicks. The truth is that you are like me, like a Celestial Entity—like, but not the same. Yes, that is it! That is what you are! A CLE: Celestial-like Entity. Close to perfection, but not quite. You are still human, so you are fallen," Timothy said while doing an extremely precise dance to a song being blasted by a distant car radio.

He spoke in a lighthearted tone, but the words fell upon Louis with grave seriousness.

"I'm fallen? What do you mean by that?" Louis grabbed Timothy's arm to stop his laughable movements.

"Yes. Not just you; everyone here is. That's why your bodies eventually fail. Anyway, remember that 'perfect' does not mean good and 'fallen' does not mean evil." Timothy stopped his crazy dance and regained his composure.

"What do you mean?" Louis asked.

"Those beings who pose a threat are perfect, but far from good. As fallen and imperfect as you are, you are good, and I hope you always will be. One thing about you humans—CLE or not—is that you are unpredictable. What fun! Evil will always be in your heart. Never forget that and let it take you over," Timothy said to Louis.

This tale was unreal, yet it was the most real thing Louis had ever heard in his life. He'd seen proof that he was something like Timothy when he'd pulled that pin out of his arm the day he woke up.

"All of this is happening because the Alorion Treaty was broken when the eNoli Arminion, Galonious, and Trife left Midlandia to attack Earth. For each eNoli CE who leaves Midlandia, a child such as yourself will change, just as you have to gain the potential to stand up to oppose that eNoli. And the same will happen for each iLone like myself who leaves. The Olivion made it so that there would be a balance if either the eNoli or iLone violated the treaty. You know all of this, but you have forgotten. You had to go through so much to even return from Midlandia. When you do remember, you will be something no one has seen before," Timothy explained.

Kind of ironic, Louis thought. Here he was on a great fall day. The sun was still out, allowing for a nice mild climate. Children could be heard playing in the distance. The fallen leaves were grand oranges, yellows, and reds. The tree shadows created silhouettes of movement on the ground. All of this was under attack. And it was his responsibility to defend it. Okay, he was with it. He was all for the adventure. He figured it would probably be like a real-life video game, but he felt he should be prepared.

"Tell me about those people you mentioned," said Louis.

"You learned all of that and far more important information on Midlandia, and you came back like a newborn baby. It is the only way, though. Oh well, it is like this . . .

"I will try to put this as simply as possible. Trife: smart eNoli CE who left Midlandia. Galonious: smart and powerful eNoli CE who left Midlandia. Arminion: mega-extraordinarily smart and mega-extraordinarily powerful eNoli CE who left Midlandia and had to have been the one to orchestrate the entire escape. Got it?"

"Powerful dudes?" Louis questioned.

"Powerful dudes!" Timothy answered.

"That's what's up?" Louis asked.

"That is what is up!" Timothy replied.

"Cool! Tell me about the Alonis. Alonis technology. If I am supposed to fight and break these guys apart, how does it work?"

"Okay! Okay! The Alonis! I am glad that we can talk about that now. This will be fun. Step back and give me some room so I can show you a few things." Louis took a few steps back, eager to see what Timothy wanted to demonstrate.

"Louis, you ready?"

"Yeah!"

"You sure?"

"Yeah! I said yeah!"

Timothy powered up and began to glow a vibrant blue. The light not only surrounded his body but also seemed to rise like illuminated smoke from a fire. He rushed at Louis with a barrage of fierce, highly skilled attacks:

Lively left hooks.
Raw right hooks.
Ugly uppercuts.
Bold body blows.
Planned power jabs with both hands.
Rough roundhouse kicks from both directions.

Each should have sent Louis flying, but none came close to harming him. Every punch and kick was blocked and stopped dead in its tracks by Louis's Alonis. It hummed as it created a compact hexagon of glowing blue light that deflected each blow and prevented it from reaching Louis. At the moment of impact each blue panel would quickly begin to fade, letting out brilliant, hot-white sparks, which fell and bounced before vanishing.

Timothy continued to attack with blinding fury and force. He came at Louis from every angle and was stopped at every attempt. The Alonis never once let Timothy close to the very special boy it was meant to protect. Louis was bulletproof and endured all of this without a single ounce of harm.

Timothy let out a laugh and stopped. "AMAZING! SUPERB!"

Louis was beyond words. This was way better than any video game or anything he had ever experienced. He'd never felt so much adrenaline. Racing cars, roller coasters—nothing came close.

"That was serious . . . so serious!" Louis finally said, beaming with excitement.

"I hope that means you are impressed. That was the Alonis in action, and it is a perfect form of positive creation meant to assist you. You just witnessed it defending you on autopilot. When the time is right, the Alonis will aid you by taking on the form most suited to who you are as a person. This form will aid you in your fight and also fulfill your truest wishes, needs, and desires. Knowing you, whatever form it takes will be extremely powerful."

Aid him in his fight?
Suddenly this was not a game.

Galonious sat on his throne with his marvelous sword at his side while he observed Louis's conversation with Timothy on the mega-huge thought-dimension screen hovering in front of him. He loved the way the image was so crisp and so clean. He felt like he was right there. Galonious cherished technology. He chose to keep his distance; if he got too close to either Timothy or Louis, he would be sensed. For now, it was best for him to go unnoticed. He would strike very soon.

"Trife, look how they aid him. How dare they get involved? Are they not supposed to be bound by laws? Their aid will only serve to hurt them. Had they not gotten involved, who knows how long it would have taken Louis to figure out what was going on and claim his powers. I would be stuck here indefinitely, so I must applaud them." Galonious clapped sarcastically.

Trife sat at the side of Galonious but positioned his upper body in front of the screen. The screen was so big that Trife did not obstruct the view. He conjured up a remote and rewound to the part when Timothy told Louis the eNoli were here to attack Earth.

"And did you hear what they said about us? We are

here to attack Earth? What do you suppose he meant by that? Midlandia forbid!"

"We are only here to make this place fun! Fun! Fun! Fun! Everyone will be free to be who they really are. Who the heck does not want to have fun 24/7? I know I do. Trife, I know you do! What about you guys? Do you?" Galonious shouted to the thousands of Crims scurrying around the Galonion empire.

The Crims cheered to welcome the fun!

"See. There you have it. I cannot wait. All of the people on this grand planet are going to be so very happy when they are freed," Galonious said.

"Galonious, I truly agree—but did you notice how they named Louis? Celestial-like Entity—a CLE. *Like us* is not *us*. Pitiful! I knew he would not be pure; how will he be able to face you in battle?" Trife asked.

"Battle? He will be of no concern once he is stuck in this dimension. Fighting gets us nowhere; that is why we left Midlandia. But if it comes to that, don't forget this gift," Galonious said, holding up a vial half-full with red liquid. "Who knows? It may turn the tide if things go wrong."

Trife rewound the image to where Timothy told Louis that he was impervious to attack.

"They will be so surprised that we can kill him easily," Trife said.

"We have nothing to worry about," Galonious agreed before changing the channel. He had developed an affinity for television. Then it struck him.

"Trife! Trife! What is wrong with you? How could you overlook this?"

"What are you talking about, Galonious? I do not miss much of anything, as you well know," Trife said as he dodged an idea that nearly hit him between the eyes.

"Well, you missed this. Since two of us are here, what does that mean?" Galonious asked.

"That we can get things done twice as fast?" Trife answered.

"True, but think: There are two of *us*, so . . ."

"Of course! Two iLone CLE are here!" Trife said.

"Yes, but think: What did we just see? Who was with Louis?" Galonious asked excitedly.

"Louis . . . and one of—yes, so if one of the iLone is here, there is a CLE who will be on our side! Of course! Those are the laws—the unbreakable laws! That child has the ability to accomplish one of our main goals," Trife shouted with glee. He had no idea how he had missed that. That was really unlike him.

"Yes. I want you to find the eNoli CLE as soon as you can," Galonious commanded.

Trife was eager to get started. It was such a pleasure for him to think about all of the Horribly Marvelous possibilities.

An eNoli CLE on their side.
Who could it possibly be?

⇒ CHAPTER TWELVE ⇐

It seemed to always be there like a noose around Louis's neck or a raspy snake constantly hissing in his ear or a scratchy two-times-thick burlap coat draped over his bare skin. It was annoying. It was haunting. It was the vacuum of confusion created by the loss of three months. Louis tried to piece together the fragmented visions of his time spent on Midlandia (wherever that was), Timothy's words, the fact that he was a CLE, and the reality of the Alonis into a skeleton key that could unlock everything. In spite of his grand effort he failed at being a locksmith.

Louis arrived at school the next day to find Brandon sitting behind Derrick Carlton once again. Apparently Timothy was gone. Timothy had mentioned something about not having much time here and having other places to go.

Timothy dropped all of that information on me yesterday and then just bounced? He's going to abandon me like that? Just great! What the heck? Who else am I going to ask about what's going on? Louis thought to himself as that frustratingly annoying feeling of confusion festered.

This day was uneventful—until lunchtime's Final Brocli Incident . . .

Out of nowhere Louis was violently pushed. He could feel the concrete and loose gravel he had fallen on, but to his surprise there was no pain. He looked around to see the until-recently-absent Ali Brocli standing over him. Apparently the Alonis did not see the need to protect Louis in this situation.

Louis breathed deeply, then pressed his palms to the ground and raised himself up effortlessly. Unexpectedly, he felt energized, as if the hit had jump-started something inside of him. He did not understand this new feeling, but he went with it as he heard Ali shout, "Who told your sick ass to come back? You're no longer the man here. This is my school. You're nothing, Proof. Nothing. Now I'm going to kick your ass. I'm going to beat you down right here in front of everyone."

The kids on the playground had begun to form a perimeter around Ali and Louis. This would surely be horrible, yet entertaining. No one wanted to miss it.

"What's going on here?" Brandon shouted as he forced his way through the crowd. He had no idea that Ali was back.

"Oh, man! Louis, what happened?" he said; then he saw Ali. Brandon was about to get Louis out of there, but Louis waved him off.

Louis said nothing. He brushed off his clothes, tilted his head slightly to the left, and looked Ali in the eyes. This would be the last time Ali would ever terrorize anyone at school. Louis would stick up for everyone, because he loved all of his friends, even if they did not love him back.

"Bring it, you punk!" Louis growled.

With those words it was on. Ali rushed at Louis, but before he could get to him, Louis delivered a back-handed slap to his face. Then he immediately made a fist and landed a mighty, lightning-quick blow to Ali's jaw.

"Whoa. You slapped him like a . . . ," said a voice in the distance.

Without hesitation or much thought Louis spun his nemesis around and jumped to put Ali into a half nelson. All of this surprised the heck out of Ali, and he fell to the ground. Louis stood behind Ali and held him in a sleeper hold, about to knock him out. The kids on the playground could not believe that the formerly chubby Louis had the hulking mass known as Ali Brocli at his mercy. Louis kept Ali in a neck lock and spoke calmly to him.

"If you ever act badly toward any kid, whether they're one of my friends or not, I'll beat you so bad they'll put me in maximum security prison. That hit was nothing. You feel that blood in your mouth? How many teeth did I knock loose?"

He squeezed Ali's neck tighter and continued. "I'll say this one time. You can try to punk another kid, but I'll not let you. It's because of your garbage attitude that no one likes you. You're the reason why you have no friends. I don't know why the hell you are so bad, but anyone can change. Don't be such a jerk. Do you hear me? You can have friends. I'll be your friend. The way I see it, you only have one choice—well, two. You try to make friends or you don't try to make friends. Either way you will never bother anyone else. You feel that pain in your jaw? That's nothing! I could beat your life backward, shake it apart, then rip it into a billion pieces. You think I just look different? I am different! Could the old Louis do this to you? Huh, could I?"

Ali tried to say something, but couldn't.

"What's that? You trying to say something, homie?"

The kids mouths hung open as if their jaws were broken in awe of how Louis handled Ali, but they had no idea what was being said between them. Louis let Ali go so that he could speak. Ali sat on the ground and did not dare look up.

"Okay, okay, you win. You're right. Louis, you're right. I'm going to try to change," said Ali.

Ali stood and faced Louis. Louis extended his hand to him. Louis did not know if Ali would try to pull something. The kids were frozen in blocks of suspense. Ali grabbed Louis's hand. As soon as he did, Louis squeezed it hard and looked Ali deep in the eyes. Ali had heard the words and felt the pain of the punch, but until now he hadn't known how serious the situation was.

As Louis continued to grip Ali's hand, Ali began to feel a tingle in his entire body. Ali let go of Louis's hand and clutched his chest as if he were having a heart attack. Silence grabbed the students as Ali fell to the ground and lay motionless. Louis stood over him in horrified confusion. He had no idea what to do. Was he dead? What had he done?

"You killed him! You killed him! You're a crazy psycho!" one of the kids who was not even close to the action cried out.

Great! Terrific! Fantastic! Even when I try to help, it all turns to crap, Louis thought.

Brandon ran up to Louis and tapped him on the shoulder.

"We got to get out of here. Come on!" Louis did not know what to do, so Brandon's suggestion was as good as any. He followed Brandon away from the school yard and out to the street.

"Proof, what did you do to him? You had him all choked up! Whoa! I know some other guys you can do that to. You do that to all of the bad guys around here and life will be a lot easier for everyone. I have never seen you that pissed off before," Brandon said as they headed for home.

"Brandon, shut up! I think he's dead. He probably had an aneurysm!" Louis shouted.

"Aw, man, quit with the drama. Dead or not, don't you know what self-defense is? It's not your fault. I mean, you know how big he is! He probably had a heart attack. People are getting them younger and younger. Shame about Big Pun. Moment of silence . . . He pushed your ass to the ground and said he was going to kick it. You were just defending yourself. If he's dead, good riddance. He deserved it after what he was doing to everyone. I would think people'd be happy you did that. I know I am. Even if he is dead, you won't go to prison. Probably just to juvi. Don't worry. After that they won't *dare* mess with you. Hey, wait—what am I saying? You don't have anything to worry about. Doesn't your uncle know Johnny Cochran? Oh man, I forgot that great man passed away. Moment of silence . . . Damn, maybe you do have something to worry about. Anyway, how'd you do that?"

Louis had no words. He had never been so scared in his life. It all seemed like a murky, sinking dream that would not release him from its grip. He thought he was supposed to be good. He really believed that. How could that be true if his schoolmate was dead and it was all his fault?

As they marched quickly down the streets, they did not know it, but they had visitors. Galonious had seen Louis on the playground and thought this was the perfect time to bait him into a fight.

On ragged rooftops, twenty or so Crims watched the two walking home. Silent and unseen, one by one they jumped onto the street. Their horrific ungodly moves were quick and jerky. Then the center Crim stepped forward and let out a horrid war cry.

Louis and Brandon quickly glanced at each other. "What was that?" They looked back and saw all twenty Crims.

"See I told you . . . weird things. Out of here!" Brandon yelled.

The boys were already about fifty yards in the lead when they began to run. The Crims gave chase.

Scared as he was, Louis did not fear for himself; he figured the Alonis would protect him. He only feared for his friend. "Brandon, turn left down Glenwood Ave," Louis commanded. Brandon turned, expecting Louis to follow.

Louis stopped running to stand strong as L. Proof — Young CLE.

"You want to fight? Come on, but leave my friend out of this! You filthy beasts!" Louis shouted at the Crims. He knew he could handle this as he felt a powerful surge that jittered and vibrated every portion of his being. It was a true rush, something that was greater than he was and that he could not control. Powerful.

Galonious observed this from every angle possible on multiple high-definition screens from the thought dimension.

"That is what I am talking about, young sir. You tell them. We need you strong! I can feel it!" Galonious yelled, admiring the young teen's courageous fighting spirit. He even stood up and cheered.

The Crims advanced toward Louis like F-18 fighter jets flying in arrowhead formation.

Did you see that?
The Crims advanced toward Louis like F-18
fighter jets flying in arrowhead formation.
*Hold up —before all of this my life used
to be so Marvelously Lovely.
Now calamity chases me
and misery loves me.
Fine, Crims want it raw,
they can get it raw—
'cause I'm from Marvelous World,
East Orange, NJ!*

*The Crims are now:
forty feet away
thirty feet away
twenty feet away
It's totally okay!*

'Cause Louis Proof—LP—
a regular Celestial Emergency
Will easily show 'em what it truly
means to be Young CLE
But is LP ready to rock? Is he ready to rock?
Hell, yeah, he's ready!

What? Those Crims couldn't even be trusted to start a fight properly. Louis had to look up in the sky as they jumped right over his head. While still airborne one of them turned and smiled at Louis with a demonic grin — an expression that told Louis all he needed to know: They were after Brandon.

Louis froze as he watched Brandon trying to get away. The Crims ran faster now, leaving Brandon no chance of escape. They were upon him. The Crim that had taunted Louis scooped up Brandon with both arms before leaping high in the air. It spun him around so it could scream wildly in his face.

Brandon looked like he was about to cry. Instead he screamed right back at the Crim, who let out a dreadful laugh worse than a scream as it saw that Brandon had wet his pants.

Then this horrific Crim did the most gruesome thing that Louis had ever seen: It pulled Brandon through its body as though it were Silly Putty stretching beyond the breaking point. Sick. Urghhh!

"What the hell is this? Help! Louis, you better come get me!" Brandon yelled.

Instead of turning around, the Crim grew a face out of the back of its head and gave Louis a look so evil that it made him want to vomit all over the street.

Meanwhile, its cohorts were getting farther and farther from Louis in leaps and bounds. They would have been totally out of sight had they not stopped.

Louis feared the worst. They had stopped to eat Brandon. Brandon was yelling at the top of his lungs, and no one could save him. No one but Louis.

Once again, Louis felt as he had on the playground such a short time ago. He was being tested and he had to react. This time his friend was in danger, and he had to silence the threat. But what would he do? He would never make it to Brandon in time. Brandon would be eaten in less than ten seconds. But he was determined. It was live-to-tell until Cocytus melts. He would not let Brandon's demise come at the hands of these blasted Crims.

Timothy was right. The world was all algebra, and he could see the equation in his head:

Speed + Grand Force = Royal Butt-Whipping
for the Crims and a Safe Brandon.

Louis wished he were as fast as his race cars, with the speed and driving skills of Dale Earnhardt Jr. and the force of a roller coaster.

Silent, pure wishes.

Wishes granted. So it began. Louis succumbed to an urge to swing the Alonis medallion completely around his neck. Alonis activated—not for defense, but for action. Unknowingly Louis had determined its form. He charged toward Brandon and a thin vertical beam of light appeared at Louis's back. It grew horizontally and moved with him. Four wheels, two doors, a hood, a trunk, two bumpers, and side panels flew out of the light. As he raced forward, a seat scooped him up; car parts effortlessly and quickly interlocked around him and built the car of his dreams. Louis was now completely inside a high-tech, nearly see-through car. Mini-sized for a kid.

Crescent moon steering wheel with the slip-free grip. Seat belts strapped him in. The windshield—ultra-Celestial digital. Plasma screens with every view of the street—ultra-Celestial digital. A visor hung overhead just like the one he used to control his race cars—ultra-Celestial digital. Totally illuminated car of impenetrable ultratheoretic etheric titanium and light that radiated an electric-blue hue.

"Get 'em, Louis! Get 'em!" Galonious cheered, pumping his fists. With Louis's power increasing at a fantastic rate, Galonious would be able to finalize his plan that night.

Louis raced toward his friend. Cars on the street were a blur. The buildings all seemed to run together. The engine had to be a V60. Sound barrier nearly broken.

Wait a minute? What do you think?
Maybe he should stop?
Maybe he should go.
Maybe it's Celestial Pole Position Grand

Turismo Fury.
The Crims have picked the wrong kids to
mess with!
Louis chase after Brandon like a bullet.
He's got a Celestial-like complex, bless it
and shoot it.

The car ejected Louis forward, sending him flying directly at the Crim who was holding Brandon. Before Louis could make contact, the car disassembled and returned to the light at his back.

Grabbing Brandon with one hand, Louis made a fist with the other that tore through the air, sending the Crim flying. It landed forty yards away, bouncing violently on the pavement, leaving scrapings of its flesh after each impact.

Now that Brandon was free, Louis pushed him to the side so that he could bring harm to each and every Crim in sight. One rushed boldly toward Louis. Louis raised his foot and kicked the Crim in the side of its face, breaking its jaw. Moving so fast that Brandon could not see his hand, Louis punched the other side of its face in midair, forcing it into a brick building, which shattered, creating an imprint of the Crim's twitching body.

The Crims were no fools and would fight no more. They scurried away. They'd rather deal with Galonious later than with Louis here and now.

"See, you mess with me, you mess with my boy L.

Proof. Remember that. L—that's short for Louis—L. Proof. He killed someone today. A big fat dude! You can't come after me and not deal with him!" Brandon shouted, not the least bit embarrassed that he had wet his pants.

Louis had destroyed the threat and Brandon was safe—for now, at least. Brandon yelled all sorts of congratulatory remarks to Louis. Louis heard none of it. He was emotionally torn between awe and disgust, standing still and silent. His new abilities had allowed him to save his friend, yet just minutes ago he had left Ali Brocli dead in the playground. He really had no idea who he was anymore. One thing was for sure, he endured it all:

The destruction of his former life . . .
　　Nothing was the same—ask anybody.

Brandon's attack . . .
　　Louis was the reason it had happened. Who was next? His mother? His dad? Lacey?

Whatever had happened on Midlandia . . .
　　Would he ever really remember?

His absent brother . . .
　　When would he be back? Louis sure missed him.

His theft of his mother's youth . . .
　　Had he shortened her life?

The sideways comments from his former friends . . .

How could they just abandon him like that? He'd even stood up for the ungrateful whelps after they turned on him.

Something was way worse than all of that: He had killed Ali Brocli.

How could Louis have done that?
No matter what, Ali did not deserve to die.
Louis would surely have to go to prison.
Louis was a murderer.

Louis looked at Brandon dancing in the street, ranting about what bad guys to go after next in Louis's phenomenal car. Normally this sight of Brandon would have made him laugh, but he felt no joy. Sorrow and pain were welling up with an intensity that he had not known was possible. Tears streamed down his face. He wiped them away but they just kept coming.

"Proof, you crying? Why you crying? Look what you did! You crying? You saved my life! What, you mad they didn't eat me? That's why you crying? Man, I can't mess with you!"

Louis just walked away. He wasn't thinking about Brandon. He wasn't thinking about anything. Uncle Albert had said to stick to the blueprint, and this was not the blueprint. He left Brandon there and headed home.

He never would have done that had he seen the lone Crim stalking along the side of a building. Louis was out of sight, and Brandon was alone. Brandon heard a thump behind him. Before he could say a word, the Crim charged at him and they both disappeared.

Just as they exited, a Crim and a clueless parent crossed over from the thought dimension.

The Crim took Brandon's space.

The parent had been sucked out of the thought dimension, reclaiming the dimensional space, which Brandon's kidnapper had stolen from her weeks ago.

The Crim knew that it would only be able to occupy Brandon's space for a short time. So what? While it was here it would try to have a Crim-load of fun. It tore down the street. The parent stood in an abandoned building — not too far from the location she had been snatched from. She screamed for reentry to the thought dimension. She felt as if she'd been torn from the greatest dream or resuscitated after dying and visiting heaven. She did not want to be here anymore, not even for her children.

Maybe you have it all wrong.

Maybe being in the thought dimension is not as bad as it seems.

Tough luck.

Life can really suck sometimes.

⋙ CHAPTER THIRTEEN ⋘

On the way home Louis finally calmed down. He had to sneak into the house to avoid any questions from his mother about why he was home so soon. When he got to his room, the familiar sight of his racetrack, cars, and video games offered no comfort. Actually, it reminded him of what had just happened. He had to get as far away from all of this as he possibly could, and his means of doing this was hidden behind his desk. He did not want to run away—just get away for the day. He knew where to go. It was not close, and he usually went with his family, but he could get there by himself.

He had about six thousand dollars saved. He never spent money irresponsibly, and he had been working with his uncle since the store had opened. He was being paid under the table, of course, but his uncle paid him by the hour as he would any other employee. He also had most of the holiday and birthday money ever given to him. For the first time he was going to use his money for something other than buying a video game or RC car part. He was about to have a real taste of the true freedom of economic empowerment. This money was going to carry him to the place where he most wanted to be.

Louis moved his desk away from the far wall of his room. Behind it was a hidden compartment he was sure only he knew of. He hit a panel at the base of the floor and the wood popped out. Reaching into the dark, vacant space of the wall, he pulled out a black fireproof box. He opened this box and his heart sank. He saw no green and white dead presidents, but rather the yellow tint of a sealed envelope, addressed to him in his brother's handwriting. He opened it to find a letter and a thousand dollars. His feelings about the missing money disappeared as he began to read what his brother had written to him.

Louis,

I do not know what to say other than the fact that I messed up and you have helped me out once again. Even if I treated you bad in ways I hate to think about, you still had my back. This time I really did it and have to leave. If I do not, I don't know how bad things would get. It's like something has been chasing me and I just cannot shake it. I even think I can see it sometimes. Everywhere I go, it seems bad things happen. I will not blame anything I did on anyone but myself because in the end the truth is that it all started with me. I am not good like you. I can only hope that after this I will be able to be.

It's funny, but you are my little brother and you have always been the responsible one. You did your share of bad kid things, but nothing like I have done. You were even able to help me when you were unconscious. One thing that I asked Mom and Dad was that I be able to explain everything to you. Well, I will not do it in this letter. I will do that face-to-face. Any other way would be cowardly. On top of that, I am trying to redeem myself. Maybe I will have done this by the time I get home. Maybe I'll write all about it. It's one hell of a story.

While I'm gone, I don't want you to feel bad or change who you are. Don't let anyone get you down. I have heard the rumors that people have been saying. I am sure they will be floating around when you get better. I wish circumstances had allowed me to stand by your side during it all, but I will only be able to support you in spirit.

If my word is worth anything to you anymore, I will say one last thing to you. Do you know what karma is? I know you do because you're a smart kid. Well, I think I totally messed mine up. Remember, whatever you do will come back to you. Don't ever get yourself into a situation where you cannot fix your karma. Learn from my mistakes. Stay good. I promise I will pay you back as soon as I can. I will be back.

Your Brother,
Camron.

PS: I didn't take most of the money without leaving you something as collateral. I left you my prized possession, and it's worth a few grand. I am sure you have grown, but it'll probably be too big. Who knows? Look in the far left side of your closet. I know Dad keeps all of his old clothes in there, so you wouldn't find this if I hadn't told you. Enjoy it-it's yours until I get back and repay you.

Man oh man, when is that guy going to get it together? Louis thought. He wasn't angry that the majority of his money was gone. His brother was always getting into some type of trouble. Never this extensive, but Louis was just happy that he could help him like always. What else was money for? Still from now on Louis was putting his money into the bank. There would be no more surprises like this.

Louis did feel a bit better after reading the letter, and he smiled. He remembered his brother's boisterous but lovable personality. He remembered all of the crazy, funny stories Camron used to tell. He remembered how Camron was so well liked. Louis remembered the love.

But when Louis thought about his own predicament, he felt angry that his brother was not there to help him. He balled up the letter and threw it against the wall.

Camron, come back! I'm always helping you. For once I need you! Louis thought.

But Camron would not come, and if he did, what could he realistically do for his beloved little brother in this situation? Nothing. And Louis still had to get away.

Louis didn't know what Camron had done, but he was pretty sure that his brother hadn't killed anyone or taken their mother's youth.

Stay good? Who is the good one now? Who has worse karma now? Louis thought as he stood to make his way to the closet to find what his brother had left him.

Suits. Shirts. Ties. Louis was still pissed off as he pushed them all to the side. The last item to the left hung lonely in a black garment bag. That had to be it. Louis calmed down as he laid it carefully on his bed and slowly opened the bag. It was indeed his brother's prized possession, the coolest thing he'd ever owned: a marvelous black leather jacket. This was no regular jacket, but something that could have been listed as ultra-exclusive in *GQ*. It was made of the finest Italian leather and worth several thousand dollars. Louis picked it up and carefully placed it on the back of the chair at his desk. He had always wanted this jacket, but it would stay there for now.

Money. He needed money. He took some money from the safe box and tucked it into his pocket. This would be more than enough for him to reach his destination and return. He thought of leaving the Alonis behind too. As far as he knew, that was not possible, and deep down, no matter how he felt, he really didn't want to.

Louis heard his mom downstairs. Nothing she could say would console him, and if he had killed somebody, he could not look her in the eyes. He had nothing to say to her. He just had to leave. The cops would be here soon. He was sure of it.

He had rushed downstairs and was almost out the door when he remembered something. "Mom, you have to pick Lacey up from school!" Lacey had not gotten out of school yet and would surely be looking for someone to take her home.

Then he was out of the door and gone.

Alone. Not even the Crim that had snatched him up stuck around as Brandon found himself in a place that was like an echo of where he had been just a few moments ago. He could still see the corner store where he used to buy oatmeal cream pies. Across from that was the dog pound and the traffic light with the faulty caution signal. Everything was familiar but covered in a distorting haze. Brandon felt as if he were waking from a dream and the world around him had not decided to make itself real yet.

What did appear with no distortion were black rectangles, which rained down, blocking his view of the city and sky. The rectangles fit together to build a tunnel of darkness with no apparent entrance or exit.

Brandon felt as if he were floating in a horrific ocean with twenty-foot-high waves of fear, terror, and dread. He stayed as quiet as possible in an effort to not bring attention to himself just in case he was no longer alone.

All of the metal rectangles had fallen into place. Brandon was enclosed in silence. He looked as far down the tunnel as he could, and his eyes saw no break in the darkness. He was sure that sooner or later something would pay him a visit. He was correct, because in the distance he could see the glimmer of two frozen blue-gray eyes focused on him from far down the dark, lonely tunnel. He could tell that they were getting closer and closer and were part of something found in the most horrifying nightmares.

Humanoid snakecrabspiderlike abomination. It walked the earth, being too vile for hell. It slithered toward Brandon, but not on the ground. It moved through the center of the tunnel as if it were floating. As it neared, Brandon could see that it was indeed suspended in the air, but not entirely. Its rear portion walked along the tunnel in a spiral pattern, like a finger in the bottom of a cup circling toward the mouth. It walked on the ground, then made its way over to the side until it was upside down on the ceiling, then onto the other side until it was on the ground again. Without pause it continued forward while its upper body remained perfectly centered in the tunnel.

Brandon could not move. His back was against a cold, black, metallic wall that hadn't been there a minute ago. Trife silently hovered directly before Brandon, perched like a venomous snake about to strike. Everything about this eNoli CE had been intensified and revamped so that it was synonymous with intimidation and terror. Trife was in rare form.

Trife wasn't the only thing Brandon had to worry about. Dozens of Crims now clung to and crawled along the walls, cackling and howling. Trife suddenly reached out and clutched Brandon's throat, effortlessly lifting him off of the ground. Trife laughed and swayed back and forth, showing off his catch. The Crims clapped and cheered. Trife motioned for quiet, then stopped to show Brandon feigned concern.

"Want to call out but cannot? Well, let me," Trife said as he dropped Brandon to the ground. With a sneer he pressed a button on a control console strapped to his wrist, triggering a stereophonic audio discharge with video. Brandon saw and heard himself: "See, you mess with me, you mess with my boy L. Proof. Remember that. L—that's short for Louis—L. Proof. He killed someone today. A big fat dude! You can't come after me and not deal with him!"

"Transdimensional TiVo. I love it. Anyway, we are waiting. Louis—or, as you say, L. Proof—should be here any minute now. NOT!" Trife's tone was in no way funny.

The Crims hissed, moving erratically on the walls. They got fiercer with intimidating gestures, and Trife got meaner with focused eyes, shredding through Brandon. They began to close in . . .

"Stand back. You might scare the boy," boomed a voice. Trife's upper body retracted to meet his lower half. All the Crims cleared a path to Brandon. Then the owner of the voice revealed himself: the Galonious Imperial Evil.

Louis had never before taken such a long trip by himself. As he sat on the bus, the world seemed to move in slow motion as he pondered everything that had happened. Nothing was the same. His life was in peril. As far as he knew, he was now some type of alien. That would be fine if the rest of his day could be regular. No friend-snatching Crims. No cars popping out of nowhere. Just an old, dull, regular remainder of the day.

It was a full bus. So loud. So many individual lives housed temporarily on the number 34. Everyone had a story. No matter how connected or disconnected, everyone had his or her own vibrant life—good or bad. A life that Louis knew nothing about, but which would continue for God-only-knew how long after these people stepped off the bus and out of sight.

So many people had stories no one would ever know or care about. Maybe people should want to know. Maybe people should want to care, if only a little bit. What if someone had taken the time to ask him why he was on the bus by himself? What story would he have told them?

"Well, my name is Louis Proof, and I just found out that I am a new type of human, a Celestial-like Entity. CLE for short. I don't even know what that really means. And guess what? I'm responsible for everything, plain and simple. And guess what else? I'm running away from home for the day, not only because this is too much for me to handle, but because I killed a kid in my school when I shook his hand. On top of all that, I am only thirteen. What's your story?"

But no one asked. No one had a clue. People didn't care. To them he was just a thirteen-year-old on a bus. No one sensed the tremendous burden that he carried for himself and for everyone. Why should they?

Louis was in peril. Everyone's life just went on.

A woman was talking obnoxiously loudly on her cell phone, telling someone that she wasn't going to buy a certain outfit since her sister had one just like it that she could borrow.

Louis was in peril. Everyone's life just went on.

A child was sitting anxiously on the seat next to his mother, begging to press the stop signal. "No, Alex, it's not our stop. When it's our stop, you can press it."

Louis was in peril. Everyone's life just went on.

A guy in the rear was hollering about how he had beaten Muhammad Ali. People looked at him as if he were crazy.

Louis was in peril. Everyone's life just went on.

He sat back and hoped that if he thought hard enough, he could wake from this terrible dream. Maybe he had the power to do so. But if he could, he didn't know how.

Louis was about to close his eyes and try to wish anyway, but then he saw a relatively young man looking at him. It was as if the man did care and knew exactly what was going on. It was as if he were in on the grand tale that was Louis's life. Louis felt that the man knew of everything that had happened and even of what would happen. Ridiculous! Louis turned away.

This familiar yet unfamiliar guy stopped looking at Louis and switched on the radio he was holding. The song had a great drumbeat, a melodic bass line, and a piano riff. It was really good. Louis had never heard it before. The bus riders, young and old, began to nod their heads to the beat; even the driver smiled and nodded his head. Everyone *was* connected. Maybe he wasn't as isolated as he thought.

"Did you not see how Brandon was not scared when he was just attacked? We are no match for you. Is that not right, Brandon?" Galonious said as moved closer. "Now, Brandon—wait, let me change our surroundings." The tunnel disappeared and an ornate metallic coliseum built itself around them from the ground up. It was creepy, and its towering size was intimidating. Countless Crims of all varieties sat in the ascending rows and looked down.

"Now, Brandon, let me tell you my name. I am the Galonious Imperial Evil. Yes, evil. Because of the freedom-robbing laws of your world, I am the bad guy. Say hello to the bad guy," Galonious said as everyone — or better yet *everything*—cheered at Galonious's words.

"Yes . . . bad guys, raise your hands!" Galonious said as he proudly raised his hand. Trife and all of the Crims raised their hands and cheered uncontrollably. They were having an uncontainable, Horribly Marvelous time. Galonious silenced the crowd so that he could continue.

"All good guys, raise your hands," Galonious said.

Brandon looked and not one hand was raised. Galonious stared into Brandon's eyes.

"Shame on you! You did not raise your hand," Galonious said.

Brandon, more scared than he had ever been before, raised his hand. "Awww . . . that just does not count. That was an afterthought," Galonious said. "Now, Brandon. I want you to do something for me, and of course it has to do with betraying your best friend. What else could it be? I know you have a price. Everyone does. What is it?"

Every Crim looked intently at Brandon, waiting for an answer. Brandon was far too scared to answer.

"Oh, sorry, don't be scared. I cannot do anything to you, at least not here. Did you not hear me say I need you to betray Louis? You are his best friend; you are very important to me, especially with Angela away. Yes, I know about everything. Go ahead, talk—be rude if you want. I know how you can be. For now you are important. Speak your mind!" Galonious said.

For now Brandon was important. As always he let something like that go to his head.

"I won't sell Louis out. That's my friend. He's got my back and I've got his. Didn't you see how he smacked your boys up when I was in trouble?"

"Riiiight. Suuure," Galonious said as he gave his cronies doubtful looks. "Okay, have it your way. Play that game. I decided for you a long time ago. You think we have not been watching you? Trife and I have been keeping tabs on you for the past three months. I know you better than you think. So, yes, what you most want will be waiting for you when you get home."

"What I most want? Man, you don't know me! I don't care what you say . . . you don't know anything about me! And how the hell are you going to get Beyoncé to be in my house when I get home? You can't do that!" Brandon said.

Laughter rocked the coliseum.

"Brandon, I am capable of all things . . . especially from here. What you most want will be waiting for you at home. I will get it right, and you will betray heaven to keep it. I know you, Brandon. Now go," Galonious said.

The same Crim that had brought Brandon here charged at him without warning, and Brandon was returned to his proper dimension unharmed.

Everything was as it should be, sort of: The street was the same, the traffic light still broken. All was normal except for the Crim that Brandon could see scurrying back into hiding.

Balance had also been restored. To its dismay, the Crim who had taken Brandon's place had been sucked back into the thought dimension. The other Crim had granted the parent's wish by swapping places with her to return her to the thought dimension. That parent had been too concerned with trying to figure out how to reopen the portal to tell anyone what was going on.

Brandon could not wait to get home so he could call Louis and tell him about Galonious.

After the bus, Louis got on the train. An hour's ride. He wasn't there yet, but he was close. In the distance he could see the biggest roller coaster in five states.

The Excitement Plus.

Marvelous mass of meticulous metal. Countless loops. Daunting dips. Scream until your lungs explode, 'cause it still won't let you go. Yellow and royal-blue color scheme. The Excitement Plus—roller coaster extreme.

He had to ride it today.

A free shuttle transported him to the amusement park. Admission cost sixty-five dollars, and Louis had it in his pocket. A hefty price to pay when all he wanted was a single ride, but he didn't care. The cashier looked at him quizzically. "Hey, where are your parents or your party? You are not here by yourself, are you?"

"Actually, I am. I'm just here to ride the roller coaster," Louis answered honestly.

"Oh yeah? Which one? The Excitement Plus? Well, since you only want to ride the roller coaster and you do not look like you are having a good day, how about this— we pretend that it is your birthday, since you missed it. This ticket will get you to the head of the line, and you can even sit in front if you like," the cashier offered.

"Great!" Louis said.

Best thing that happened all day. He reached in his pocket to pay.

"Oh, no, free of charge. Remember, Louis, it is your birthday!" the cashier said, refusing the money. Without thinking, Louis took the ticket, thanked the cashier, and entered the park. Maybe he should have wondered how the cashier knew his name and that he had missed his birthday. Who could it have been?

Brandon hesitated outside his apartment door before entering. He didn't know if he was ready to see Beyoncé or whoever was on the other side of the door. Finally, he took a breath and turned the key.

Brandon stepped into a whole new world:

The apartment clean.
The dishes done.
Food cooking on the stove.

"Brandon! I'm glad you're home," said a voice so mellifluous to Brandon's ears it was almost heart-shattering. So unfamiliar, yet familiar. So close. So welcome.

Galonious had looked deeply into Brandon's heart — into his soul. He had seen past any frivolous or childish request, and what Brandon Davis most wanted was indeed waiting for him when he got home.

✦ ✦ ✦

Louis remembered when he hadn't been big enough to ride; now he had no problems getting on. He couldn't wait for the marvelous feeling of secure, calculated, yet calming peril. Once he was strapped in, it was only moments before he was carried slowly but steadily toward the sky. He could hear and feel the clanks under the roller-coaster car. It reached the apex of the first hill. Falling toward the earth. For the first time since he'd woken from the coma, he was at peace. It was funny how he had to give up all of his freedom to gain his freedom. He was speeding at more than 100 mph, and he was not in control. His life was in the hands of the ride. No choice but to surrender. He was at peace on this roller coaster because there was nothing he could do about anything.

Loop upside down. So high in the air. Death drop. If Brandon was in trouble, he could not help him. His brother was gone—there was nothing he could do about it. He was strapped in. The ride owned him. It threw him around any way it saw fit. The wind slapped him wildly in the face. His heart was forced into his throat.

Front seat, view of everything. No matter how great the world appeared, it all looked small. Others screamed wildly. Louis relaxed and was finally calm. If the world was under attack, what could he do from these heights? Nothing. So why worry?

Roller coasters: the forty-three-second freedom.

"Mom, is that you?" Brandon asked.

"Yes, Brandon, who else would it be?" a woman said jokingly.

Who else could it be?

It could have been the mother who looked at Brandon with hate and resentment. The mother who saw a smaller version of a man who had found her unbearable. The mother who blamed Brandon for sins that were not his fault. The mother who lived oblivious to Brandon's innocence and accused him of impossible atrocities. It looked like the same person, but it wasn't. This was someone different. Brandon was not fooled. Brandon knew this was not his mother, and he was exultant. He felt no loss because his mother was gone. He couldn't, because she had never really been there to begin with.

He hugged this woman with both arms. She hugged him back the way Louis's mom hugged her son. This mother and this feeling could not have been real, but it felt real. Inside, Brandon wished the feeling to be authentic, so it was. Anything was better than what he was accustomed to.

"Brandon, I know it's early, but I made your favorite dinner. Everything is going to be different now. I have one job now. Do you know what it is?" she asked.

It did not take Brandon long to figure out what it was.

"You are going to make me the happiest son on the face of the planet!" Brandon said with enthusiasm.

Louis's time at the amusement park was over, and he was about to face whatever fate awaited him. He'd had his last moments of freedom.

On the bus ride home Louis noticed that something was wrong. The bus was not following its regular route, and he was the only passenger. He had never been the only rider on this usually very busy route. What a funny feeling. He passed the vacant tattered seats, the large windows that would only open slightly, and the metal poles riddled with stickers to reach the front, where he saw a familiar face. Timothy was older, wheeling the big old bus without a care.

"Timothy—you're older again. What are you doing driving this bus?" Louis demanded.

"Hey, while I am here I am going to try everything I can. You ever jump out of a plane? I hope you got it all out of your system. You cannot hide from anything. It is going to get rough on these streets, and no matter what, you will only do what you will do. You cannot change who you are."

"Who I am? I can't change who I am? Well, I have news for you—I'm a killer. I killed Ali Brocli. The only thing I have to do this time is get arrested," Louis said.

Timothy slammed the brakes and looked at Louis.

Both were silent. Then Timothy let out one of the biggest laughs Louis had ever heard.

"I had to stop the bus. I would have gotten into an accident. You think you killed Ali? You did the exact opposite. You saved that kid. He is doing better now than ever."

"I saw him have a heart attack. He's a big dude. I know his favorite food is bacon. He grabbed his chest. I had him in a headlock," Louis said frantically.

Timothy shook his head and began to drive again.

"No, Louis, had you stuck around, you would have seen him get up. What you did when you shook his hand was seal his promise. He made a promise to an iLone CLE, and he meant it. Ali had to immediately wash any idea of revenge or double-dealing out of his entire soul. You forced most of whatever it was that made him act the way he did out of his heart and body. It can come back, but it is up to him. He has a whole new start. That is why he grabbed his chest. That is why he fell. The experience knocked him out. That's not all. What happened next may sound crazy, but it is true. After you ran away, Ali got up, and for the first time in a long while everything seemed brand-new to him. He went for a walk and did not say a word. Hey, look where we are—this is your stop."

Louis looked outside the window and could see that they were at the JunkYard JunkLot.

"This place has been shut down. I can't get in. You

need to just take me home," Louis said.

"Well, maybe no one else can get in, but it will always be open to you. I am sure you will get some inspiration in there. No better place for you to be right now. Go ahead—I would not lead you in the wrong direction. You see that light? Where the first obstacle is? The cars, pipes, and elevator are shut down, but all you have to do is step into that light to enter. Go ahead. I have to get back on schedule. Got to pick up people and take them where they need to go. Go ahead."

As soon as Louis stepped off the bus, Timothy drove away, but not without waving good-bye. Louis walked to the light just as Timothy had told him to. After riding a roller coaster without screaming, stepping into a light wouldn't be hard. He did and found himself instantly inside the JunkYard JunkLot.

CHAPTER FOURTEEN

The place that had been so brilliant, marvelous, and majestic was now nearly dark. The huge screens were no longer lit. The skyboxes were dim. No hip-hop came out of the speakers. None of the elaborate rides had any life. Worst of all, there were no kids there. Louis was all alone. What had happened to cause this? How could the best place that a child could go be so lonely and vacant? The new sadness of it all crept into Louis.

As Louis walked around all of the magnificent rides and attractions, he thought that he was alone, but he was mistaken. He was being watched by two pairs of eyes. They tracked him to the center of the JunkYard JunkLot. The DJ booth stood high and silent. Everything was still except for footsteps coming from behind the door at the base of the tower. The door that had been sealed tight during his first visit was now ajar. Before Louis could investigate, it swung open, inwardly.

There stood another teenager, a little older than Louis but nonetheless a child. He was thin like Louis, but with straight black hair he had to keep sweeping out of his eyes. He wore a charcoal-colored lab coat and underneath sported a black Orchard Street shirt and baggy khaki pants.

"You finally got back here? So what are you going to do about all of this? I had to shut this place down. You know why? You should. You were here when they arrived. I know you saw them too. When are you going to fix this?" The teen said all of this with authority. Louis could tell that this guy was serious about every word that came out of his mouth.

Louis now remembered vividly what had happened the first time he'd been there. This boy was one of the three people he'd believed had seen the "weird" stuff. He had forgotten all about them.

Louis was not going to get caught up in another conversation about what he should or shouldn't do or what his responsibilities were. He sidestepped it.

"You shut this place down? You did this?"

"Had to. All of that bad energy would hurt the kids. I made sure that I built this place like you wanted and that if a kid fell, he would not get hurt. But bad energy and the likes—not a task for me, for you!"

Louis was confused. Four months ago he'd had no idea this place even existed.

"I had nothing to do with this place being built. That's im—" Louis had to stop midsentence. He could not say the word "impossible." It no longer seemed to have any meaning.

He looked around once again and thought about

everything that was here: the roller coaster, the race-track, the DJ booth, all of the rides, the elaborate skyboxes. Everything that he would wish for in his wildest dreams. *Maybe I did*, he thought reluctantly. But how was that possible?

"Of course you did. The Branch family doesn't own this place. One of the elevators just happens to be in their junkyard," said a voice coming from behind Louis.

Louis turned to see who'd spoken. It was a girl four-teen or fifteen years old, about the same height as Louis. Her hair was pulled back in a ponytail. On her head was a designer bucket hat tilted to the side. Louis liked her style. She immediately haunted him, but in a good way. Something inside of his body wanted to jump out and grab her. He felt uniquely, peacefully warm, calm and anxious at the same time. A true emotional first for Louis.

"I'm sorry. He has no manners. He's Prolif and I'm Glitch," the girl said, extending her hand. Louis took it and felt as if he had come in contact with ethereal per-fection. It was like winning his first race. It was like being cheered and congratulated by all his friends. Louis almost lost his composure. He had to focus his thoughts on something other than the way he felt as he reluctantly let her hand go. Glitch genuinely smiled at him, and that multiplied Louis's feelings ten times, but he kept them subdued.

What type of name is Glitch for a girl that looks as good as she does? She sure wasn't a glitch—or maybe she was, the best kind possible. A mistake that was better than everything else. An anomaly in the matrix. Then it clicked.

"You're the Magnificent ProliFnGlitcH?"

"Yes. His ideas are prolific, and I fix all the glitches. We built all of this—with your help, of course," Glitch said.

"With my help?" Louis asked.

"Yes. You and a few other kids would send us ideas, and Prolif would expand on them until they turned into what you see here. He's great at designing and constructing, but sometimes—well, always—he ignores the details, and that's where I come in. I fix all the things he overlooks so that everything works properly," said Glitch.

Louis hung on her every word. He could listen to her all night.

"Yes, yes, yes. Thank you, Glitch. I would like to take credit for everything, but no man can create the world on his own. Louis, I get your thoughts, embellish them as I see fit, then construct the plans. Glitch . . . well, she fixes the glitches. Other than that, it is all me. I do everything else. It is all me. Thank you. Thank you. Thank you," Prolif said quite prolifically.

"My thoughts. You get my thoughts?" Louis asked.

"Why, yes. Of course, we're here to assist you. We needed something to do until this war started. So we just read your mind to see what you would really like and built this place. Don't you know about our roles in the Earthbound Celestial Wars?" Prolif went on.

"Prolif, if he doesn't know, it's not our place to tell him. I am sure someone from Midlandia will. They know far more than we do," Glitch said.

"Midlandia, schmidlandia. That's the place of all places and crazy as, well, Midlandia to boot. If it were their place to tell him everything, we wouldn't be here. There are a few things I think he should know that no one from Midlandia will tell him," answered Prolif.

"Like what? Do tell, brother. Please do," Glitch said.

"First of all . . . ," Prolif began, as if this were the most important discourse Louis was ever to hear. "Do you think Arminion, Galonious, and Trife were able to do all of that on their own? Of course not! If you ask me, the Olivion knew this was going to happen, may even have been behind it, and helped the eNoli escape. Everything is too convenient. The virus being part of a contingency plan. The fact that so much happened for Louis and Cyndi to be Olivion's Favorites. What about the fact that they both just happen to be alive now? Oh, and let's not forget—this is the biggest one! The messages we mysteriously received from who knows who and where preparing us for this war some time ago. You tell me, Glitch, what do you make of such convenient little facts?" Prolif finished.

"Well, it's all really deductive reasoning when you consider what the Olivion is assumed to be. If you go by that, it is impossible to think that anything goes down without the Olivion knowing about it. I've had those same thoughts myself," said Glitch.

Louis's head swam. Prolif and Glitch said so much and so little all at once. On top of that, Glitch had him in an instant heart-lock. One thing was for sure, though—Louis wanted to know about the Olivion. He had even used the term *Olivion's Favorite* to get the Alonis. Timothy had not explained what the term meant, nor had Louis thought to ask with so many things being thrown at him.

"Prolif . . . Glitch, Timothy told me about Arminion, Galonious, and Trife. I'm guessing the Olivion is the same as one of them."

"The Olivion? You surely met the Olivion while you were on Midlandia. You should be able to tell *me* who or what the Olivion is. But of course you don't remember. You don't even know what it means that you were able to go to Midlandia and return. After that, handling this should be as easy for you as a fifth-grade math test would have been for Einstein or even better yet me.

"But anyway—the Olivion. I'm in no way ashamed to say that the Olivion is one thing neither I nor my sis knows everything about. Who could? It's like a true myth. It definitely exists, but no one knows the exact facts. It's said that the Olivion is neither eNoli nor iLone, but beyond both. Some say the Olivion is the Midland Isle or the Midland Isle is the Olivion. One thing is for sure: There's no way the Olivion didn't know or even want this to happen," Prolif explained. Glitch seemed to be in total agreement.

Louis turned his back on the two and walked away. He thought about his wild visions, searched them for something that might seem like this Olivion, and came up with nothing.

"I don't remember anything like an Olivion. I'm sorry I don't have any info."

"Don't worry. It's all part of the process—your memories returning and all. You came back with great power that you can immediately tap into. We have something for you to do that will be very helpful. You have to get rid of the bad elements that forced me to shut down this place!" Prolif said.

Louis had no idea that this was where Galonious had his alternate dimension stronghold. Because so many Crims were gathered here, the negative energy was so concentrated that it was able to seep through dimensions. It shorted out the energy used to power the JunkYard JunkLot and caused all types of problems.

"You are not an iLone from Midlandia. Get involved. Do something. Clear this place out. Go ahead!" Prolif said, then stood back and waited. Louis had no idea what to do, so he did nothing.

"I want to see what this virus does to you, and you are a Favorite, so I know you have an Alonis. That's it around your neck. I'm waiting," Glitch said.

They were builders, not super action fighters, like Louis was supposed to be. They really wanted to see what he could do. Louis still did nothing—not because he didn't believe he could or because he didn't want to, but because he simply did not know how and refused to fake it.

"Sorry, guys, it's not going down. What you are talking about sounds like fun. I like the idea, but no dice. When I did all of that other stuff, it was a mistake. I want to help, but I don't know how it all works. I'm just remembering pieces. I need more time to figure it out. I mean, hey, I'm only thirteen years old."

"Thirteen years old? Thirteen years old? I am not much older, but at age eight we graduated from school and left home to travel all around the universe as we saw fit. Then we came here, just her and me. You guys stay home sometimes into your twenties and thirties. Matter of fact, some of you never leave. You guys take so long to jump into life. I graduated from school when I was eight—," Prolif said, before being interrupted by Glitch.

"No, Prolif. I was eight; you were nine. You had to stay an extra year. Louis, he messed up on his final project. He had the best quantum inventions among the greatest minds in the universe. He got so full of himself that he thought that he did not need to get help from anyone. Mind you, we've always been a team. Well, Prolif the absentminded created a project on his own that had no glitches. This was the first time, and I was proud of him. But numbnuts over there handed it in and did not sign his name to it. He got no credit, and there was nothing that could be done. He disregarded a specific rule. He had to stay an extra year because of that. In the end it was not a bad thing. He is much better for it. To this day he is the most prolific student of the academy. He may forget some details, but his ideas are prolific. That is a special kind of genius. His mishap did much to humble him. Be happy you did not meet him before it happened. That story is the reason you see our name on everything now."

"Yes, yes, yes. Where would I be without my sister, Glitch? The sign of a true intellectual is to know one's strengths and weaknesses. Glitch and I are a team, but I remain super, super, smart," Prolif said.

"He's totally a genius. Can't deny that. He's got a point. So smart that the minor details escape him," Glitch said with a sly smile.

Louis thought. Glitch had to be smarter than Prolif if she could double-check everything he did and fix the problems. How considerate and humble she had to be. She looked out for her older brother just as he did for his. They had that in common.

"My point is that I'm sixteen years old, and look what I am able to do. I was able to make all of this come to life for you. Age? Do you think that age means you can't do things?" Prolif said.

"Yeah, I do. My mom and dad tell me all the time I

can't do things because I'm not old enough. I don't think so, but hey, that's the way things are."

"Well, Louis, when you're out on your own, you're going to have to step outside of what you think you know and do what you have to do. Even if it's nothing like what you're used to doing. Everything is different. Totally different. I know you know this," Prolif said, smiling for the first time.

"He's right. Even you're different now. You've been outside; you know what's going on. We saw you save Brandon on the street. We don't know what you have to do to get rid of the negative aura creeping around us, but we know you can. So just do it," Glitch said, walking Louis into the ProliFnGlitcH lab. She turned on a monitor that displayed Galonious's stronghold.

"This is where we are. All of these things are here, but we cannot see them. They are in a different dimension, and their negative energy is so powerful that they are affecting things here. You can get rid of it all. Trust me. I know you can," Glitch said. Louis could hardly believe his ears.

She spoke to him, gentle and assuring, making him feel as if he could do anything, even trust—both in her and in things that he could not see.

As Louis walked outside of the lab with Glitch, he willingly accepted the power within himself for the first time. He didn't make the slightest effort, didn't even concentrate, but everything around him began to stir.

Then, in a flash, all of the dim light that illuminated the JunkYard JunkLot was sucked up into Louis. It was now completely dark. Then Louis began to project this light outside of himself. It started as a blue vertical beam that grew behind him—just like when the Alonis appeared. Louis could see the smiles and wonder on the faces of Prolif and Glitch. The glistening blue light was both warm and amazing but harmful to those who threatened Young Mr. Louis Proof. In this light, Louis thought Glitch looked outrageously beautiful. He had to find out more about her. How had she gotten him to do this?

The light began to grow around Louis until it covered him in a domelike structure. He gently raised his arms, then quickly took a defensive stance and pulled them in close to his sides. The light contracted around him. Then with immediate speed he extended his arms straight out. After a second of silence, all of life's wonder rushed in as the light went ballistic. It spread in all directions and rippled through dimensions. It collided with the dreadfully grand buildings of the dark stronghold and toppled them whole. Success! Not a single one left standing. They had been ripped from the ground like houses in a tornado. Hundred-story buildings had been flipped straight up in the air and thrown out of sight. Others had fallen as if they were sets of wooden blocks that a child had carelessly dumped on the ground. The legions of Crims that inhabited this city were also hurled through the air, spinning, but they fought to return. As soon as they landed, they rushed back to the former Galonion empire to reclaim it, even though the buildings were gone. They would meet the worst fate. The wave of energy that sought to cleanse this area broke into disks of light. Each disk hunted down one of the henchmen. When the light met its target, it broke the Crim's body apart by infusing it with an energy so positive and pure that no being of negative energy could withstand it. Then each disk returned to the perimeter of the JunkYard JunkLot, rejoining the domelike wave of light. Galonious's imperial domain that lay invisibly over the JunkYard JunkLot had been dismantled and forced far away.

Louis had used his power to influence events in an alternate dimension. Just as the extreme negative energy had had an effect on the JunkYard JunkLot, the extreme positive energy of Louis had been able to counteract this and set things right.

Louis felt as though a shell around his body had been broken. As if for his entire life until this moment he had been slogging in mud, moving at half speed. Glitch had triggered something inside of Louis, and now he was free. *Free to do what?* he wondered.

Prolif, Glitch, and Louis hadn't seen what had happened in the thought dimension, but they could sense that Louis had done something. Prolif pulled a keypad out of his pocket, and with a press of a button all power to the JunkYard JunkLot was restored. The elevators were working. The huge TV screens once again beamed and radiated in full glory. The skyboxes were fully lit. Xenon lights bathed the park in brilliance. Music poured from the speakers. The roller coaster began to thrust itself down the track. It was marvelous once again. The light that had swept over the JunkYard JunkLot now formed a protective barrier that would hopefully keep it safe for boys and girls for an eternity. No matter what, kids would be able to come here and have fun, unharmed and unafraid of anything that was going on in the outside world.

Glitch grabbed Louis's hand and led him back into the tower. They both saw that the screen that once had been flooded with Crims was all clear. Only here, on this screen, could the protective barrier be seen.

"See, Louis, you should never doubt yourself. You did do it!" Glitch said as she hugged Louis and kissed him. Louis went into orbit. He felt a strong connection with Glitch that he felt with no one else. Not even Angela. It unsettled him.

"Whoa, what time is it? I have to get home. It's 10:50 p.m. You guys may not have to get home, or you are home, but I have to. See you soon," Louis said.

"Louis, see you soon," both Prolif and Glitch said as Louis exited the same way he had entered.

Louis was physically in the junkyard but mentally in the clouds when he stepped out of the light. Cars were parked on both sides of the street, and he looked up at the flickering streetlamp that seemed to be begging for attention. Louis thought of the Alonis in action, the JunkYard JunkLot revived, who he truly was on the inside, and the way that Glitch made him feel. What an experience!

Louis surveyed the street and saw that, apart from a cat that had just toppled a garbage can, he was alone. This was lucky, because he desired motion. Not the act of walking home—total extreme motion. The street was long. The lights were all green. So why not?

Movement. It started as a walk, then a jog, then a sprint. Nowhere near fast enough; he had to run. He ran as he had when he'd rescued Brandon, but this time it was different. This time it was for a peaceful reason. The street could barely contain his speed. His feet left smoke rising from the pavement. He swung the Alonis Medallion around his neck. Instantly the Alonis was activated. Pieces of the phenomenal car once again flew from the light that was at Louis's back, connecting around him. With Louis inside, the Alonis traveled faster than any land vehicle ever had before. Just as quickly, it disassembled and dashed back into the light. Louis once again ran on foot. He slowed down. Then, as if he were dancing to an unheard song, his steps stuttered on beat, and the Alonis reactivated and surrounded him. This time he traveled twice as fast.

Louis would not be tied to the streets. As long as there

was a surface, the Alonis would travel on it. He drove up buildings, the Alonis's tires hugging their surfaces. Gravity was no longer a factor. Alonis, deactivate. Now he was running straight up the side of a building. Alonis, come out and play. He rode up the building until there was no more building, and he was launched into the sky. In midair the Alonis deactivated, and Louis flipped, bathed in moonlight. Arms out, body extended, perfectly balanced, he spun above the building. He fell back to it in the Alonis and rode down the side faster than he had ridden up, sparking light trails behind him.

The best experience of his life and it was his and his alone. Urban streets had never before seen the likes of Louis Proof, CLE. He gripped the wheel and stepped on the brakes to slow down to 30 mph. He stopped for a red light. Rules were rules. He was not alone at the stoplight. A car full of girls in their early twenties or late teens had stopped right next to him. They could see the vehicle, low to the ground. Alonis technology, unlike any other car. Sleek lines emitting bluish neon light. Semitranslucent finish. The most desirable car that had ever existed, just a bit smaller than most.

Louis wondered if they could actually see him in the car. In an instant the window went from opaque to clear solid light. He looked over and tilted his head as if to say, *What's good?* They smiled and responded with all sorts of greetings. Louis loved their fascination and intrigue, but . . . green light. He was off again. Zero to 80 mph in one second.

He heard a siren. A cop was now chasing him. He was relieved to know that it was not because of Ali Brocli. He sure as Midlandia wasn't going to stop! Instead he slowed down to make things interesting. He dipped through the streets. Grand Theft Auto without criminal intent. Then three more police cars arrived. He could easily have lost them, but he was having fun. Still, he didn't want to cause an accident. He had an idea. He took it up to 110 mph again to create some distance and made a sharp turn.

Louis stopped dead in his tracks, but the Alonis continued—or so the police thought. The Alonis created a holographic image of itself at Louis's request. The real Alonis deactivated. Louis was astonished by how perfectly his plan was executed with just a thought. He ran to the sidewalk as the police cars raced past. Within moments the hologram disappeared just as Louis had wanted, leaving the cops in a state of total confusion.

The Alonis came out to play.

He once again became the roller coaster that moved with the force of steel and fought a winning battle against gravity.

He once again became the NASCAR racer who would never crash and burn.

The Alonis was amazing!

Louis made his way home at a reasonable speed. He was oblivious to the fact that Galonious, unseen, hovered high above the rooftops in his dimension of thought. His shadow looked like a cutout as he stood in front of the full moon. Galonious could hardly contain his enthusiasm. He knew that Louis was ready. His own stronghold had just been destroyed, and Galonious was ecstatic about it. This was glorious proof that his plan was about to enter its final stage. Louis's power—though not his knowledge—rivaled that of Galonious. This would make it possible for the most powerful eNoli Earth had ever known to make his grand red-carpet entrance.

It was time for Galonious to call upon Mr. Brandon Davis.

⇒ CHAPTER FIFTEEN ⇐

Louis had never returned home at such a late hour by himself before. He knew that he would be in trouble, serious trouble. No good mother would tolerate a thirteen-year-old being out this late on his own without reason. That's enough to serve a mother a plate of heart attack with a side of aneurysm. Louis paused as he put his key in the door. He hesitated to face his mother's wrath. He opened the door, then locked it behind him. His father was upstairs in bed, but his mother was in the living room watching TV.

"Mom, I'm home. Sorry that I'm late. I didn't mean to make you worry. I just had to get away," he said, ready to absorb the verbal bashing his mother was about to pour over him. He waited. It did not come.

"Mom, are you okay?"

She is so angry that she cannot speak, he thought.

He was standing behind the sofa and he couldn't see her face, so he had no idea what her reaction was.

"Louis, come sit down next to me," Mrs. Proof said.

When he did, she pulled him into a tight hug.

"Louis, you are no longer my little boy like you used to be. Don't misunderstand me. You will always be my little boy, but now you are the world's little boy. I knew this as soon as you said those words to me. I would make myself sick if I was always worrying about you every time you left here. Actually, the truth is that I no longer have to worry about you. You will always be fine. Whatever it is I gave you today will ensure it. Your grandmother told me that. She didn't tell me which one of you it would go to, but she promised me that whoever claimed it would be free from harm. Also, you think I don't know that darn near half this town has lost their minds? This is somehow related to you, and you are going to make it right. Louis, it is not my job to stop you. It is my job to support you. That does not mean that you can become an unruly brat. You have always been responsible, and I don't think that will change. Don't lose yourself when you are trying to save others. Whatever you have to do, just make it happen, and let me know what I can do to help. Oh, and one more thing—don't think this means you can slack off in school!"

In the face of the "coma," Camron leaving, the crazy events in town, her sudden aging, the Alonis—just everything—his mother saw the situation as it truly was, and she was in his corner. He looked over at his mom. Her previous aging had begun to melt away. She was now the same mom that he had always known. The nearness of the Alonis must have been the cause. If he stayed close, she would always be young. He loved his mom so much, but he could not always stay close; he had to be Louis Proof. And part of that meant he had to deal with his mother's aging and everything else just like all people do.

He held his mom tightly. Then he suddenly felt ill, like he was about to vomit. They had attacked Brandon because they were not able to harm him. What if they came after his mom? What if they came after his dad? What if they came after his cousin, or even Angela when she came back? They were his weakness as well as his strength.

No matter what he did, even if he saved the world from all grimy and bad things, Mom would not always be here. She had aged visibly right before his eyes. She could be harmed by someone trying to harm him. Neither she nor anyone would be here forever.

Louis closed his eyes and grabbed this moment in time. The feeling of the sofa supporting his body. The feeling of the sneakers on his feet. The sound of the *Late Show* and Letterman's laugh in the background. Most important of all: just being with his mom. She was here; he was here; they were here together. He had to remember what this felt like. He took so many things for granted:

He hadn't known how important summer was until he had lost one, but he would have another.

He hadn't known how important Brandon was until he was in trouble, but he was safe now.

He hadn't known how important his brother was until he was gone, but he would be back.

He hadn't known how important Angela was until she was gone, but she would be home soon.

What about when there were no more summers as a kid? What if someone he cared about could not come back? What then? What if, for whatever reason, he lost someone? Would he be able to recall a special moment with the person and remember every detail so that he could relive it whenever he wanted? Would he be able to say it was okay that he or she was gone because his memory clung onto marvelous moments like this?

He would be able to say this about his mom. He would have this moment forever. He would always remember what it felt like.

"I love you, Mom."

"I love you too, Louis."

Aside from being attacked by a horde of Crims, Brandon had had a wonderful day. He had the mom he'd always wanted. Not only did she cook, take care of Brandon, and clean the house, but she'd also bought him twenty video games at the same time, which was unheard of. What's more, she'd managed to avoid buying duplicates. She'd even purchased a big expensive TV just so he could play them in superhigh-definition. He'd tried to call Louis earlier, but he couldn't reach him. Brandon wanted Louis to come over to his house for a change.

Oh well, I'll just have to find someone to play with online, he thought.

Dinner was excellent. Fake Ms. Davis talked to Brandon about trips they could take and how proud of him she was. After dinner she even offered to play some of the new games with Brandon. His mouth dropped as he got the pixels beat out of him by his own mother. She didn't even fuss with him about going to bed. For Brandon, suddenly it was single-parent bliss.

And then he went to his room. As soon as he entered it, the same Crim that had harassed him before charged at him, flinging him and itself into the thought dimension. Just as before they swapped places with one excited Crim and one terribly upset human from the thought dimension.

"BRANDON DAVIS. How are you? Have you been living it up? I bet you have had more fun at home than you have ever had. What you most wanted—did I not deliver? Now you have it. Nothing better than a great mom. She is as good as Louis's—maybe even better? What do you think? Will you keep it all, or go back to what you had before? All you have to do is one thing. Now let me think, what could that be? Oh, yes—betray your best friend. What else *could* it be?" Galonious said.

"If I say no, can I keep all of the games and toys, but you take the mom?" Brandon asked.

"*Whaaaaat?* Boy! You must be kidding! No, and it will be worse. Way worse! Remember, I am the Galonious Imperial Evil. I am my own brand of evil, not the generic kind that you can just buy off the shelf!" Galonious shouted.

In that instant, Galonious changed into a truly heinous demon. His skin turned deep gray and began to peel to reveal his demon insides. He grew coarse hair through his back. His teeth became razor sharp and dripped an acrid black liquid. He towered over Brandon and grinned for a second.

"You know what? That is played out. I am tired of this. I have been watching too much TV. Let us try a fresh approach," Galonious said in a semidemonic voice.

Galonious became a baby. There was something familiar about this baby. It looked Brandon in the eyes with a hatred and scorn that no normal baby could ever feel. The baby slowly stood up and became a toddler. As the toddler took a step toward Brandon, he became six years old. As the child advanced farther, he grew even older. Brandon knew this child like he knew no other. The boy stood eye to eye with Brandon. Brandon was looking at himself. But this was an evil Brandon. Wicked like no other child had ever been — as if every dark quality within his true self had been extracted, mutated, distorted, and amplified like a speaker turned way up and about to crack its subwoofer.

If a mother is what Brandon most wanted, this is

what he wanted least. It could move and think on its own and take on Brandon's life, and Brandon would have no control. Who knew what that Brandon could do? Who knew what evil actions it could perform while people thought that it was indeed the original Brandon?

"We have a deal. You returned unharmed and you got what you most wanted. A deal is a deal," Galonious said, reverting to his chosen form.

Galonious walked away. Then he paused to face Brandon. "Or you can forget that deal. If you don't keep the bargain, you will be right back here and you will never return. Think about anyone—people you like, people you don't like. I will do the same to them and worse. You know not what pain is! You know not what evil is! You will do what I plan for you."

Brandon had no idea that Galonious had been replacing adults all summer. Nor did he have an inkling that being trapped here might not be the worst of fates.

"Louis. Louis, wake up," said a distant voice. It was late at night, and Louis was sure he was dreaming. He thought that he heard Brandon's voice.

"Louis, wake up." Louis heard the voice again, then felt a slap. Now Louis was awake and Brandon was standing at the side of his bed.

"What are you doing here? What's the deal, Brandon? How'd you get in here? You climb up the drainpipe again?"

"Never mind those whats and hows! This guy Galonious. He . . . ," Brandon said, sick about what he was about to do.

"Brandon, what's the deal?" Louis said, prodding him to continue.

"Louis . . . Louis, there's this girl in trouble like I was. You have to . . ."

Brandon thought of all they had been through and all that Louis's family had done for him. Then he thought about the time he'd spent with his mother. She was not real. She was not his mom. She was way better than his mom, but Louis had always been his friend, and Mrs. Proof was his mom, as far as he was concerned.

It was some real nonsense that he was about to do. If he were to go through with it, he would actually turn into the person that Galonious had shown him. That was who he might have been had it not been for Louis and his family.

"Oh, hell no—hell no! I won't do it. I'm no rat. He can't make me do anything. Louis, Galonious, he gave me what I most wanted, and that was my mom. She, like, really loves me now, like your mom does, but mine is not real. He said that if I didn't trick you and bring you to where he said, he was going to hurt me and a lot of people. Louis, forget what he wants me to do. All I know is you have to shut the imperial evil down. You have to shut him *down*. I've seen you against a whole bunch of those freaks. You can punch holes through him. Take him out. If you do, maybe I can at least keep all of my stuff," Brandon said tirelessly.

"What? What stuff?" Louis asked. Brandon was still speaking at a frantic pace.

"Ohhh, that's not important. What I was saying is that you can take him. I don't know how I can help, but you can take him. You can run him over or shoot him with that car of yours. I know that thing has to have weapons. That's my word! You can get this guy. I know you can. You can do anything. I mean you built those cars . . . you ride the roller coasters without screaming. You are the only one who ever fought Ali Brocli—and you took care of him so easily! You're the man, Louis. No, Louis—you're the kid! I mean, what's different this time? Sure, you don't know this guy. He's evil and proud of it. Oh . . . and he's got an army. But really, what's different? People need help and you always help and someone is helping you. You wouldn't have gotten that car thing if you weren't going to have to use it. He doesn't have anything like that. You have got to merc that dude. Take him down! I know where he is! Let's go!"

The room went silent. Brandon looked Louis straight in the eyes. Louis had to be bigger than what his body gave him credit for. He just had to. All things considered, Louis was feeling confident and truly invincible. He sat there listening to Brandon as an inextinguishable fire burned inside of him, fueling those feelings. His mom had even said that she had no reason to worry about his well-being anymore.

Now he was the "world's little boy." His blueprint was to help. It always had been. Louis said, "Okay," in a way that only a thirteen-year-old who had no idea what he was about to get himself into could.

"Yeah, that is what I'm talking about!" Brandon said excitedly.

By this time Brandon was going through Louis's dresser drawers and getting clothes for him to put on. Brandon threw shirts and jeans on the floor until he found the clothes he was looking for. Brandon knew it was best to coordinate. Trouble or no trouble, there was no need to leave the house looking like a bum.

"Get dressed. You can't do this sort of thing in your pajamas. Let's go." Brandon handed Louis some clothes.

That would have been enough, but Brandon noticed the leather jacket that Louis's brother had left for him. He quickly grabbed it. "You have got to put this on. You would look so cool if you took Galonious out wearing this. No joke!"

Louis paused for a second, then put the jacket on. Louis must have been feeling invincible if he thought it was safe to fight in the leather coat. It was a little too big, but it looked great on him—as if it really were meant for Louis and his brother had only been holding it for him.

Louis may have been cool in his regular clothes, but

in this jacket, paired with the Alonis, he looked ultra-official.

"See that. Now you look like somebody. Galonious better watch out!" Brandon said.

Louis quickly scribbled a note to his parents and placed it on the bed. Under the shield of night he and Brandon climbed out of the window and slid down the drainpipe to the street.

All of the commotion had awakened Lacey. She'd been listening just outside of the door almost the entire time. If Louis was going, she was going too. She was dead set on that. But by the time she'd gotten dressed, Louis and Brandon had already left. That wouldn't stop her. She went into Louis's room and climbed out the window and down to the ground the same way Louis and Brandon had—but before she did, she read the note left on the bed.

Dear Mom & Dad,
Off to save the world.
Will be back soon.
Love,
Louis

Lacey ran after Louis and Brandon. She was in stealth mode, making sure that she did not step too loudly or get too close. Brandon led Louis toward the destination that Galonious had specified. That was part of the plan, but what was different was that Louis was ready. At least as ready as any inexperienced CLE could be.

"Louis! Brandon!" Lacey called.

She knew that they were too far from home for them to take her back or tell her to go back on her own. They stopped in their tracks as she caught up to them.

"Hey, Louis, I told you I wanted to help. I told you I *can* help. Don't count me out!" Lacey shouted.

"Lacey, why are you here? You're going to get hurt. Go back. You know what? You both should go back so I can handle this on my own. This is my job! My responsibility!" Louis shouted.

"Louis, we have to get there. I say she comes. I say we both come. What do we have to worry about? You're going to shut this guy down like one! two! three!" Brandon said.

"Yeah, Louis—one! two! three!" Lacey said.

"No time to take her back. He said I had to get you here by a certain time. Let's go!"

Hubris replaced Louis's better judgment and his fear of Lacey and Brandon getting hurt. He was CLE and supposedly had endured the greatest challenge imaginable, which was Midlandia. Plus, going by the way he was handling everything instinctively, this would surely be a cakewalk. Besides, it would be cool to have an audience. He'd show Brandon and Lacey what he could do.

In a quick motion Louis tossed Lacey in the air. She landed on his back. She wrapped her arms around his neck and looked straight ahead. Louis and Brandon ran and ran. Lacey could see something in the distance. In this specific place where Louis was to be led, the dimensional fabric was ill woven and being torn. Right before the three kids' eyes, Galonious ripped into this dimension.

His dimensional birth caused reality to fragment and break apart. This section of the city seemed as if it were morphing wildly back and forth from the never-could-happens and the pure-impossibles. A cold torrential rain pounding the children was soon replaced by arid desert air that left them dry and thirsty. Now pitch-black midnight was punctuated by the light of the streetlamps, which soon went out. Total darkness and complete silence, until the wind began to blow wildly and they were assaulted by wet, sticky cold. Being caught in a blizzard without being able to see anything was terrible, but suddenly it was a marvelous summer day. No it wasn't. The heat grew so intense that the great heaps of snow melted and flooded the streets. As the water rushed away, the pavement trembled.

Galonious had just screwed everything up. Not even he wanted to suffer the consequences of breaking the laws of dimensional balance much longer. On top of all of this he was being pulled back to the thought dimension because there was no space for him here. He had to struggle, but he was dead set on initiating his plan. He would not go back.

His militia on Earth was roughly two hundred strong and finally came out of hiding. These maniacal menaces hurried past the three kids, paying them no mind. They only wanted to reach their commander in chief and await his orders.

"This is where he told me to bring you. That big bastard is him. Are you ready?" Brandon asked without fear.

Louis thought that since he was supposedly impervious to harm and had tackled every challenge without knowing what to do, this too would be no problem. "Sure. Why not?" he said.

Lacey held tight to Louis. Still on his back, she wasn't going to let go until she had to.

"Galonious, you punk! We're here, but L. Proof knows what's up. He is going to wipe the floor with you," Brandon screamed.

Galonious looked at Louis with a sense of both disdain and pride. Louis was indeed as powerful as he'd expected, and Galonious was the reason for this. He had provided the challenges of rescuing Brandon and reviving the JunkYard JunkLot, which had allowed Louis to channel some of what he had learned on Midlandia.

"Louis Proof! So glad you could join us. Come get me and meet your fate!" Louis put Lacey down and ran at Galonious. The Alonis came out to play.

"No!" Lacey yelled as she ran after him. Even she knew that this was probably not the best thing to do.

Brandon stood still in anticipation of Louis's victory. Just before Louis was about to meet Galonious, Galonious effortlessly expanded, then bent and stretched himself into the form of a dark, elaborate tunnel. Louis could not stop and had no choice but to enter this tunnel. He was only inside of it briefly, but on the walls he could see Galonious's evil image both laughing and clapping for him. On the other side of the tunnel was the dimensional portal. Before Louis knew what had happened, he'd disappeared into the thought dimension.

Galonious returned to his normal form, victorious and surrounded by his cheering Crims. Lacey would not stand for any of this, nor would Galonious and his Crims frighten her. All she wanted to do was chase after Louis. She set pace for the portal and it closed shut after she entered it, leaving Brandon alone with Galonious and the Crims. A Crim cheered as it was able to enter this dimension by taking Lacey's place.

The city was now calm again.
Galonious had won.
It had been that easy.

MARVELOUS WORLD

≫ A.K.A. ≪

The Marvelous World
of the Supposedly Soon to Be
Phenomenal Young Mr. Louis Proof

BOOK 1: THE MARVELOUS EFFECT

✦ LEVEL VI ✦

⇒ CHAPTER SEVENTEEN ⇐

Louis and Lacey were mesmerized by a world that was a weird version of the one that they had lived in all their lives. The two were still on the same block as before, with U.S.A. Barber Shop and all the other stores and buildings, but everything looked like flat, stained-glass cutouts. Louis gazed at Galonious and was surprised by how he appeared to be like the 2-D characters of *South Park* would have been if they'd been realistic-looking people.

This just would not do. Louis knew that he was supposed to put Galonious down. He had no idea where he was or how he'd gotten here. What he did know was that he could still see Galonious. Yes, he looked different, but he was right there. Louis ran to attack him and threw what would have been devastating punches, but each strike went right through its target. Galonious was oblivious to the attack.

Useless. Louis kept punching. He wouldn't have stopped if Lacey hadn't called him.

"Louis, stop! It's not working! Forget about him. How are we going to get back home?"

Louis stopped punching, but he had no answer for her. They could see Brandon calling out to them, mouthing their names—"Louis! Lacey!" Louis quickly ran up to him, shouting, "Brandon!" but just like everything else from their dimension, Brandon was now flat and fading away. Lacey tried to grab Brandon, but her hand met nothing but air.

Louis once again rushed at Galonious, throwing rapid and powerful punches. He was so angry that his fists flared up and began to glow. He hurled fists of light. The glowing streaks trailing each punch soon faded. Such power. Such force. All wasted, with no effect on Galonious—he just walked away. Louis did not chase him. Instead he slumped to his knees, defeated and without a clue as to what he should do next.

Lacey looked again at Brandon, who had not yet faded completely. What she saw was odd. Brandon, who'd once been full of fright, had changed his attitude entirely. He no longer looked desperate, upset, and frustrated. He looked as if he'd just figured something out. He seemed unconcerned with Louis and Lacey and began to follow Galonious.

"No, Brandon. Stay away from him! Run! Get away!" Lacey called out. Brandon kept following Galonious.

Soon, all images of their original dimension faded away, and they saw only the thought dimension. Hot white comets and fiery red, yellow, and orange meteors blazed overhead in the dark night sky. Nebulae twisted and rotated beautifully. Stars twinkled and randomly changed patterns. It was as if the stars were being led by a single one that danced about as it saw fit. Ships, boats, aircraft, and other vehicles that Louis had never seen before darted fantastically above. The ground was firm, but Louis could not tell what it was—certainly not sand, dirt, grass, concrete—or anything to leave footprints in. It was quite odd. There were no buildings and no landscape, not here at least.

Louis and Lacey soon realized that they could no longer worry about Brandon or gaze at this new dimension. They had a much more pertinent issue to deal with.

Hundreds, possibly thousands of Galonious's Crims were creeping in like bad habits. Louis and Lacey did not have to think twice about whom the horrids were eager to meet. More and more scuttled near, creating a tidal wave of threat. Lacey and Louis stood side by side. Louis had no idea what to do. He did not know if it was possible to fight so many. Simply put, their numbers were unthinkable.

Before, he had faced only twenty Crims.
Before, he had stood up to only one bully.
Before, he had outrun only the cops.
This was in a class by itself.
It was a menace of epic proportions.

Lacey looked at the countless Crims and then at the dazed expression on Louis's face. She looked back at the Crims and showed no fear.

"Louis, there's something that I didn't tell you. You know how I can play basketball?" Lacey asked, as the Crims approached. There would be no escape.

"Yeah," Louis replied, wondering why she would bring that up now.

"Well, I can fight like a hundred times better than that," she said. She grabbed her long, curly hair, pulled it back, and gathered it together with a scrunchie she snatched from her pocket.

"We can take 'em," she said as she got into her Short Moon Rising stance, just as she had on the day Louis had woken up. Louis knew that it was wrong and that he'd sworn he'd never do it again, but in this situation he felt it was acceptable: Louis looked at Lacey as though she were crazy.

Lacey didn't care what Louis thought or believed. She just closed her eyes to focus on what she had to do and how she would do it. It would be hard, but she knew she could handle it. Eyes open. Without warning she was off. Her seven-year-old footsteps carried her directly toward her enemies. Her face showed nothing but determination. Her fists clenched. Her thoughts were pure. Only a few yards away. She would attack upon arrival. Arrival was now.

Of course Louis tried to chase after her, but he couldn't. Prickly hands and bonds extended from the ground, clenching his legs, arms, and chest. He fought them restlessly but could not break free.

Lacey was unaware that Louis was not backing her up as she leaped into the air, landing on the face of an unsuspecting Crim. It fell under her weight, but before it went down, she used its face as a launching pad to flip forward and land on another Crim's head. It fell just like her first victim. Every Crim that her feet made contact with was pounded into the ground. Lacey fought fiercely underneath the marvelous night sky.

They attacked her in waves. She defeated them in waves. With her seven-year-old fists she carved paths through their hordes. With each turn her roundhouse kicks connected with four, five, and six Crims at a time. Elbows blasted them back if they got too close from behind while she showered pain on selected targets. It seemed that with each blow, something happened in sync overhead. A nebula would explode when she punched. The stars would take on a new formation when she kicked. Comets would speed up when she ran. A star would go supernova when she sent her enemies to the ground.

After beating all that were near her, Lacey paused and gathered herself, shooting cold glances at the Crims. They did not attack but began to circle. Then they rushed at her from all angles. Could she hold this down? No question!

Lacey, beat 'em up!
Lacey, beat 'em down!

Lacey, go on and beat those Crims like you
own 'em.
Lacey Proof the truth and here to bring it
for real!
Divine intervention mixed with little-girl
Celestial skill!

Her method was to punch with so much strength that
when her fist met a Crim dead on, the force of impact sent
it flying backward, knocking down every Crim in its path.

She hit a Crim at twelve o'clock.
It went flying, knocking all the Crims
behind it twenty yards.
She hit a Crim at three o'clock.
It went flying, knocking all the Crims
behind it thirty yards.
She hit a Crim at six o'clock.
It went flying, knocking all the Crims
behind it forty yards.

It was something like amazing. It was something like
extraordinary. It was something like Young Miss Lacey
Proof, the marvelous seven-year-old little cousin of the
supposedly soon to be phenomenal Young Mr. Louis
Proof. Apparently, it ran in the family.

Louis was transfixed by shock as well as by the
restraints that prevented him from moving.

How is she able to fight like that? Louis wondered between struggles to break free. It was as if he'd found something that he'd been searching for.

He was the reason. It all came back as he remembered the past summer.

He was on Midlandia. He was staring into what he could only judge to be a mirror, but it did not reflect himself. It echoed the sounds and sights of Lacey, and she was in grave trouble. Crims were surrounding her and her friends on a playground, and there was no help anywhere to be seen. She called to her big cousin Louis, and he heard her, but from here he couldn't do anything—or so he thought. He would use this mirror. He reached into it and touched Lacey to transfer a bit of himself to her so she could defend herself and her friends. That was not all. This transference was also the reason she would become a basketball star when no one would let her play. He would have to ask Timothy how all of it had been possible when and if he saw him again. There was no time to think about any of that right now.

Louis finally broke free, followed his little cousin's lead, and fought his way to her location. Divine skills directed his punches and kicks. He reached Lacey and they stood back to back. The Crims withdrew and surrounded the two. They were obviously trying to decide on the best method of attack. Silence.

"Lacey," Louis said.

"What's up, L. Proof?" Lacey asked, eyeing the Crims that were staring her down.

"We trying to lose tonight?"

"Hell, no!"

"That's what I thought. Let's go!" Louis said, about to set it.

The Crims attacked. Louis and Lacey met the challenge. They would not lose! They would not back down! The two Proof children dismantled the Crim army in an extraordinary display of grade A martial artistry and superhyperfighting.

The Crims were falling one by one, but Louis would not be fooled. No matter how well they were doing right now and no matter how many Crims Lacey sent flying on her own, Louis knew how it would end. There were far too many to even count. He would not be able to stand the consequence of seeing Lacey struck from behind with a single mortal blow. He had to get her to safety. He had to send her home where there were far fewer Crims.

Sometimes your worst worries are bound to come true. At other times something can happen to make you realize that your worst worries were really not all that bad compared to what can actually happen. This was one of those times.

Fewer and fewer Crims came at the two, until the attack dwindled to a complete halt.

"Well, I guess you guys learned your lesson!" Lacey yelled.

Although it seemed highly unlikely, Louis thought for a moment that maybe they had. The Crims began to laugh. The laughs came from all directions at once and sounded like the high-pitched screeching of a million crazy clowns.

Surface shake. Terrain tremor. Louis and Lacey had a hard time keeping their balance during what was turning out to be an earthquake. The entire landscape was changing to become rocky with jagged plateaus. It looked like something from a twisted and demented Road Runner cartoon. Lacey would no longer have to worry about falling, because metal clamps reached out of the ground and snatched her ankles. She could not move either foot. The ground she was standing on began to rise into the air.

"LOUIS!" Lacey shouted.

Call his name and he'll come running!

Louis set out after Lacey, and his fists began to feverishly glow blue. Sparks flew from them as thoughts raced through Louis's head:

How could I let my little cousin fight?
But she was doing so well . . .
I should have been focusing on protecting her . . .
Now she's being lifted far away!

Louis was sick with the love that he felt for his little cousin—his little sister. This sick feeling was replaced by something Louis had never felt before. It was not just anger—it was pure rage.

How dare these Crims hurt a member of his family and carry her away! Louis would make them pay; then he would go after Galonious for starting all of this.

Crims jumped at him from every angle. Teeth showing. Once-hidden claws extended. Eyes glaring with hate and disdain. They tried to prevent him from reaching Lacey, but Louis blasted anything that came near him into the sky. The Crims would not fall until they were miles away.

Lacey was still being abducted by the craziest-looking contraption, which continued to grow out of the ground. It started out straight, but then it began to go in all directions as if it were a wild vine. The wicked, wild portion of the pillar had grown horizontally at the huge section Louis had reached. He ran. Alonis, come out and play. He was in the Alonis, riding and twisting along the crazy-shaped pillar. It went straight, upside down, to the left, to the right, and all directions in between. Crims still tried to attack, but they were either run over or shaken from the Alonis. The crazy pillar finally stopped growing, and Louis could see Lacey far away at the top of it. Winged, airborne Crims came at Louis from every direction, but they would not stop him. The Alonis would swerve to miss the impact of the attack yet stay affixed to the surface of the pillar.

Ahead, Louis could see many Crims climbing up the pillar, trying to reach Lacey—at least twenty, unlike the others. They were lanky but fierce, with shoulder blades that angled out of their hides like razors about to tear through their own skin as they extended their strong, bony arms and thrashing claws. The Crims were pulling themselves up to the top of the pillar. Lacey could see them now, and her shrieks echoed in Louis's ears.

Stop. Stare. Show claws. Pounce. The Crims tried to tackle Lacey from all sides. She was scared, but she was still Lacey Proof. She could not move her feet, but her arms were free, and she attacked. She sent them flying from the limited surface of the crazy pillar with the strongest punches she could muster.

Louis could see it all. He had to get there. Lacey was safe for the moment, since she'd blasted back each of the Crims that had just tried to attack her. But a vicious Crim was creeping up from behind her.

"Lacey, behind you!" Louis yelled, but it was too late. The Crim struck Lacey down, grabbed her by her head, and shook it violently to taunt Louis.

That was it. Louis had arrived at the very top of the pillar and didn't stop there. He rocketed right past it, flying in the Alonis. The Alonis retracted as he extended his arms and flipped. Both fists left streaks as he fell like a heat-seeking missile toward Lacey.

His rage continued to build. He aimed to permanently silence the Crim that held his cousin. As he pulled his fist back, Louis did not strike the Crim to send it flying—he purposely struck it to end its life.

Even though the Crim did not bleed, it was hit so hard in its face that its neck snapped back. Louis could feel his attack breaking the Crim's bones. The glow that was once only on Louis's fist now surrounded the Crim, who screamed in anguish and disintegrated.

Louis touched down on the pillar as Crims crawled up its side to get to them both. Louis could not get Lacey free from the restraints. The Crims would be there in an instant. "Damn it!" Louis shouted. He crouched down on one knee, pulled his fist back, then punched the pillar. It began to shake and crumble. The restraints opened and Lacey was free. But they were falling. Louis grabbed Lacey into his arms and jumped from the toppling pillar. They were miles up in the sky, but that did not matter. The Crims would fall with the pillar and get crushed by it.

Dropping out of the sky, teaching meteors how to plummet to the earth with proper style. Moving so fast he burned colors of bright white, brilliant blue, and the boldest black. Hit the ground. Dimensional shake. Louis landed with such force that the vibrations could be felt through all dimensions. Louis still held his family in his arms. All Lacey could do was look at her cousin with smiling amazement. She knew that everything Timothy had told her about her big cousin was true. All true! The Marvelous Effect!

Louis ran. Crims were everywhere, still leaping and swiping at them. The Alonis created shields of solid rectangular light that blocked every Crim attack. Each rectangle disappeared when struck but regenerated to meet the next hit.

"Louis, I thought this would be easy. It was for a while, but I got hit and it hurt. For real it hurt! I can't believe that I got hit!" Lacey said, rubbing her head as Louis carved a way through the attacking Crims.

"Lacey, I am going to send you out of here. I'll send you back home."

Louis had run past all the Crims. He had an idea that would save Lacey but leave him stranded here. His safety was secondary to Lacey's. It was his responsibility to protect her, and he would not fail at that.

He stopped running and put Lacey down. The Crims were leagues behind them.

"Lacey, you'll be home in no time. You'll be safer there, and you can get help."

"No, Louis, I won't leave. We're a team. I can help! Didn't you see me lay the smack down? I won't get hurt anymore," she said.

Louis just looked back to make sure the Crims were still far off. He concentrated. He began to glow that usual blue hue. The blue light seemed as if it were solid, surrounding him like a gel. Then it began to reach for Lacey, until it left Louis, creating a sphere around her. The Alonis was no longer around Louis's neck and nowhere to be seen. Louis had expected as much.

"Louis, don't make me leave you alone here!" Lacey

screamed, as tears rolled down her face. Lacey was tough, but on the inside she was still a little girl, and Louis had to keep that perfect part of her out of harm's way.

Louis Proof loved his family eternally and would sacrifice anything to get her home safely. So good-bye, Lacey.

Louis only smiled and blew her a kiss. The sphere totally encompassed Lacey, and it moved backward. The Crims finally began to catch up to them, but they could not stop the Alonis. Lacey was now speeding toward the Crims. Each one unlucky enough to be in her path was destroyed.

Lacey continued to accelerate until she began to flicker as she ripped back into her own dimension. The Crim that had taken her place was sucked back into the thought dimension. Lacey did not know exactly where she was, but there were no Crims here. It was a regular street, and no one was out. It seemed she was now safe in her own dimension. The Alonis collected itself from around Lacey until it was just a single point of blue light in front of her face. Then it was once again a medallion, which glowed and floated until Lacey grabbed it. With her touch it went to sleep. Lacey could only think of one thing to do.

"Timothy!" she cried at the top of her lungs.

Galonious was not only greeted by Crims on his arrival. His generals also showed up for the grand occasion. There were seven generals of the Imperial eNoli Earthborn Army: Elon, Ar9nine, Keyon, Messeya, Kantia, Kenchi, and Frank. They had been ordered into hiding, and their existence had been kept secret until now. They leaped onto the street from undisclosed locations to meet Galonious. They paid attention to no one but Galonious.

"Well, generals," Galonious said, "you know very well what must be done. As I foretold, this moment would come. This is our time!"

The generals nodded in unison.

"Seven of you. Seven continents. This will make things quicker and easier. Take flight. I will summon you when it is time for the second wave of this plan to go into effect. Until then, feel free to have fun. Make me proud, my children!" Galonious said.

Six of the generals leaped into the air and out of sight in six different directions. Each was followed by a small number of Crims. The last one did not leap. He and his set of followers just ran very quickly out of sight. They would not leave this continent.

Trife had free reign to observe all of this from the thought dimension. He, of course, was CE and still did not have a way to cross over and maintain the dimensional balance. Either the laws of physics had to be rewritten or Trife would have to swap places with the second iLone CLE. There was no way to rewrite the laws of physics, and neither he nor Galonious had a clue as to where the second iLone CE child was located. So Trife would have to remain here, which was not such a bad thing.

Galonious turned his attention to Brandon, who was eagerly standing near him without an ounce of worry or fear.

"You thought you could pull one over on me? Me, of all people? The Galonious Imperial Evil? Never will you be able to outwit me! Everything worked out as I planned. You may have changed the formula, but it still worked. How could it not? Did you forget that I am the bad guy and there is no real good guy here to stop me? That is why we left Midlandia. Besides, Young Brandon, you know that everyone loves the bad guy. Tony Montana, Michael Corleone, Darth Vader, Freddy Krueger. All bad but good guys. Actually, what I say is that good and bad are a matter of perspective. You love the bad guys. Brandon, you know me well. Do you not?" Galonious said.

Brandon looked at Galonious as if for the first time. He

was nothing like he'd been in the other dimension. There, Galonious was menacing, but like a thought or whisper in Brandon's ear. Here, Galonious was not menacing at all. He was like an undeniable truth, and there would be no going against him. Brandon felt no reason to, because it seemed that Galonious belonged here and had always been here. As a matter of fact, Brandon could not remember Galonious ever *not* being here.

"Walk with us, Brandon. We are all good friends. I am sure you can see that by now," Galonious said as they headed down the street.

Brandon had a smile on his face. They stopped when they reached the huge church on Central Avenue. It was an elaborate structure with ornate steeples and towers and huge stained-glass windows of deep, rich blues, yellows, oranges, purples, and reds all outlined with black. It took up a full block.

"You always wanted to throw a brick through that stained-glass window, but you never did. Brandon, why didn't you?" Galonious asked.

"I don't know," Brandon replied, puzzled.

"Come on, Brandon, tell me," Galonious insisted.

"I don't know," Brandon said, feeling even more puzzled.

"Come on, Brandon, why not?" Galonious said.

"I don't know," Brandon said.

They kept going back and forth like this as if performing a comic routine, until Brandon came to an epiphany. "I can't think of a reason why I shouldn't do anything that I want, now that you mention it," Brandon said.

A smile crept onto Galonious's face. He had freed Brandon. It would not be long before he would have the entire world enjoying the same type of freedom. He stepped away from Brandon and picked up a stone. It was neither a big stone nor a small one. It was just right for a thirteen-year-old to hold in his hand and launch forward with a commanding force.

"Well, Brandon, I know you wanted to use a brick, but here is a stone and there is the window. You can throw this stone harder than a brick. This is much better. Have you ever seen a stained-glass window break before? It is a splendid sight. So many different-colored shards of glass raining to the ground. And the sound . . . Brandon, the sound is *extraordinary*." Galonious handed him the stone and pointed to the biggest and most elaborate stained-glass window of the church, above the main entrance.

Brandon held the stone. It fit perfectly in his palm; his fingers clutched it with a tight, sure grip. It seemed as if it were made for this task. Brandon cocked his arm back, then hurled the rock at the window.

There was no huge sound as Galonious had promised. Shards of glass did not come tumbling down. Nothing that Galonious had said came to pass. The stone went right through the window, leaving only a hole the size of itself as proof that it had even been thrown. Brandon was disappointed. He could not understand why Galonious would lie. Maybe his throw was too weak, he thought. He picked up another stone. He would try again.

He was about to throw when Galonious put his arm in front of him.

"Wait for it. Just wait," Galonious urged.

Everything seemed to go silent. Brandon's gaze was locked on the window. The hole produced by the stone created an intricate network of cracks that began to spread. Crackles, creaks, and pops played like the beginning of the crescendo on a hit record. The window shattered, and Brandon leaped three feet off the ground with excitement.

In the moonlight, the colors of the falling glass shimmered, catching every bit of the mischievous moonlight. Just as Galonious had said, the glass breaking into countless tiny pieces was a beautiful thing. On top of that, the crashing sound was chaotic, yet symphonic. It was ridiculously loud, and Brandon loved it.

No sadness. No remorse. No guilt. A new feeling inside of Brandon grew and grew. It was a rush of excitement and freedom, a freedom that he had never experienced before. His life now moved at full speed. Brandon was sure that this was the beginning of something Horribly Marvelous.

Brandon looked at Galonious with admiration. Galonious gave him a proud smile back. Brandon could not understand why he had thought this guy was a bad guy, even though Galonious had confessed to being one. It was as if Galonious were just the other side of a story that he had been reading his entire life. And those Crims—what was so weird about them? Nothing now. He felt as if they had always been here waiting for him to play with them, but people like parents and teachers would not let him. Whenever he had gotten a chance to play with them, he'd had to sneak around and do it without getting caught. They, like Galonious, weren't odd at all. They were all old friends.

Brandon picked up more and more stones and threw them at all of the stained-glass windows of the church until not a window was left unbroken. He felt great, but unsatisfied. He had to do more things like this. His head swam with everything he wanted to do but couldn't have done before:

Steal video games from the store.
Grab the backside of every girl who had one worth grabbing, even the ugly ones.
Never study again.
Get back at everyone who'd ever wronged him.
Drive a car.
Go to the wildest strip clubs imaginable.

Galonious was leaving, but Brandon didn't need to follow. He was too concerned about living life by the new rules, which were that there were no rules. Besides, he now had two Crims of his own to keep him company. The Crims took on forms similar to Brandon, and they looked like they had been hanging out with him forever. This was the first night of a new life for Young Mr. Brandon Davis.

He had responded to her call. Out of nowhere Timothy appeared behind Lacey and put his hand on her shoulder to get her attention.

This startled Lacey.

"Lacey, I am here. What happened? What are you doing out so late? Where is Louis?" Timothy asked.

She hugged him, buried her head in his chest, and then backed off to punch him in his arm.

"Timothy, where were you? Some job you're doing! How could you let this happen? It's bad, Timothy. Real bad!" Lacey screamed.

Timothy had noticed that Lacey was holding the Alonis in her hand. "You have the Alonis? What happened?"

"Louis is trapped somewhere . . . he used this to get me out. This medallion wasn't like this—how it is now—it was something else. That's not important. Where have you been? How did you let this happen? I thought you were here to help!" Lacey said, backing away from Timothy.

"I am sorry. I was distracted . . . well, not distracted;

there is so much I have to do. You see, there are others like Louis. There is Cyndi, and she is the result of me being here. That is the way it is; for every iLone or eNoli who comes to Earth there will be a CLE created to bring balance. I was keeping an eye on Cyndi. I have to. Louis and Cyndi are equally important, but she is not on our side. She is already a titanic threat. I do not think she will waver from the eNoli, but . . . oh, we have other issues to deal with. We have to help Louis. There is only one place that we can go for help. You have to come with me," Timothy said, as he reached for Lacey's hand.

Lacey wanted to ask about this Cyndi person. Was she the same Cyndi the world was going crazy over during the summer? There was no time, though. She just nodded as if she knew what was going on and grabbed Timothy's hand. They both knew that they had a world of work in front of them as they ran off in pursuit of help for Louis.

≫ CHAPTER NINETEEN ≪

Things that were not here:

One Alonis Apparatus Amazing
One Little Cousin with a Mastery of Martial Arts

Things that were here:

One Louis Proof, CLE
One-Thousand-Plus Imperial Army Members

No problem.

Louis's back would have been against the wall had there been one, but there wasn't. Nothing but the wacky terrain was around him, and nothing but Crims was in front of him. He would not run. All that mattered to him was that Lacey was safe; if they wanted a million-to-one war, he would serve it up, and he would not allow himself to be on the losing side. He had no Alonis, but he still felt as though it were with him. With or without the Alonis he was a CLE and ready for battle.

The army rushed in his direction, but it stopped a

few yards from him. One of the Crims stepped toward Louis. It stood perfectly still and looked Louis straight in his eyes. It was weird—as if they knew each other. Nonetheless, Louis was sure it was going to belt out a war cry, urging the others to charge. But instead the Crim spoke.

"Allow me to introduce myself. I am Quinlin. Please, Louis, no more fighting. No need for fighting. We have a message," it said.

Louis had had no idea that the Crims could speak, let alone that they had names. They had given no hint of either. No matter what the Crim said, Louis did not believe that he and his brethren would sidestep a brawl when they had him severely outnumbered.

Quinlin signaled to the massive army. Louis could feel the power welling inside himself. This would surely be an epic workshop on destruction . . .

There would be no fight. There was only a huge rumble as thousands of Crims hurried away, leaving about forty behind. Quinlin stepped back to the remaining group, who huddled together as if hiding something. Some looked back at Louis periodically to see if he could hear what they were saying. They soon broke from the huddle to reveal a perfectly square TV. It was about twenty-one inches on all sides. It was an image cube, to be precise. The cube showed a crystal-clear image that Louis could not decipher. Quinlin carried it toward Louis and placed it about twelve feet in front of him. Thirty-five other Crims dragged similar cubes near Louis, making a total of thirty-six cubes. Each had what seemed to be a different piece of the same image. The Crims fit the cubes together until they had built one big screen about ten feet high by ten feet wide.

Louis looked at these screens and knew immediately that something was wrong. The Crims had noticed this sooner than Louis and had already begun to rearrange them. Quinlin was not like the others. He looked like them but was in control. He stood next to Louis and barked orders and directions about where the cubes should go to make the complete picture. The rest of the Crims moved at a very quick pace, swapping the screens around. They stopped and looked at the big screen. Close, but not quite.

"That's not what I said! Just stop. I am going to do it."

Quinlin stood directly in front of the screens and appeared deep in thought. His next move was an electrifying display of acrobatics, strength, and speed. He tossed screens high and straight into the air. The top two from row six. The top three from row two. The top four of row three. While they were in the air he snatched some of the remaining screens and swapped them with others. He became a blur as he worked.

"Do I have to do everything? I always have to do everything. Is it too much to ask for some help?"

The cubes that he'd thrown straight up in the air had not fallen yet when he once again took a place next to

Louis. Soon, they plummeted to new positions. Now the picture was complete: the Galonious Imperial Evil. Who else?

Galonious was looking away at first, talking to his cronies, but soon turned directly to the screen. Quinlin gave Galonious the thumbs-up. Galonious acknowledged this gesture with a nod and a grin, then began to speak. Galonious looked as though he were deep into what he was saying, but in actuality it was a big fat waste of time because there was no sound. Louis motioned to his ears.

"Speakers—and I'm not getting them!" Quinlin ordered. Almost instantly, two Crims whipped out two huge rectangular cabinet speakers with exposed subwoofers. More speakers soon came out of the ground. They were small and rested on stylish metal stands. Some speakers even floated in the air above Louis's head.

Galonious could now be heard in crystal-clear, high-fidelity audio. "I trust that is better. I do love surround sound. Don't you? I want to make sure you hear me with no problems. I think I have even fixed the static. Well, Louis, thank you. And what for? For being you. Without your help, I would have never been able to escape that dimension properly. You have no idea how I did it, so you will never be able to come back. No matter what you are, you are too young to match my intellect. The main thing, even if you do find your way back, is that I am here now and you cannot change that. So, thank you once again!" Galonious said exultantly.

Louis saw that Galonious was near his school, with his army standing obediently behind him. Galonious was the reason for every bad event that had happened to him and to everyone in his city. He was even the reason the virus was no longer dormant in Louis's body. "I'm coming after you. I will get out of here and nothing will hold me back. You're through, you hear me?" Louis barked at the screen with an anger that he was beginning to know quite well.

"You are going to come after me? I seriously doubt that. But where are my manners? We have not been properly introduced. Let me divulge upon you my full and proper name. Are you ready, young sir? Of course you are! My name is the Galonious Imperial Evil. Your friend Brandon knows me well. And you are Louis Proof. What do you call yourself? A CLE?" Galonious said with a sarcastic laugh before Louis cut in.

"Whatever, man. You better not hurt anyone, or that's game over. I will get out of here, and when I do, it'll be on. I'm telling you now. When I'm not unconscious I always keep my word!" Louis shouted.

"Hurt anyone? Louis, what have you heard about me? I have no intention of hurting anyone. With all of my power, why would I even think about hurting anyone? That would be like fighting a baby—a crippled one at that. Simply ridiculous. That has never been my way. I want nothing but fun, fun, and more fun! I know that is what everyone wants. I only want everything to be so very Horribly Marvelous. Young or old, everyone should do whatever they want. Why should they not? That is what we, the eNoli, wanted on Midlandia, but the iLone just wanted to hate and hate on our desires to live without restriction. Here it seems you all deep down want what we want. That is why we are here. It was as if we were invited. So, no more rules. No more fear of authority. Yes, everyone will be free."

"Everyone free? This is America; we are free. You are talking about chaos and disorder. You are talking crazy!" Louis shouted through the screen.

"No, it is you that's talking crazy. Your freedom is an illusion. You have no idea what freedom is. It scares you, and some will consider the freedom I bring to be evil. That is untrue, but I have proudly claimed the name Evil. Many things that were once considered evil are the norm now. So "evil" is just a word that I happen to like, and its meaning is relative. I will give it an entirely new meaning!

"I will leave you now, but remember, there is no need to fight. What is the use? You will get nowhere. You will be there forever and ever and ever and ever, and . . . the sad thing is that after a short while you will not even want to leave. I know you humans so very well. Matter of fact, if I were human, I do not think I could be trapped in a better place than where you are. Louis, farewell."

The screens went blank and the last of the Crims were also gone.

What did Galonious mean when he said that this was the best place for a human to be trapped in? One thing Louis did know was that he was alone and lost.

Hold it together, Louis. You have a long road ahead of you.

CHAPTER TWENTY

"The junkyard? Why are we here? Louis isn't here. You said we were going to help him," Lacey said to Timothy as she looked around at the Branch Family Junkyard, which she thought was a pointless place to be.

"Lacey, you have to trust me. You did before, and it is going to be really important now," Timothy said without looking back while he navigated through the junkyard.

"Yeah, I guess I wouldn't have called you if I didn't trust you."

Timothy led Lacey to the spot that he had directed Louis to after he let him off the bus. There was no longer a light there. Timothy began to focus, and the light reappeared. He and Lacey entered and were in the JunkYard JunkLot.

"Prolif! Glitch!" Timothy said, and almost instantly Prolif and Glitch popped out from their lab.

"Oh, well, if it isn't Timioosiyon from Midlandia! What made you break the Alorion Treaty? I know why the eNoli did, but why did you? Guess you were forced to, because aren't you guys all about balance? You know what that means. This is going to be very dangerous—

of course. You're probably the only one here who can. Louis and the Alonis are connected, and if you activate it, we could reverse its energy flow—," Prolif said before he was interrupted by Glitch.

"And create a dimensional vacuum to suck Louis right out of that dimension. Like a transporter, but between dimensions instead of locations," she added.

"Right! Right! Glitch is always right. Right like me!" Prolif said.

"I can activate it, but will what you say work?" Timothy asked.

"With my sister and me on the case? Don't insult us. You know very well what we are capable of," Prolif said.

Prolif and Glitch were not CE, CLE, or Midlandian. They were technically human but had not grown up on Earth, so this would be the first time they or any non-CE or non-CLE would deal with energy as pure as that found in the Alonis. If they were to mess up, the results could be catastrophic.

Could they mess up and make it impossible for anyone to watch TV again?
Yes.

Could they mess up and create perpetual day or night?
Definitely.

Could they destroy this universe and countless others?
Oh, yeah! That was just how powerful the Alonis was.

What did this mean to Prolif and Glitch?
Only one thing: 110 percent pure excitement.

Prolif and Glitch were beyond eager to get started, and their heads swam with all of the possibilities of harnessing such energy. They began working on plans for an elaborate device that would use the Alonis to make dimensional transport possible. They had no idea how long it would take or what the design of the device would be, but they would not stop until they were finished.

Any direction was as good as any other to Louis. He started walking. North? South? East? West? Who knew?

The sky was as intriguing as it had been when he'd first arrived here, but it told him nothing about his location or anything else. Louis would not have known he was getting anywhere had he not seen a few structures in the distance. He had no idea what they were. Maybe whatever it was could help him. Maybe it would be the location of a fortified enemy fortress. Louis did not care, as long as it was something more than the bland environment surrounding him.

To Louis's amazement he heard something behind

him. A bell. Louis turned around to see a bell attached to a bike with five and a half wheels. It was warning him to move out of the way. It passed quickly by him, riderless. Now Louis heard a loud sound from above. He looked up and saw a marvelous aerial display. Fantastically elaborate spacecraft and airplanes flew overhead. The spacecraft were unlike anything he'd ever seen.

They did not seem otherworldly, like UFOs—just super-high-tech and unlike the ones used by the armed forces or even NASA right now. They were sleek, like something from a futuristic sci-fi movie. What was this place?

He signaled to one of the smaller planes, thinking the person flying it might be able to help. To his surprise it landed. It taxied to a spot not twenty feet from him. The cockpit opened and no one was in it. The vehicle, like the bike, was operating solo. Louis had no idea how to fly a plane and was not about to try. The plane closed its cockpit, turned on turbo boosters, rose straight up in the air, and sped off. It was soon a pebble in the atmosphere and then gone.

Farther away, the night sky seemed to have a hole in it, a patch of perfect, bright-blue sky and wispy blotches of arctic-white clouds. Under this patch of day was a building.

Louis soon saw that the distant structure was his school—but it wasn't his school. Perfectly clean on the outside. No trash anywhere to be seen. No random graffiti. In every way perfect. He entered through the main doors. Freshly painted hallways. No chipped paint anywhere.

Even the air smelled perfect. Platinum and gold plaques on the walls documented academic excellence. Trophy cases. Unlike the one that he had seen every day at his school, these were filled with nothing but first-place trophies in every sport from basketball to debating. Louis was astonished.

He could not wait to get to his own classroom. He wanted to know if he was in class and if the same students at his school went here. Only a few classrooms down and he was there. He looked into the classroom, and it was nothing like the one he was used to at home.

It was a large, spacious room. The light from outside was broken apart by yellow blinds hanging in four wide windows. The blue walls were a deeper shade than in his own room at home. Colorful posters on the topics of literature, science, and math hung on the walls. His class was even fortunate enough to have a mini library. Books lined the bookcases at the back of the room.

New desks had been specially crafted for comfort. On each rested a brand-new Mac laptop for high-tech note-taking and instant Internet access. There were a good number of students in the classroom, about sixteen. Louis saw himself among them. This Louis was sitting at a desk paying close attention to the day's lesson, but it was the old version of himself, the one who was nearly the most popular kid in school. How he wished he could go back to those days. Everything was marvelous here.

Yes, everything was marvelous indeed. Angela was at her desk, not too far from Louis. She looked just as he remembered her. It was the first time he had seen his friend in months. But he knew she could not be real.

Every child was focused on the teacher. They took notes and seemed to be enjoying everything. Now and then the entire class, including the teacher, would laugh. All hands rose when there was a question.

Before long the bell sounded, and the students funneled into the hallways. They didn't pay Louis any attention, not even Brandon as he walked by. Louis knew he could not be the real Brandon and just let him pass. Louis waited until his other self exited the room. He wanted to meet him face to face.

"Please excuse me—I don't want to be late," fake Louis said as Louis stood in front of him.

The official Louis politely stepped out of the way and walked alongside himself.

"Late for what?" he asked.

"Late for the assembly. Principal Hanks is the greatest principal ever, and the president is honoring her today. No one deserves an educational congressional medal of honor more than Principal Hanks," the nonauthentic Louis said.

Louis let his old self walk ahead and enter the auditorium, which was perfect, like everything else. No seats with stuffing coming out of the cushions. No faulty PA system.

The kids were now sitting, and no one spoke. No rustling voices. No giggles. No yells. No whispers. No peeps. No nothing. It was sort of eerie.

The lights went dim, and the window curtains were pulled shut. There was a clank above as the spotlight switched on and pointed dead center at a person on the stage. It was the president. The one and only commander in chief of the United States. Louis knew this could not be real, because nowhere could he see any Secret Service. The president began to speak.

"It is not every day that I am able to honor someone as important as your beloved principal. I mean, who else could have led all of her students to perfect scores on all regional tests? Not to mention that every student and teacher has a perfect attendance record. Her commitment to excellence is unmatched. So much so that I do not even deserve to be out here introducing her. I really am not worthy. Without any further delay, here is your principal, the one and only Principal Hanks," said the president.

The lights went up, the window curtains were pulled open, and then the blue velvet stage curtains parted to reveal Principal Hanks. There she stood in a pink, white, and black designer suit, elegant jewels around her neck, beaming. All of the kids cheered uncontrollably. As she began to speak, Louis stood in the main aisle of the auditorium near the door. The principal was thrown off by his presence. She kept pausing and looking at him. The president was about to hand her an award when everything stopped. No one moved but Louis and the principal. Things were no longer perfect.

"Who are you?" she shouted to Louis, holding her hand above her eyes to shield them from the lights.

"Principal Hanks, it's me, Louis. Louis Proof. What's going on here?" Louis replied.

"Louis, is that you? I didn't know any kids were brought here. I have only seen adults. You're all better. You look so different. You're in shape," the principal said. As those words exited her mouth, Louis's fake self was changed to look as he did now.

"Yeah, I know. Tell me about it. Not as great as it seems!" Louis shouted back, hearing his voice echo in the auditorium.

Principal Hanks stepped off the stage and met him halfway. She gave him a hug and told him she was happy that he was okay. Before, she'd been frustrated and tired. Now she seemed gloriously content. Maybe she was not real, like everything else? Louis struggled with this idea but knew he had no choice but to play along.

"What is this place? This isn't our school. I know you know that. What are you doing here?" Louis asked.

"Well, Louis, I was arguing with parents about the crazy and wrong things the students were doing, and the next thing I knew it felt like someone had snatched me up, and then I was here. I was by myself and began to panic. When I thought about where I would rather be, all of a sudden the school built itself right in front of me! When I walked in, everything that I imagined was here. This is all that I ever wanted to achieve — right in front of you," Principal Hanks said.

The students immediately unfroze. They turned to focus on her current position. They looked at her with doting, respectful, and loving eyes and cheered for her as if she were their hero.

"I am so happy you are here. You will be the first real student. Louis, you should stay," she said, before turning her attention to the other pupils. "Students, look who's back! It's Louis. Tell him how happy you are to see him. Tell him how you want him to stay," she said to the entire student body.

All six hundred of them stood up. "Hey, Louis! Where have you been? You're all better. We were worried. We want you to stay. Louis, you were the best. School will be no fun without you. *Louis! Louis! Louis! Louis!*" they shouted, overlapping one another's voices. They showered Louis with cheers, smiles, and pumped fists. Louis was speechless. No foul looks. No whispers under the breath. They did not gaze at him as a sick kid. They didn't look at him as if he had lost his mind. This surpassed any welcome that he could have ever expected. They all wanted him to stay. They were all happy to see him. Oh, the things that he could learn. The fun he could have. The new friends he could make. He was sure it would be great. But real? The jury was still out on that.

No matter what, he could not stay here. He had to remember what he was supposed to do. He had to stop Galonious.

"Thank you. I'm happy to see you all, but I cannot stay," Louis said. He then told Principal Hanks, "I have to go now; this just isn't real."

"Louis, touch the chairs, feel the floors, touch anything and tell me this isn't real. I do not know how, but this is real, like anything from our other lives—only better. Much, much better."

She paused and turned to look at the fake Louis. This Louis disappeared, leaving behind a vacant seat.

"Go ahead, Louis—you can take your seat if you want. If not, that's okay. Don't make any trouble . . . you know how I don't like trouble. If you want to make problems, go somewhere else; this is a big place. You have no reason to rain on my parade. I don't believe you were ever that kind of person. Don't start now."

Louis did not know what to say.

"Well, Louis, you think about it. I have an award to get from the president of the United States," Principal Hanks said.

Taking a seat was not an option. Louis knew what he had to do. "I can't believe that you won't come with me."

"No way, Louis. You should see my house," Principal Hanks said as she walked to the stage.

She then stopped. "Louis, are you sure that you do not want to stay? I mean, I know you will love it here. You could learn on a college level. You can learn anything you want here. I mean everything. Math. Science. The universe. Any language. Cooking . . . I know you love to eat . . ."

As sure as death and taxes, Louis loved to cook and eat. If he was not watching the Cartoon Network or the Speed Channel, he was probably watching the Food Network. He had not been hungry or satisfied by food since he'd woken up from the "coma." Maybe he would be here. That would be great . . .

Amazing. Louis stood still as the auditorium began to spin. He saw blurred colors of blue, white, and gold. When everything slowed down, the auditorium and most of the students were no longer there, and Louis was in an elaborate kitchen—like one he had seen on the show *Secrets of the CIA* but much better. It was a classroom with six rows of stadium seats. No way! To Louis's surprise, world-renowned, superfamous Austrian master chef Wolfgang Puck was the teacher. Whoa! He could take cooking classes from Wolfgang Puck! That would be awesome!

Wolfgang stood behind a countertop island in the

center of the floor. It had a grand stove with electric burners, a sink, master cutlery, and everything else a master chef would need. Shiny pots and pans of all different sizes and colors hung overhead. Each kid had a smaller setup in ascending rows which circled around in front of Wolfgang.

The students had their own miniature chef hats. Some wore them tilted to the side. Others had to keep adjusting them so that they wouldn't obstruct their vision. They all wore stylish chef uniforms with their names monogrammed on them.

Kids were pulling soufflés out of their ovens. They were pouring special sauces over uniquely designed dishes with single pieces of meat and stalks of asparagus. Brandon held a pan in each hand, flipping their contents into the air. He also had vegetables and pasta over high heat. He gave Louis an enthusiastic smile and a nod, then focused back on what he was doing. Angela had pulled the pans of a quite tasty-looking double layer cake out of the oven. Now she was putting strawberry and raspberry filling on the bottom layer. She also had a bowl of vanilla icing, ready to go on top.

"After I get my grade, I want you to have the whole cake," she told Louis with a smile.

Just for me, Louis thought. It seemed that anything was possible here. And what was that? It was Louis's friend hunger. He was ravenous, and he knew that eating that cake would be the only thing to satisfy him.

This was one of the best kinds of anticipation.

"Louis, so glad you are finally here to join the class. I have heard so much about you. Everyone told me how you like to eat. Don't we all?" Wolfgang said, while the class laughed. "Why don't you start with this cake after I grade it? Angela made it because it was supposed to be your favorite. What a great friend she is." Wolfgang took a slice of Angela's cake and began to examine it closely.

"Density . . . excellent. Texture . . . excellent. Aroma . . . excellent." He then took a bite. "Flavor . . . marvelous. No, beyond marvelous. A-plus. Excellent work, Angela." The whole class clapped for Angela, who smiled and took a bow.

"Louis, I got an A-plus. Now the entire cake is for you. I bet it's the best you'll ever taste. I know you love this kind of cake. Here, take it," Angela said. She handed Louis a fork and then the whole cake, which he held on a plate in one hand.

Golden yellow cake with delightfully red fruit filling! It smelled so good. Buttery, with a hint of vanilla, complemented by the subtle aroma of fresh fruit. The wavy peaks of icing were so creamy and fluffy. Heavonic. Wolfgang was right.

Louis stared at it, grabbed a fork, then took bite after bite after bite. He always enjoyed the taste of food, but this was a whole new experience. The flavor was like having the most passionate love letter written on your tongue. When he was done, he was perfectly satisfied. Everything was *real*. Before he could do anything else, he heard the voice of the principal.

"That was a good one that you came up with. Just think, that's only the beginning. You can have a class on building those cars that I know you love—no, how about a racing class? If you want it, it can be real. Just think about it . . . ," Principal Hanks said.

Then, in a wink, he was no longer in the kitchen. He and the kids were outside at the Daytona 500. Louis had had no idea the stadium was this huge. He could never quite get the grasp of it all when he watched it on TV. The spectator seating rose high in the air, and the crowd cheered so loudly that it could even be heard above the roaring of fifty NASCAR engines.

The students were dressed in racing gear and all part of Team Earnhardt. The cars were lined up and ready to peel off to begin the race. The kids jumped into their cars and were off. Louis was in the driver's seat of the number-eight car, and to his side was Dale Jr., speaking into a headset and giving him instructions on how to take the turns.

The wind and engine sounds were nearly deafening. The heat was almost enough to melt your clothes off. The smell of burning rubber from the tires was everywhere. The speed would make a normal person have an accident on the track and in their pants. It was great. What could be better?

Brandon was in the number-three car driving at top speed. Dale Sr. was right there beside him in the passenger seat, giving him instructions just as Dale Jr. was to Louis. They were racing neck and neck, battling for position going into the curves. This was nothing like racing his cars with the visor.

"Louis, ease up on the turn. Great, you got it. You're doing fine. Couldn't do better myself," Dale Jr. said.

Louis focused on the track and was stacking up excellently against all of the other NASCAR racers. He was currently in third position, and Brandon was in fourth, right behind him. Brandon and Dale Sr. crept up alongside Louis and Dale Jr. They were now neck and neck along the straightaway. What a time he was having. It was life-threatening and intense, but fun nonetheless. Louis had never thought this could happen. No way was it possible for him to be thirteen years old and drive a car in this fashion in a major competition. He couldn't even compete in the Alonis. Wherever he was, it was a great place to be. Maybe he could stay.

Louis was barely able to maintain his current position as he completed the lap.

"Louis, that was lap fifty-five. We have four hundred forty-five to go. You have to drive with your head right now. I know you can handle it," Dale Jr. said to Louis.

"Oh, yeah! Junior, you know I'm here for the win!" Louis shouted.

Louis was now a real NASCAR driver . . .

"Well, if that's not enough, how about this? You can learn anything and everything here." Louis again heard Principal Hanks. Suddenly, Louis found that he was no longer at the Daytona 500, but inside one of the most elaborate planetariums imaginable. Comets streaked by overhead. Supernovas exploded. Stars gleamed in astounding patterns. Galaxies of planets, asteroid belts, comets, moons, and suns were formed. It was as if he were in the center of the cosmos.

All of the students were sitting in stadium-type seats looking at all of the sights. "Go ahead, Louis, ask any question about anything in the universe. You will get an answer," Principal Hanks said.

Louis could not remember a time when he was in a position where he could ask any question and get an answer. What would he ask?

When will I die?
Where is my brother?
Who shot Tupac?
Who shot Biggie?
Who shot Kennedy?
Will there ever be another cartoon series that will run as long as The Simpsons?
Why is Robin the most powerful Teen Titan when he has no special powers?
When was the universe created?
Was the feeling that I felt when I met Glitch love?

Did I hurt my mom when I took the Alonis?

What are tomorrow's lottery numbers?

Will I ever be rich?

What the heck happened during the summer?

Will I ever be as happy as I was before all of this happened?

Will I be able to do what I am supposed to do and make everything right again?

Louis thought and thought until his mind went blank except for one question. It seemed like it would be the most important thing to ask, considering all that had happened to him.

Louis looked up at the planetarium sky, and it went calm as if in anticipation of Louis's question. "Tell me about Midlandia," Louis said.

The cosmos disappeared and the word MIDLANDIA floated overhead.

"No known place. Is this the correct name of your inquiry? If possible, be more specific," a voice asked.

"I do not know if that is the correct name. I know it is a place at the center of the universe," Louis said.

"Where is this place, Young Mr. Louis Proof? Which universe is it at the center of?" the voice said.

Louis had no idea there was more than one universe, and he did not even know the name of this one. He then came up with a clever way to rephrase his question.

"I believe that it is at the exact center of all existence," Louis answered.

"The exact center of existence. This place has no actual name. From now on, if you wish, you may refer to it as Midlandia. System updated," the voice said. The light of the planetarium changed to a brilliant shimmer of reflected light and motion. Louis was soon whisked away to Midlandia. It was beautiful and scary at the same time. There was war unlike any he had ever seen on the news or in movies. Louis watched a young male and a young female with gray-blue eyes lead countless warriors valiantly into battle with weapons much like his Alonis. He knew them. The woman was Vivionya and the guy was Kiyonrae. They had been two of his protectors while he was on Midlandia. Remembering them, he found surprisingly that he missed them. This image soon froze, and he heard words resonating from all directions.

"This is the origin of all existence. The origin of all things positive and negative. The outcome of all events is influenced by all of the iLone and eNoli's actions that take place here. Louis Proof, the explanation of this place will reveal all that you have ever wondered about and all that you have never dreamed of wondering about. The complete explanation will take approximately 922,080 hours, twelve minutes, seven seconds. Young Mr. Louis Proof, do you wish to proceed with this explanation?" The voice was waiting for an answer.

Louis paused. Did he wish to proceed? He began to realize what he had within his grasp. The knowledge of all things past, present, and future. He had asked the question of all questions.

Did he really wish to know everything? Would it even be right for him to know everything? How did he know this would be the truth? How would he ever know? How many days were 922,080 hours, twelve minutes, seven seconds? He would have to listen to everything. How could he stop? He would never be able to leave.

This is what most people search their entire lives for. He, Louis Proof, was at the threshold of knowing everything possible. He would truly be like no one else in the universe.

"No. I do not wish to proceed," Louis said.

He would leave this place alone.
Not everyone would prove to be as strong as he.

CHAPTER TWENTY-ONE

The Galonious Imperial Evil was overjoyed and about to live a life without limits. He had left Midlandia and arrived on Earth some time ago, but it was not until recently that he had reached his true destination. He brought no war. He brought no famine. He brought no disease. All he brought was a feeling of freedom that made people think there was no reason they shouldn't do whatever they really wanted to. No matter what it was or whom it would hurt.

Now that he was here, there would be no more feelings of guilt, remorse, compassion, or sympathy in those who encountered him. Those were useless emotions that everyone should be happy to be rid of. Everyone would put their own personal desires first. Brandon had done so and was euphoric. Galonious could not wait until he had liberated everyone just as he had Brandon.

Galonious and his Crim cronies flooded most of the street that they were walking down. It was late night and not many people were around. Galonious strode in total freedom and happiness. Some of his minions danced humorous Crim dances. They would jump up and down, shake, pat the ground, get up, then shake again. Galonious followed their lead. He did not dance per se, but he did do a few steps to the left and right here and there.

Soon he just let it all hang out, because the world was now his and no one here could possibly take it from him. Why not celebrate with a dance in the street? He'd be a new type of bad guy. So he, like the Crims, danced to unheard music, because his time had come.

A tall and well-groomed man was coming out of a building and caught a glimpse of Galonious in the midst of his celebratory dance. The man walked up to him and shook his hand. He had never met Galonious, but somehow he recognized him and even knew his name just as everyone soon would. It seemed that Galonious had always been here.

"How have you been?" Galonious asked.

"I have not been too good, actually," the man said.

"What is wrong? I am sure you can fix it," Galonious said as the Crims circled the man. Two even jumped on his back. The man welcomed them. He, like Brandon, could see that these Crims and Galonious had always been there, but he had not been allowed to play with them until now. How much fun they were. To the man they were not oddities at all; they were old friends that he would have great adventures with. His Crims soon shed their gremlinlike appearance to become handsome and elegant, fully clothed in a similar but more stylish fashion than the man. They were a perfect fit for him.

"My wife got custody of my kids and now she's remarried. She is going to move across the country with my kids. So what that I drink? So what that I was a little heavy-handed? Look at me. I take care of myself and I took care of my family. I loved them. That wasn't enough; she had to leave, and now my kids have a new dad. The judge would not even listen to me. He said that I was abusive and awarded her full custody. He didn't know the whole story. He wouldn't listen. You know how that feels?" the man said.

"Well, no, I do not, because I would never let that happen to me. But I honestly do not see the problem. You are capable of making things right, aren't you?" Galonious said with a smile.

"Galonious, you're right. What was I thinking? There is nothing stopping me from getting my kids. I've got a gun! There will be no saying no. I am simply going to get my kids. I feel sorry for that new dad. He is history. I cannot think of why I didn't do it before. I will just take them. It's going to be my kids and me. Those are my kids. My kids!" the man shouted as he turned to get into his car. The two Crims that were with him immediately split in half to become four complete Crims—two to stay with the man and two to remain with Galonious. The original ones now had natural places in the world. They now belonged to the man and were bound to him through his true intentions and thoughts. They would not have to worry about being sucked back into the thought dimension. Crims—such Horribly Marvelous entities for all to play with.

Galonious was happy for the man. He was going to get his kids. There was nothing better than a father who wanted to be with his kids. As Galonious walked, he could see that more people were experiencing a brand-new freedom:

A kid spied Galonious from his window. He disappeared for a moment, then used a few sheets to climb to the ground to go God-only-knew where.

A woman stood in front of an apartment building with her boyfriend. She hadn't planned to do this because it was not considered proper. But now she would do what she wanted. She would wait no longer. "I love you, and you know we're right for each other. I want to get married; if not, we're through. So, will you marry me?" she said to her boyfriend's total surprise.

"Yes!" he responded.

An older man who sat on a sofa next to his excruciating nag of a wife saw Galonious in the reflection of his TV. She had sucked the life out of him and all those who came into extended contact with her. He got up and went into the kitchen to retrieve a pointy object. His wife would no longer nag him or anyone else.

Excellent!

Now Galonious needed a car. In the thought dimension he could have just thought one up, but here he had to actually get one. No problem. Anything that he could get there he could get here, with some resourcefulness. He was eNoli, and eNoli always had a way of making things happen.

What did he want to drive? Powerful. Classic. High-tech. He remembered all of the TV that Trife had had him watch. He knew what he wanted: a new S-Class Benz. But he didn't know his way to a dealership and couldn't drive. He needed help, and Trife was not around. Trife knew the ins and outs of everything. Galonious was too important to concern himself with the details.

Without Trife, Galonious would have to come up with a way to get around on his own. He would not fly. He would not run. He would not walk. Instead he sat on a bench near a corner surrounded by a horde of his minions and waited for the bus. He had never ridden a bus. He hoped one would come by soon. That would surely be an experience.

The JunkYard JunkLot amazed Lacey. With all the excitement and confusion she did not have a chance to take it all in. She was still worried about Louis even though this was the best place to try to be happy in. There were so many rides like nothing she had seen before, yet she wouldn't ride them. If Louis was not safe, there was no way she could have fun.

The Magnificent ProliFnGlitcH were hard at work. What they had created before was nothing compared to what they were hoping to accomplish here. Plans and drafts. Drafts and plans. Every equation was mentally calculated instantly, then written out for double-checking. Prolif did not make the plans by himself. Glitch worked on this project just as feverishly as he did, and Prolif was happy to have the help. Any other team of scientists might have taken years to accomplish what the Magnificent ProliFnGlitcH achieved within a couple of hours.

They had completed plans for the device that would hopefully work. Theoretically it was flawless, and they had everything on hand needed to build it.

"Supplies," Prolif said to Glitch.

"Yes. Supplies," Glitch said with a smile.

The center of their lab featured a large Magnificent ProliFnGlitcH emblem. The emblem split apart vertically to reveal a platform, which lowered Prolif and Glitch underground. This room was as huge as the upper level and filled with all types of supplies. Rows and rows of metallic shelves towered some thirty feet in the air. These shelves housed everything used to build the JunkYard JunkLot. Junk was carried in on conveyer belts and fed to machines that turned it into all the parts used to construct the rides.

Many of these parts and devices could not be found anyplace else. In fact, besides building and maintaining the JunkYard JunkLot, Prolif and Glitch were in the business of selling these rare parts throughout the universe.

Waiting for them on the lower floor was a vehicle that looked like a brand-new Range Rover. The back, however, was wide open like a pickup truck but much longer.

Prolif and Glitch eagerly hopped into the modified platinum Range Rover. Glitch drove and Prolif looked at a digital screen that showed a layout of the entire place and an inventory list. Here were replacement parts for every ride in the park. Tracks for the roller coaster, huge HD screens, and countless other things seemed to be in unlimited supply.

Row C, section three. Glitch drove the car to that section. What they needed was high up on the top shelf. A control panel opened in front of Prolif. He pushed a button and a huge retractable arm came out of the back of the vehicle. He grabbed a joysticklike controller and used it to direct the arm, which reached up to the first part needed.

"Row H, section nine," Prolif said.

Glitch got them to that section in a blink. As they went

down this row, another arm came out of the back of the truck. Now Prolif was controlling two arms that snatched items from both sides of the aisle. And so they went, item by item, until the back of the truck was completely full.

"That's it. We have everything," Prolif said.

Glitch drove to the spot where they had come in. As they got out of the vehicle, the mechanical arms placed all of the supplies on a conveyer belt which transported them to the upper level.

The plans were drawn. The parts were gathered. It was time for the Magnificent ProliFnGlitch to start building what might be the only device that could bring Louis back.

The bus driver opened the door for Galonious and his minions. She looked at the familiar unfamiliar figure until she remembered that she did recognize this guy. Yes, he was an old friend. Like Brandon, she knew him well.

"The Galonious Imperial Evil and the crew! You all ride for free," the bus driver said as Galonious stepped into the bus. The driver knew not only Galonious but each and every one of his friends. She remembered that they rode the bus every day.

All of the Crims that could not fit in the vehicle climbed on the roof or found somewhere to hang on. Others followed on foot. Nobody seemed to find any of that odd.

"You know what? From now on everybody rides for free. I don't give a damn," the driver said.

A few people on the bus applauded. "Matter of fact," the bus driver said as she pushed a few buttons on the fare collector, "everybody take your money back. Isn't any heat on this bus. The shocks are shot. I haven't gotten a raise since I don't know when. My boss is a pain. Screw him. Matter of fact, I am going to tell him that I quit, along with a few other things."

Everyone cheered as they went to the front of the bus to get their money back.

The driver called her boss, "Hey, Hodge, guess what? I quit. Oh, and your wife is doing Smith in accounting and your third junior is not your junior."

The bus driver had just done what she had wanted to do for years. She no longer thought about the bills she had to pay or about her four kids. She would not sacrifice anything for anyone ever again. So what if they could not take care of themselves financially? So what if her husband had to go to work in the morning? She was going to have fun from now on and spend the money that she'd set aside for her children's future. It was her money, so why shouldn't she spend it? Vegas was calling very loudly right now.

"Hey, this is my last route, but where the heck does everybody want to go? Y'all want to go to your stops or have some fun? I don't want to go home to my whining kids and nagging husband. Always nagging like a bitch!

They all stay up late! I can't even come home to a quiet house. Name the place and we're off, if you have the heart for it."

A teenager cried out, "I want to go to New York. Hell, yeah—New York!"

How convenient. New York was exactly where Galonious wanted to go.

Louis knew that more people he knew had to be here. But where were they? He had been walking for a good while and had seen no one else. He'd encountered only a flock of fantastic, wandering ideas waiting to become realities—fascinating, but no help.

If it had been an option, Louis might have given up. He would not give up, but he wouldn't walk anymore. He started to run. Run until he collapsed. Run until his heart exploded. Run until . . . wait, he could stop. He was finally near the structures he'd seen long ago in the distance along the horizon.

There have to be more people here, Louis thought. "Yes!" he shouted, excited about getting to this city as fast as he could. As he got closer and closer, he could feel something was terribly wrong. Nonetheless he kept his head up and walked without fear.

Louis stood small within the darkly ornate city, which towered against the sky. The buildings were dingy and halfway decrepit. It looked like it was a mélange of different eras:

The time of knights and dragons.
The time of horses and carriages.
The time of Internet and advanced cell phones.

The streets were unpaved and muddy. Cars, horse-drawn carriages, and bicycles drove by, splattering the mud. People's clothes were from various time periods:

A young guy was dressed like Charlie Chaplin but wore a brand-new pair of sneakers and a basket-ball hat.
A woman was dressed like she was from the Elizabethan era, but she carried a Gucci bag and wore expensive jeans and heels underneath her dress.

Unusual.

"Kill him! You should do it. You can do it. He should not have done that. He deserves it," a woman whispered sinisterly into her wireless headset as she walked by.
"Come on, what does it matter if you steal that? Just make sure you have your gun so that if you get into trouble, you can go out blasting. No better way to die," a man was whispering into a phone.
"You will show them. Teach them all a lesson. Get in the last word. They will see how serious you are. The pills are in the drawer and the alcohol is on the table.

Get them out and take them all. You will win. Show them how unfair they have been. Come on. Come on— yes, that's right. Yes, yes, yes," a woman said right before she ended the call. Soon she would need to find someone new to talk to.

Louis was sickened. He tried to block it all out.

Everyone speaking into their cell phones would get very noisy, then suddenly become eerily silent as they walked by not saying anything. Then again, in unison, they would begin talking all at once. Eerie.

This was a place of despair and darkness, horrible and like no other. A place of murderous mayhem, death, thievery, cheating, suicide, and demons. All of the worst ideas imaginable inhabited this place. The discouraging, incorrigible thoughts of the unmoral lived here freely and unashamed.

Louis saw something that did not seem to belong in this place and among these people—a lone old woman sitting in a rocking chair in the middle of the street, rocking with a smile on her face. She looked nothing like the others. She had no phone or headset and seemed like a caring grandmother. Louis approached her, but she paid him no mind. People kept talking, and they too paid him no attention.

"Hello, excuse me," Louis said to the old woman. She didn't reply. Louis spoke louder so that he could be better heard over the people in the streets.

"Hello, can you tell me where I am?" Louis said.

With that, everything went silent, and the woman gave Louis her undivided attention.

"Why should you get that answered from one person if you can get it from all of us?" the woman said as she looked at Louis. Her eyes then glazed over as if she were possessed. This frightened Louis to his innermost fiber. He had never seen such a vacant and evil look before, not even when he fought the Crims.

The woman appeared to be in her eighties, but she got up out of the chair as nimbly as if she were a young girl. She looked deep into Louis's being and approached him with her hands behind her. Louis instinctively backed up.

"Sorry, I didn't mean to bother you," Louis said, trying to edge away.

"Oh, my dear, it is not a bother. No bother at all," the woman said, leaping at Louis as she pulled two very large razor-sharp kitchen knives from behind her back. She took broad, ferocious slashes at Louis, like a master swordsman. She was very quick, but not too quick for Louis.

Louis could see that he was in trouble because the other people were walking slowly but attentively toward him from all angles. They had stopped speaking to whoever was on the other end of their phones and headsets to zero in on their new visitor. Louis began to run down a side street while the nimble, homicidal grandmother chased him, brandishing her knives.

"Oh, yes, all paths lead there. They lead there. And when you are there, you will get nowhere. You will soon see," the woman yelled frantically as she ran like no other eighty-year-old woman could. Her footing was sure and her strides were pure. If Louis hadn't been CLE, she would have caught him effortlessly.

Louis was nearing a large building. It was nothing like the rest of this place. It was a glass building, beautiful and spotless. Inside, Louis saw that there was a woman sitting at a desk in a grand hall.

The closer he got to it, the more his pursuers slowed down. When he reached the door they stopped, about forty feet behind him. They resumed whispering and sneering into their communication devices. Louis had no idea what they were saying and did not care. The only one who actually spoke to him was the incredibly athletic and insane old woman.

"Young one, you will get nowhere. You will find your true doom there," she said, staring maliciously at Louis.

If this building is going to stop them from following me, it must be good, no matter what she says. It has to be better in here and that's why they're not coming after me, Louis thought.

He had no idea how wrong he could be.
No idea at all.

CHAPTER TWENTY-TWO

The Magnificent ProliFnGlitcH were in extreme building mode. They fit together every part that they'd gathered from their super supply room to create an apparatus with an elaborate control panel. Lights flashed and digital dials glowed with blue numbers. As far as transdimensional chambers went, it was quite stylish. On the control panel was a very small compartment with nothing in it as yet.

"Okay, we need the Alonis," Glitch said to Timothy.

Timothy eagerly and happily handed it to Glitch. She marveled at the splendor of the blue and platinum medallion just as Timothy had done, then placed it in the small, empty chamber.

"Timothy, you have to activate it now," Prolif said.

Timothy closed his eyes, concentrated, and spoke foreign words that rained marvelously on Lacey's ears. Soon the medallion began to glow. Illumination flooded the entire lab. Timothy had to grab Lacey and shield her eyes. What happened next was totally unexpected, and no one knew what to do.

The Alonis broke out of the small chamber. It flew

around the room as if it were looking for something. It flew swiftly, searching the shelves, the desks, and all the devices in the room. It circled and examined Timothy, Lacey, Prolif, and Glitch. No Louis. It spun around, then hurled itself out of the lab. It broke through the wall and raced forward, gaining more and more speed. Everyone ran out of the lab to see what it was going to do.

It flew all over the JunkYard JunkLot. It zoomed along the amazing RC racetrack. It sped above the spectacular roller coaster as it looped and circled along its rails. The Alonis went high and low without making contact with anything. If it had, it would have destroyed whatever it touched just as it had wrecked the wall.

Timothy, Prolif, Glitch, and Lacey figured that it was searching for Louis to no avail.

There was no Louis to be found here.

The Alonis returned to the center of the JunkYard JunkLot and simply floated, weightless, as if it were thinking or devising some sort of plan.

The Alonis motionless.
The Alonis focusing.
The Alonis light pulsing.

It had to find Louis, but he was not here. Therefore, it would have to go to where he was. It sped forward and was about to crash into one of the huge plasma screens when it disappeared.

The Alonis was gone and with it almost all hope of rescuing Louis.

"Aw, man, what are we going to do now?" Lacey said.

CHAPTER TWENTY-THREE

Louis walked into the building and up to the reception desk. "Hello, young man, welcome to the museum. Oh, the things you will see here. Are you a student with ID? If so, you get a discount," the beautiful woman behind the desk said.

"I'm a student, but I don't have an ID," Louis answered.

"No school ID? Well, you have to pay full price. Give me your hands," the lady demanded.

"Why do you need my hands?" Louis asked. He was not extending his hands in the woman's direction under any circumstances.

"Well, you are not from here, nor are you a student with ID, so you have to pay full price: a finger from each hand. Such a small price to see what is behind those doors. So, hand me your hands; I get to choose which fingers and to cut them," the woman said, growing very sinister.

Louis stepped back and noticed a glass jar that stood on her desk. It was filled with fingers and toes. Some bloody, some blackened with rot, some being eaten by maggots.

"No way," Louis answered. The woman pushed a button on her desk, causing the locks to bolt and the windows to shut.

"The building has been locked down. There will be no escape or entry," an ominous recorded voice sounded over the PA system.

The woman rose and, like the old lady, charged at Louis. Louis evaded her. There was only one way he could go, and that was deeper into the building. If he went outside, he would have to face the killer grandmother and the evil city he had just escaped. There was just one enemy right now. Although Louis was sure he would encounter more, he'd rather take his chances in here than face an entire demented city.

Louis leaped for the only visible door. Once through, he shut it behind him. The woman banged and yelled, "Pay your fee! Pay your fee! Out here or in there, you will pay!"

Louis locked the door, but soon the ruckus subsided. There was an unnatural calm. He did not let his guard down, but he stopped bracing the door and began to look at the room. He was certain that any minute a crazed battalion of lunatics would be after him, but he saw no one. Only empty, elegant glass cases about eight feet tall, wide, and deep. Nothing inside of them, but they were locked tight with padlocks. Weird.

Why are they locked tight with nothing to lock in? Why

would the fee be two fingers to see this stuff? There is nothing here, Louis thought.

As Louis moved among the cases, peering into them, his image was distorted and refracted. Rows and rows of glass cases as far as he could see, the lengths of multiple football fields.

The building was very high with nothing but a huge glass ceiling above him. The large space reminded Louis of how small he really was. Louis had no choice but to walk, so even though it was kind of creepy to be here, he continued in a straight line. The light from outside shimmered in the glass and created rainbow-colored refractions on the ground.

Louis pretty much zoned out as he walked. He was tired and still had no idea how to get home. Then he could have sworn that he saw something move in one of the empty boxes. He turned to look at it directly but nothing was there. Louis chalked it up to being tired and continued to walk. Once again he saw something; he was sure. Dark figures. Quick actions. Out of the corner of his eye.

Louis leaned closer to the peculiar box and scrutinized the interior. He got so close that he could see the condensation of his breath on the glass. Louis stared and stared. Nothing. Louis blinked and continued to stare. As if it were being developed, Louis began to witness, ever so faintly, a moving image. Not clear, but coming into focus. Louis once again breathed on the glass, wiped it away, and looked harder. He squinted and looked even harder—so hard that he wished he had not.

What came into focus was something a child should never see—nor anyone, for that matter. A woman was using a knife to do unspeakable things to another woman while demonic children watched. Louis jumped back in terror, but not before the murderous woman threw what had to be a body part of her victim at the glass in front of Louis's face. It hit the surface hard, splattering redness. The two children and the woman, still clutching the knife, rushed the glass wall. They beat on it viciously, trying to shatter it. *Escape! Attack the child!* These thoughts tore through their ravenous minds.

Louis had never seen such manaical looks on the faces of children before. They could not get to him, but their hate-filled eyes attacked him as he had never been attacked before. Then the woman and children were no longer at the glass. They had returned to the same bloody deed they had been committing when Louis first looked into their box. They were like a recording that had been rewound and restarted.

Louis wanted to vomit and fell to his knees. While down, he sensed what was all around him. He did not have to look, but he knew the contents of all the glass cases.

Within them were the worst acts imaginable:

Acts against men, women, children, and animals.

Acts against the human spirit.

Acts against God.

Acts too evil to speak of.

Acts too horrid to think of.

Acts that Louis was forced to bear witness to.

In every direction he looked he saw an act more abominable than the last. Thousands and thousands of vile boxes. An infinite index of pandemonium and carnage. Louis got to his feet and tried to run to the door he'd used to enter this room. He was sure that he had been walking in a straight line, but he had lost his way, and there was no apparent exit. Even when he tried to run to the glass walls of the building, he could not get any closer to them. He was trapped.

It did not help when the lights began to flash and he heard clicking sounds. Some of the boxes had begun to glow a deep crimson red, and their locks had unfastened. The lids sprang open, and Louis could see demons leaping straight into the air. While they leaped, the lids closed. Demons were now perched above the boxes and had their sights set on Louis.

The evil was out and had contaminated the entire building. The glass walls became darkly stained. Light could no longer shine through. Louis knew that once again he would have to fight.

The Crims he'd met earlier were nothing like these

abominations. The demons would never capitulate. They wanted to destroy in the worst way imaginable. They longed to carve Louis down the center and eat his insides. What a delightful treat! Little did they know that Louis possessed the ability to remove his name from the menu.

If ever there was a time that he would have to pull himself together, it was now, but after what he had seen it would be difficult to impossible. Louis was on his feet but felt as though he were sinking. Every sight that he had glimpsed in the locked cases dragged him deeper into the undertow. He had not been up for air once since the descent began.

Now twenty of the most fearful entities stood ready to torment and mangle Louis. They would come from above and from the floor. Some would slither, some would fly, and some would stomp, causing everything to tremble. They encircled him from the sides and above. Louis could not pull it together.

The only way Louis could try to gather his resources would be to close his eyes. That was not an option.

Louis was caught off guard and thrown by a demon who had sneaked up from behind. Had the Alonis been here, he might have been protected, but it was not. His body flew through the air and slammed into the side of a glass container, which shattered and released a dark gray mist. A nearby demon smiled a sinister smile, inhaled a small portion of the acrid mist, and grew stronger and even bigger. The rest of the plume zipped up to the top of the high glass ceiling, where a small section opened to let it escape. What had he released? He could not think about that now.

Everywhere Louis turned, there were malevolent demons. He was able to hit one and send it flying, but it shattered some glass cases, releasing more noxious vapors. Like the other demon, it inhaled the fumes and doubled in size. Once again, Louis was struck and sent flying. As he banged the ground, his leg was grabbed, and he felt himself being dragged away. This fiend signaled to a hideous spear demon, which configured itself as a wall studded with rusty, deadly spikes. Louis could not shake himself free. The demon spun Louis around faster and faster. He would gain momentum and hit the spiked demon wall with a force that would cut his body into ribbons once he was let go. Without the Alonis as armor, Louis seriously doubted he would be able to survive the impact without harm.

The room became a blur as Louis swung in circles. His body crashed into and smashed glass boxes that were in his circumference, releasing still more evil vapors. The demon swinging Louis inhaled some of this, and with his increased strength swung Louis even faster. The spiked demon inhaled, and its spikes grew longer and more pointed.

Release. The demon let Louis go and sent him flying toward the spiked demon wall, and he had no way of stopping himself. There was silence as Louis closed his eyes and hoped for . . . Death would be such a godsend.

Louis's fate was out of his hands, just as it had been on the roller coaster and on the elevator during that first trip to the JunkYard JunkLot.

Everything began to shake. An earthquake rippled through the entire area and a magnificent light broke the wall behind Louis.

The Alonis had come for him, leaving a blazing trail of light as it soared forward to reunite with Young Proof. The Alonis fused itself with Louis's body, and it was as if he were being doused in glowing water. It did not splash or drip. It was absorbed and disappeared.

But the force of Louis's horrible trajectory continued to propel him toward the spike demon. The Alonis activated and created a brilliant armor of light. Louis hit the demon and destroyed it. He did not land after the impact, however, nor did he continue to fly through the air—Louis disappeared entirely.

No longer would he be captive in that terrible place. The Alonis's split-second arrival had ended Louis's suffering. Just as the Alonis had brought Lacey back to the proper dimension, it now brought Louis. Galonious had greatly underestimated the power and abilities of the Alonis, even in the hands of the inexperienced Louis Proof.

With Louis's return, the dimensional balance was once again disturbed. Since there was a decent distance between Galonious and Louis, the effects were not catastrophic, but still they were noticeable. Even if Louis and Galonious stayed away from each other, it wouldn't matter. That would only postpone the onset of total dimensional chaos.

The winds began to sporadically blow debris around. Candy bar wrappers, leaves, and dust circled Louis. There was no thunder, but jagged streaks of red light began carving pathways in the sky directly above Louis. The paint on houses began to rapidly change colors as it cracked and peeled away. It was fall, but the grass began to grow a bright orange color. And the strangest thing happened: Trees went into bloom, and their buds were precious jewels that fell to the ground. The bricks and concrete of buildings began to accumulate surface cracks as they changed to different materials—everything from plastic to aluminum. These were just warning shots of what was soon to come.

Louis didn't notice any of this. He knew that he was back in his dimension but didn't know where he was. In exhaustion, disgust, and revulsion, he fell to the ground and lay in the fetal position on the concrete. He could not move. He was in shock, still unaware of the effects of the dimensional imbalance.

Louis's thoughts flew to the last time he'd seen his

mom. The perfect moment, stored forever. That brilliantly true Celestial feeling washed over his body and began to comfort him. He started to radiate vibrant light. He recalled traveling on the bus with Brandon and Lacey to see Uncle Albert in his new office for the first time. He remembered crossing the finish line first during one of his RC races. He remembered Glitch. He remembered how his cousin had greeted him the day he woke up, making everything seem fine. He remembered how he'd felt the first time he met Angela.

These thoughts fought the horrific ones that had shocked him, and they made Louis glow with radiant colors. He was now able to stand and think about what he had to do. Everything seemed different to him. He had a new understanding.

Before, he'd been ready to fight out of anger. He'd wanted revenge for all that had happened and on all who had wronged him. No longer did any of that fuel him. He was not concerned with revenge. After experiencing firsthand so much irrational hatred, he had no use for it inside himself. At least not right now. He was concerned with love. Love for the world in which all great moments happen. Love for the world in which everything wrong can be made right. This fragile Marvelous World.

He would fight to prevent the evil thoughts locked inside those glass boxes from becoming realities stalking the Earth. If they did, because he had released them, he would fight them back to where they'd come from.

Before, his foe had been seen but unseen. Now he'd glimpsed his true enemy and would be able to fight it.

GET READY!

CHAPTER TWENTY-FOUR

Galonious in the big city. It was his for the taking. He would start downtown, move through midtown, make a few appearances, and then head uptown. He could not think of a better way to spend his first day in NYC.

All who saw him knew and greeted him. He was a superstar without need of introduction. No one had time to gawk, though, because they soon realized that they had more important things to tend to. Some went into stores and took what they wanted. Some parked their cars in the middle of the street, got out, and ran around naked, screaming at the top of their lungs. Some were more reserved with less outlandish desires that would be fulfilled later on.

Galonious loved every moment of it. He only wanted everyone to be free. Why work when you don't want to? Why be confined by laws? No reason at all. The more people Galonious came in contact with, the more people realized this. They were finally free. Galonious was proud of his accomplishments. And to think this was only the start. Just wait until he got on TV.

Through a store window Galonious saw a teenage girl. She was a child of great power. She was familiar, yet he did not know her. She was looking at clothes while a boy about her age stood by her impatiently until he finally left for another part of the store.

Galonious tapped on the glass to get the girl's attention. She looked to see who it was, but she was unaffected by Galonious. He was preaching to the choir.

Soon everyone near the window saw Galonious and felt the effects of his presence. Now he knew who she was.

She was Cyndi Victoria.

Galonious entered the store and spoke to the child. It would be a short conversation. Galonious left because he felt a wrenching pull at his body. He looked at the sky and in the distance could see pulsing red cracks slowly tearing it up. He knew this could mean only one thing: Louis was back. He had escaped Galonious's trap and was getting closer, and he wouldn't have to deal with any dimensional pull working against him. Where the cracks originated was ground zero, and the effects were spreading. They would soon reach this city, so there was no time to waste.

Galonious had work to do and did not want Cyndi to become mixed up in the fight that he was sure Louis would start now that he was back. Galonious gave her information that would cause her to leave this continent to discover and activate her Alonis. Oh, and most importantly, call hordes of eNoli to Earth.

Cyndi Victoria was sent on her Horribly Marvelous way.

Louis could think of only one place to go to find people who would know what was going on. After he figured out where he was, he made his way back to the JunkYard JunkLot. Upon entering he heard an unexpected but very welcome voice.

"Louis, you're back! I can't believe it! How'd you get back?" Lacey hollered. She ran up to hug him, as did Glitch.

Louis didn't know why, but he knew that Glitch was very, very important. Lacey saw the outrageously goofy look on Louis's face. She was not the kind of girl to blow up someone's spot by saying, "Oh, you're in love," but she grinned and gave Louis a look that said she knew the deal.

"We tried to get you back, but we had no luck. The Alonis disappeared. We lost it. Sorry, Louis," Lacey said, still trying not to laugh at Louis's face.

"No, Lacey, I have it. It came back to me. It saved my life just in time," Louis said as Glitch let him go.

Lacey was ecstatic when she heard this. "For real? I should have known better. I'm happy you're back. Next time don't get so worried, 'cause I won't get hurt. You saw me! You know I'm official with my fighting skills, so don't send me away. Just let me fight!"

"Lacey, come on—you did get hurt and it could happen again. But you can fight for real! You're serious! I'm sure you'll get even stronger and better. The way I see it, you'll be the secret weapon. No one will see you coming," Louis explained.

"If you say so, Louis. So what're you doing now?" Lacey asked.

"I have to talk with the resident geniuses and Timothy," Louis said, looking at the other three.

"Who? Oh, those guys," Lacey said with a smile.

Louis kissed Lacey on the cheek, then said to the others, "So where's Galonious? I want to go after him right now."

"Slow down, Louis. You need to take it easy. I don't think that you're ready to take on Galonious. Do you really know who he is?" Prolif asked.

"Prolif, you have no idea where I've been and what I've seen. The only thing on my mind is getting Galonious out of here as soon as possible. Do you know what might happen if I don't?" Louis asked.

"Yes, I do. Look at this," Prolif said, pressing a button on his control pad. One of the large screens showed the outside sky. "See those small red streaks in the sky? They are the effect of reality breaking apart because both you and Galonious are here in the same dimension. They will only get worse. It happened during the summer, too. You have that on top of the effect Galonious has on everyone. So yes, you have a job to do, but don't rush into anything without thinking. You are too important to just go flying off without a good plan."

"All I know is that it is my job to fight him, and that is what I have to do. Plain and simple," Louis said, feeling confident. Maybe he was too confident. He seemed to forget what had happened when he'd last rushed off to meet Galonious.

"Yes, Louis, but you're not ready to fight him. Who knows what he has up his sleeve? You don't even know the extent of your abilities or how to use them properly," Glitch said.

"Yeah, but everything has been automatic, and I feel so good inside, like I'm supposed to meet and take care of this problem right now. You have no idea what he put me through. I can't even think about what he'll do to the world. I'm back, and it is time to seek him out," Louis said.

"Louis, we are all for that, but you can't just power up and fight this guy. . . . We need a plan. We need to be organized," Prolif said.

"But you guys told me to clear this place out before. You told me to just do it and I did and it worked. Now you want me to wait and plot everything out."

Timothy had no idea what to say. He knew that Louis was in no condition to fight Galonious. He also knew he was the one destined to do so. The world was in Louis's hands, and the thought of that just seemed crazy.

Brandon had a bag of candy, video games, and DVDs. He'd acquired them from various stores that his Crims had granted him after-hours access to. His new buddies were very helpful. What Brandon wanted to do now was have some super fun. That meant the JunkYard JunkLot. He was sure it was still closed, but he was also positive that the Crims could get him in. They'd been able to get him into all of the closed stores, so why not the JunkYard JunkLot? He was eager to go back. The rides. The fun. The games. The excitement.

"Come on, hurry up," Brandon said to his Crims as they were about to enter the Branch Family Junkyard.

They walked ahead and appeared to hit a glass wall. The barrier around the JunkYard JunkLot did indeed work. They could go no farther. Brandon walked on, telling the Crims to stop playing and get him inside.

"Fine. I'll go in myself. Stay here. I'll be back," Brandon said as he stepped to the first obstacle.

Brandon was surprised when he hit the car bumper and the doors of the car swung open.

"Yes!"

He was already on his way back to the JunkYard JunkLot.

I'm going to move in here with my new mom. I'll eat the best food and have fun all day and night. I'll get fat, like Louis used to be, Brandon thought to himself.

He continued to the pipes, and when he reached the elevator, he rang the bell. While Brandon waited, he opened a new portable gaming system and popped in a new game.

"What's that sound?" Louis asked.

"Someone is at one of the elevators," Prolif said, surprised.

Prolif pressed a button, and they could all see Brandon on one of the screens.

"That's Brandon. Let him in," Louis said.

"Wait. Something is wrong. I am afraid your friend has come into contact with Galonious. Can you not tell, Louis?" Timothy asked.

Louis looked at Brandon. Now he could see that Brandon was different. He didn't need to hear his voice or see him move. This was his friend, but he had changed. Once again, it was one of those familiar-yet-unfamiliar situations.

"Yeah, but he looks like he's unhurt. At least that's good," Louis said.

"I would be willing to bet that he has been having the time of his life. Wait here. I'm going to get him myself," Timothy said as he went to the elevator.

In no time at all he was opening the door to greet Brandon. Timothy could see that this child no longer had a conscience nor the desire to tell right from wrong.

"Timothy. I never thought I'd see you here. You disappeared, and now you're operating the elevator. Where's Derrick, or is it too late for him? I hate that farting kid. If I ever go back to school and he farts in front of me, I am going to throw him out the window. No, matter of fact, I'm going to get him right now. I'll be back," Brandon said.

"No, you are here. Are you going to let that guy slow you up in having the most fun you can possibly have? You might as well come in and have fun, then get him. That makes the most sense to me," Timothy said, using a bit of his influence over Brandon.

"Yeah, why should I leave and then come back? I'm here! Let's party!" Brandon stepped into the elevator. They were off. After the elevator's wild ride they stood in the center of the JunkYard JunkLot.

"Louis, you're here. Good, because we got stuff to do! By the way your life was easy as hell and I hate the way everyone likes you. It was kind of cool when you were no longer number one. Serves you right, Mr. Perfect," Brandon said with a laugh. "I don't know why I never said that before. Wait, wait, wait—I got more stuff to say. Let me think."

"What?" Louis said. He'd known Brandon would be different, but he hadn't expected that.

"What do you mean, 'what'? You heard me—I said it. It's not that serious. Let's move on. I wanted some new video games, and guess what?—I got some. My new friends got me into the store and I was able to take whatever I wanted. Why weren't we doing this before? If you want something, you can just take it. It's that easy. You can come with me next time," Brandon said, showing Louis the contents of his bags.

"Timothy, is this what happens when you meet Galonious?" Louis asked.

"Galonious? That is one cool dude. I am going to ride some rides now. Don't mess with my stuff," Brandon said as he put his bags down to walk to the roller coaster entrance.

Louis wanted to question him some more to get to the root of Brandon's new attitude, but Timothy stopped him.

"Louis, let him go. You see, that is what Galonious's presence does. If you come into contact with him, you no longer want to do anything but what pleases you. Brandon wanted to get some video games. He did not care that it was stealing or that he could get caught. Deep down inside, Brandon is still a child, and a normal one at that. He is not vicious, so he did not want to do something like kill someone. When Galonious comes in eyeshot of those who are rotten, that is when everything will really collapse. Who knows whom he has met? What is worse is that Galonious is not the real threat. You probably found out what is really going on while you were on Midlandia, and you may know more than I do. Let us hope you will remember it all. This is just the beginning. There is no doubt about that!" Timothy said.

"I don't care what the real threat is. I'll fight anyone. Let them come, but I'll deal with Galonious first. Wait! Before anything else, can we change Brandon back?" Louis asked.

"See, that's the problem. Brandon has no conscience or any type of social or moral restraint. If I did what Galonious has done to him, I would have the opposite effect, and he would be artificially virtuous. I will never do that. The most I will do is briefly influence people. You have to help him. I don't know how, but you can," Timothy said. Brandon was screaming on the roller coaster.

Louis waited for Brandon to finish his ride, then called him over. As Brandon walked toward Louis, he smiled at Glitch and grabbed her backside. She smacked him, but Brandon just laughed and told her that it was worth it and that that wouldn't stop him from doing it again. Louis was ready to scream at Brandon, but he reminded himself that Brandon was not in his right state of mind.

"So, you ready to go get some stuff? We can get anything you want, even cash," Brandon said to Louis as he pulled a few hundred dollars out of his pocket.

"See, my friends can even get us into cash machines. No problem. If we get some credit cards, it's over," Brandon said with a laugh. "Look at this. I even got a few of these." Brandon pulled out a magazine featuring women of the unclothed variety. "Louis, it's all wide open for us. We can get everything, but we need a head start on it all. I mean, sooner or later everyone is going to find out what I know, and then we'll have competition. Think of all the places we can go and people we can meet. We're free to do whatever we want. With all that stuff you can do, we can take really big things. We can snag crazy ice. Get the Maybach. We could go to mad strip clubs and roll into the VIP rooms even though we're underage. Forget that! We can just go to Vegas; everything goes there. No one can come after us. We can have everything on lock. Think, you could show everyone at school. Just like you wanted to when we went to your uncle's office. We could get cars. Ice. Whatever. We could get it. We could get it!"

Louis said nothing; he just looked at Brandon. Brandon wasn't evil. He did not want to hurt anyone physically. Most kids could not do the things Brandon wanted to because of money issues or simply because they were kids. Brandon could see that nothing could stop him, especially if Louis were willing to come.

Okay, as good as all of that sounded, it was just not a choice with the world about to fall apart! Louis had no time or patience; he needed his friend back right now. He jumped in front of Brandon, grabbed him by the shoulders, and shook him. "Brandon, snap out of it. I don't have time for this!"

"Get off of me," Brandon growled in an acerbic

voice. His every dark thought and desire had been intensified, and Louis could see the true effect of being exposed to Galonious. Louis was wrong to think that Brandon wasn't evil. Brandon's face began to warp. He began to look like an unholy pit bull that wanted to rip Louis apart. If Brandon kept doing whatever he wanted, he would get worse and worse.

Louis was shaken by the Brandon standing in front of him. He had to get rid of this evil. A shock of brilliant light passed from Louis to Brandon.

"Hey, Louis, get off of me. I knew that knowing you would be bad for my health. Is that any way to treat your best friend?" Brandon said in his normal voice. Louis let him go.

Brandon fell silent as he recalled all of the things that he had done: stealing, breaking the church windows, playing with the Crims. It had all been great! In his head it was ridiculously loud, and he loved every minute of it. Nothing would ever change that feeling, but now mixed in with the fun was guilt.

He had only done things that he'd wanted to do, but he now knew that it had been wrong to do them. He had never been perfect, but he knew that this time he had stepped out of bounds. The new guilt was rooted deep in him and growing, but not so much so that he would turn himself in or take any of the goodies back.

"Brandon, you okay?" Louis asked.

"Yeah, I'm fine. I was a real badass the past few

hours. Cool!" he said with an embarrassed smile. "But I'm okay now. You just disappeared! How did you get back?" Brandon asked, realizing that up to now he hadn't even been concerned about the well-being of his best friend.

"It's a long story. Hey, did you mean that stuff that you said? The stuff about how the kids were treating me?" Louis asked.

Brandon paused and a guilty smirk crossed his face. "Yeah. But I didn't mean it like that. I mean, come on, you were like perfect . . . of course I thought about that stuff. But I didn't mean it like that. I just thought about it and it never came out. I think a lot of bad stuff. A lot of stuff about everyone. Everyone does. I just never said it like that. Don't get mad about that. You should judge me by what I do, not by what I say. I always had your back. I always stood up for you. I just thought that stuff and felt it a little bit. You understand? No matter how cool you are with someone or how much you'll do for them, you should never think that person is perfect. You're not perfect. Neither am I. You get it? No need to forgive me. Maybe I just shouldn't have said it like that, but the truth is the truth. No need to apologize for that," Brandon said.

"Brandon, where did Galonious go? You were with him when I last saw you," Louis said.

"Well, I would have stayed with him, but I had so many things that I wanted to do. I don't know where he is right now, but I know where he was going," Brandon said, looking at his watch. "Hey, it's two in the afternoon. I had no idea it was so late. He wanted to get on TV, and I told him that if I were him, I would get on *TRL*, then I would bounce up to *106 and Park*. So there you have it. He's going there," Brandon said.

"So he's going to *TRL* and *106 and Park*. Not to NBC, ABC, CNN, or *Oprah*?" Louis asked.

"Hey, he asked what I would do and that is what I would do. He'll do well with that target demographic," Brandon said.

"If he gets on TV, he is going to get into the heads of millions of people. He is going to have every kid acting like, well, the worst kind of kid imaginable," Timothy pointed out.

"Well, I'm going to New York," Louis said.

"You're going to fight him by yourself? Damn, Louis, get a clue. Didn't you just learn anything? You tried that and got tricked. Now he's got an army and he's focused. You better not step into a fight without some kind of support and plan," Brandon said.

"One hundred percent true! You're just running on emotions right now. We're sure you can get the job done, but not without a plan. With no plan you're going to get torn in half," Prolif said.

"What? He's been out in the world for hours, and who knows what he's been doing? No one else can do anything to stop him. So what choice do I have? This is my responsibility. Timothy, you're the one who told me this. Now everyone is saying that I have to wait. Come on, which is it?" Louis insisted.

"Yeah, Timothy, you told me that it was his job to set everything right. So what's up now? Did you lie?" Lacey asked.

Timothy could say nothing. Louis was supposed to fight Galonious and the eNoli threat. That was the purpose of the virus and of the Alonis. This was all true, but it just didn't seem right for this child to take on so much responsibility by himself. There would be others to assist him, but even with their help, the responsibility for everyone's fate rested squarely on Louis's shoulders. That was his purpose. Yet, with that being the truth, Timothy knew that Louis was not ready. He needed time. So of course that was one thing he did not have.

"No, I did not lie. That is his job," Timothy said. It was out of his hands. Louis, as always, would have to make his own decision.

"Yeah! So Louis, let's make a plan and then fight Galonious," said Brandon. Lacey nodded in agreement.

"Okay, fine. But I have to let my mom and dad know I'm okay. I'll be back in twenty minutes. Just wait here," Louis said. He knew that he had to do this himself, and that if Lacey and Brandon were to come, they would most likely be killed—and he could never let that happen.

Louis was ready to begin his quest to beat the crap out of Galonious.

As he turned to exit, Louis looked for Timothy, but he had disappeared. Great! Timothy always seemed to be gone when Louis needed him. Louis didn't care. He just made his way to the elevator.

"Louis, wait!" Glitch yelled as she ran up to him. She knew he was not going to see his mom and dad. She gave him a kiss right on his lips. Louis could not think of a better way to be sent off to battle. "For good luck, of course," she said.

Louis stepped onto the elevator, and without another word he was gone.

"Go see his mom and dad? Yeah, right," Brandon said sarcastically.

"He's not coming back for us, is he?" Lacey asked Brandon.

"Nope, not a chance," Brandon answered.

⋙ CHAPTER TWENTY-FIVE ⋘

Louis stood in the Branch Family Junkyard and looked at the sky. It was easy to tell things were getting worse. The cracks had extended much farther. The wind blew a junked car directly at Louis, and sparks flew as he instinctively punched it back to the farthest corner of the lot.

He had to get to NYC immediately—darn near instantaneously. Louis knew that in this case public transportation was not an option. The PATH train was definitely out. Even the New Jersey Transit train that went directly to Penn Station would take too long.

The quickest way to get anywhere was a straight line, so he climbed to the highest pile of junk to find it. He could see the New York City skyline across the water. He now knew the right direction. Jump down. Hit the ground running.

Run out of the JunkYard JunkLot.
Run through busy streets.
Run through empty streets.
Run at hyperaccelerated speeds.
Run and run.
Run without even activating the Alonis.

He cared not if people saw him running at speeds unheard of. He would run until he reached the port.

"Kid, what are you doing? You can't be here. This is a restricted area!" a foreman yelled.

Louis ran right through the gate and left it hanging on its hinges. Ships were coming into port; big containers were being lifted off the docked ones. Huge cranes raised wooden and metal crates and swung them over Louis's head as he ran. Louis didn't notice any of it. He just kept running toward the water. Workers screamed at him; he would soon run out of ground. It did not matter; he had no need for it any longer.

Small splashes got his pant legs wet. He was doing it. He showed no sign of sinking or losing pace. The water would not swallow him up. Louis Proof, the water walker, the H_2O hoofer. By land or sea, he was going to get there.

There was no time for personal praise. The only thing he could do right now was focus. He knew that if he stopped running, he would fall into the water. He had never been a good swimmer. Not even being thin would change that. Drowning was not what worried him, though. Falling into this filthy water would be the worst . . .

He was about halfway there. New York was closer and closer. What would happen if he swung the Alonis around his neck? The Alonis came out to play—he was now absolutely afloat and thrashing through the water at twice the speed. There would be no sinking. The Alonis infused radiance into the dirty water. The rapidly spinning tires sent waves and a churning wake shooting out from the vehicle. So far by land and sea the Alonis had him covered.

Timothy was gone and the Magnificent ProliFnGlitcH were in their lab. It seemed to Lacey and Brandon that Louis was going to have to do this on his own. They didn't think they'd be missed, so they left the park.

"Brandon, why are we going home? We have to help Louis," Lacey said.

"I know. We are, but we're not going to be able to do it alone. We're going to need help—and lots of it. Timothy is gone again, and who knows what those two kids from the JunkYard JunkLot are up to? We have to do something now. Louis needs to realize that he's not thinking correctly. He used to make such good decisions, but now he's just making wild moves," Brandon said as they walked down the street.

"So, where we are going get help from?" Lacey asked.

"Don't worry; just come with me. We're about to find out how much of a slick talker I really am," Brandon said.

When Brandon and Lacey reached the school, the students were outside, even though school was still in session. They were all looking at the crazy streaks in the sky. No one knew what they meant, and they seemed to be growing in number, length, and red-hot intensity. It was a very cold fall day, but scorching winds were blowing, creating a bit of steam. Kids would not have to take their jackets off in the heat, because all of the jackets tore themselves from the kids' bodies and walked away on their sleeves as if they were alive.

The barren tree in the playground went into full bloom, but with money, jewels, and shrink-wrapped apple pie. Chaos broke out as the kids forgot about the freakiness of the crawling jackets and trampled over them to get to the money and jewels. Under these circumstances they were not worried about the pie, even though it was probably the best they could ever have tasted. Everything was out of whack, just as it had been during the summer. This was not the first time events like this had happened.

In the midst of the blatant bedlam Brandon climbed to the top of the jungle gym. He knew this would be the best place to try to address all of the students at once. He would have to speak quickly, because some of the kids had already run off the playground with the money they'd collected. He stood tall, knowing that he was going to have to make the most flawless speech in order to help the friend who had always been like a brother to him.

"Everybody listen up! You know all of this is crazy!

The sky! The jackets! That tree! There is only one person who can set everything right. That's Louis Proof, and we have to help him! I know you guys have been fronting on him, but you have to help—"

"No way."

"We're not helping him."

"My mom said that he's still sick and shouldn't even be in school."

"Yeah, my dad said to stay away from him no matter what."

"Yeah, he was, like, dead for three months."

"What? You're going to believe what your bogus parents are telling you? That's why you've been fronting on Louis? These are the same people that are letting you do whatever you want. Don't you think that's crazy? Those aren't your parents. A guy named Galonious kidnapped—no, adultnapped—no, parent-napped—oh, he just took 'em. They're somewhere. I don't know where, but they're not here, and those people you think are your parents aren't them. My mom was replaced too. I even like my fake mom way better than my real mom. She's a huge improvement. But I was never tricked. Don't you guys know your own parents? I know one thing . . . if you don't help Louis, you'll never get your parents back, and things are just going to get worse," Brandon pleaded.

There was no answer, and Brandon had to listen closely to hear the muted discussions the students were having among themselves. He only caught fragments of sentences:

"I don't want things to go back . . ."
"I knew something was up . . ."
"I like my parents way more now . . ."
"I am not giving all of this up . . ."
"He's crazy. My parents are fine . . ."
"Louis—no way!"
"I like driving cars and staying up late . . ."
"Louis was our friend . . ."
"Galonious who?"

"Brandon, if we help Louis, can we get our real moms and dads back?" a kid finally asked.

Before Brandon could answer, he was interrupted.

"Forget that! I don't want my real dad back. The way he beat me and my sisters?"

Everyone gasped.

"Yeah, I said it! What? I don't care, 'cause he's gone. I hope that beast rots wherever he is. If you see this Galonious or whoever, you make sure you thank him for taking my dad, and for these diamonds! Life's never been better. Louis *was* cool, but screw him if he's trying to change all of this! I'm out of here!" Chuck Avery said, leaving the playground.

"Yeah, well, I never liked Louis, and my parents are fine. I'm out of here. I'm not helping Louis either,"

Donna Sims said. She too left the playground.

"I don't know, all of this crazy stuff can't be good . . ."

"Things may be crazy, but I like it that way. I'm livin' it up! And this apple pie is outrageous! Forget about helping Louis!" John Ebren said. He had jewels and money in his pockets and pieces of pie in both hands as he followed Donna.

About thirty other kids left the playground. They had no desire to help Louis or change the madness that was going on. This was not going to be easy.

"So that's what's up? You want to live in this bedlam? This is only going to get worse. You clowns don't deserve to have a friend like Louis who's trying to make all of this right on his own! Go ahead, take your ignorant, hatin' butts home!" Brandon said.

"Yes, that's what's up, Mr. Davis. You get straight Fs. Matter of fact, you're expelled. There is no need to change any of this. Anyone who helps Louis will also get an F and face expulsion. Straight As to those of you who stay in school. You all know that's the proper thing to do. I have another class trip planned. Universal Studios!" The bogus Principal Hanks had finally come outside. All of the bogus teachers had her back, with menacing and intimidating looks on their faces.

Brandon knew he was in over his head and began to climb down from the jungle gym. Time was wasting, and if he would get no help here, he and Lacey were going to have to help Louis on their own.

"Wait, Brandon . . . Louis is the best. He's the best out of all of us!" a loud booming voice shouted. Everyone turned around. It was the last person they would have expected: Ali Brocli. The one kid who'd hated Louis before any of this started. The one kid they thought would have wanted to see Louis in dire peril.

"What? I thought . . . You're not dead? Awwww, man!" Brandon said in confusion.

"Sorry to disappoint you, Brandon. Louis was the only one who stood up to me to protect you all. Did you forget that? You owe him. He helped me. I owe him. He was the first one to offer to be my friend. He did it when he had me beat. He's got the most heart out of all of us. Brandon, I'm going to help him. You can count me in. Principal Hanks, or whoever you are, you can fail me all day. I already have straight Fs," said Ali.

A chattering soon arose. Kids began to really think about the Louis they had known before the summer. They thought about the seriousness of the crazy sky and all of the reality-bending events. They thought about their unparentlike moms and dads. It was all true—everything was spinning out of control, and Louis was a good friend they'd turned their backs on.

"When I wanted to get into racing model cars, Louis gave me one of his old ones," said Jeffrey.

"I remember when I lost my money and he got me on the bus so I could get home," said Lola Z.

"When I lost my PDA, Louis found it for me. It had everything in it," said Erica.

"I remember when I was going to fail social studies and Louis helped me study one weekend," said Marquis.

"Louis was the most fun in class. He would make it interesting with the things he would say," said Chris B.

"Louis helped me figure out that I was a spoiled whiny brat and that that was quite unbecoming. I was headed down a path of loneliness and discontent, making it in my best interest to change," Kasey said.

All of the kids looked at her with weird expressions on their faces.

"Well, he did," Kasey said.

"Yeah, Louis was the best," Ed said.

"No, Louis *is* the best. What are we waiting for?" Ali yelled.

"Yeah, we're going to help him, and then he can help get our parents back. Where is he?" many yelled.

"He's going to New York to fight Galonious and his army!" Brandon said.

"Aww, I thought he was around the corner. How are we going to get to New York, and who is Galonious? You didn't say anything about an army!" Carol said.

"Galonious is the person who makes it possible for you to do what you want. Galonious only wants you all to be free. Galonious is the best friend that you have. Galonious does have an army—an army to protect you.

Why would you want to go against him and his army?" Principal Hanks shouted.

"I've had enough of you. You're not even real," Lacey said, and then she drop-kicked the principal in front of everyone. It wasn't easy for Lacey because she was attacking an image of an authoritative adult, but she had to prove a point.

When she made contact with the holographic image, she met resistance. It was solid light, and Lacey had to use serious strength to penetrate it. She was only able to disrupt the hologram, but when she did she was able to see the ultrahigh-tech projector floating where the principal's heart should have been. Lacey regrouped and prepared to square off against Principal Hanks.

"Straight Fs, Ms. Proof. Straight Fs and expulsion! This infraction is going on your permanent record!" shouted Principal Hanks.

"Noooooooooo! Not the permanent record!" shouted Sara Bright, a straight-A and perfect-attendance student.

Lacey charged, leaped, and planted her two feet on the principal's stomach. She grabbed the hologram's neck with her left hand. The principal tried to shake her off, with no luck. Lacey pulled her right hand back, then forced it forward through the light that created the principal's chest until she was able to grab the projector. Lacey crushed it in her fist until it crumbled into pieces that fell to the ground. To everyone's surprise the projector rebuilt itself and hovered away, leading the teachers out of sight. Lacey had no time to chase them. She hoped she had proved her point.

The students were amazed both because the principal had been fake and by the way Lacey had handled the situation.

"See that. None of this is right. The principal, those teachers, and most of your parents are fake. Galonious is behind this, and we have to get to New York to help Louis take him out! Those buses have been taking you guys everywhere else, so let's go!" Brandon said.

"Yeah, let's go," said Derrick Carlton.

Not all of Louis's former friends, or better yet acquaintances, would come, but more than half did. They piled into the buses and headed to New York. Luckily the holographic drivers were not aware of their plans.

Along the way they saw Jolee Jenkins, walking her dogs, and other kids who knew Louis and had not been going to school. With so many people now in support of Louis it was easier to convince others, but still some would not climb into the buses. They were not bad kids; it was just that even with all of the weird events of the dimensional imbalance, the temptation of their new freedom proved to be too much.

They would have gone straight to New York, but they needed supplies. They stopped at various places to pick up things that they felt would come in handy:

Bats to knock the bad guys the heck out.

Heavy-duty ropes to tie the bad guys up.

Various implements of destruction that had best go unmentioned.

Bikes in case there were traffic jams in the city.

After loading everything onto their buses they headed out, hoping they would be in time to make a difference.

No one should have to protect everything all by their lonely.

CHAPTER TWENTY-SIX

Louis was about to reach land. Before it disassembled, the Alonis ejected him into the air to touch feet on a New York City pier. He was far downtown, near the financial district, and he had to get to midtown. Everyone who saw this phenomenal spectacle looked at Louis as if he had just ridden over water in a crazy car that then flung him onto the pier. Oh wait, that was what had happened.

He was not the only oddity the normally unshakable New Yorkers were able to see. In addition to the growing red streaks in the sky, gigantic water sumo wrestlers had just taken shape and started having matches in the Hudson River. Each time they made contact, they splashed, and their drops created smaller sumo wrestlers who immediately went into honorable battle. Whoa! What a sight, but Louis had no time to be a spectator.

"Excuse me. I need some help. I'm kind of confused. Which way is midtown, Times Square?" said Louis.

A few dumbfounded people pointed in the same direction. They could not believe what they had just seen him do and what they were watching in the river.

"Thank you," Louis said.

He began to run. He swung the Alonis around his

neck. He was again enclosed in the high-tech car of ultratheoretic etheric metal, energy, and light. Startled people cleared out of the way. He was off.

Past Wall Street. SoHo. The Village. New York University. As Louis drove, he could see Crims everywhere. There were so many more than before; obviously Galonious had been busy. Some people had one, some had two, and some really mischievous people had five. Some people walked hand in hand with them. Some had them riding on their backs.

It seemed these Crims did not have the same philosophy of fighting as those who had set up the multiple TV screens. Several who weren't traveling with humans called to one another and began to chase Louis. They flooded the streets behind him in pursuit. They jumped on the hoods of cars, swung from streetlights, and leaped from building tops, landing within inches of the Alonis. All of Louis's years racing his RC cars came in handy as he maneuvered, wheels hugging the streets, to avoid his assailants.

Swerve to the right. Pass the car in front. Swerve back into the lane. Horns were blowing at him, but he had no choice but to slice haphazardly through the traffic. He had to get to Times Square and stop Galonious, for the sake of these drivers and everyone else.

As Louis whipped through the traffic, the ground shook. Louis felt it, and the Alonis bumped into the air for a second.

What was that? Louis wondered.

It was Keyon, one of Galonious's generals, the one destined to remain here while the rest left for other continents. Louis could see him on one of the TV screens in the Alonis. Keyon stood seven and a half feet tall. He was hulking like a gorilla parading as a man in a business suit. But he did not wear one—only battle fatigues. He had a raw, arrogant, nonchalant aura emanating from his being. Keyon was ready for battle and destruction yet calmly sophisticated about the entire process. Debonair.

The impact of his landing was what had made the ground shake. He ran toward Louis with clean, brisk, effortless strides and the obvious goal of catching him. Louis sped forward; he had no time to confront him.

Just what he needed—the general Keyon giving chase with Crims everywhere. He was in trouble.

"Proof, fight me. You will not make it to Galonious!" Keyon shouted. He set the challenge off! He crashed his fist against the ground as a way to attack Louis.

Shake. Tremor. Seismic disruption.

The street began to crack apart from the point where his fist had hit it. The crack sought the Alonis, tried to swallow it up into the crevasse. Louis had to accelerate, but there was a problem—the cars in front of him had stopped due to an accident.

Alonis, deactivate. The car disassembled and disappeared into the light at Louis's back. Louis, running on foot, was only a few feet from a car. Two steps. Jump. He landed on the roof. Jump from there onto the side of a white moving truck in the next lane to the right, then launch to flip sideways but forward onto the side of another truck two lanes to the left. Crims from above. North. South. East. West. From every direction and in between they came. Louis sent them flying back with lightning punches and kicks.

Land on a truck. Move quickly to avoid the caving street. The widening crack was at his heels, swallowing up the cars and trucks in his wake. Louis had to stay ahead of it. Soon there would be no street, just a crater.

Almost clear ahead. Just have to get past these last cars to be able to drive again. Jump onto a taxi roof. A shower of Crims! Jump again with fist extended, spinning like a top. Mini tornado. Suck Crims in and force them out to send them flying. Stop spinning. Land forcefully on the roof of a BMW. The glass of the windshield shattered. Louis grabbed the Alonis and swung it around his neck as he leaped forward off the car. Alonis, activate!

The familiar light appeared at Louis's back, and the car parts emerged around him before he hit the ground. Once again in the car of energy, metal, and light. The Alonis landed smoothly and surged forward as soon as it touched the street. He'd avoided Keyon's attack! Welcome to Louis Proof City!

Thirty-fourth street and the mission was still at hand. He had to get to Times Square. He realized, though, that he'd have to settle up with this general in a full-out battle. He didn't know the scope of Galonious's powers, but it would be best to fight him one on one. Avoiding Keyon now might force Louis to fight him and Galonious at the same time.

Louis swerved the Alonis around to meet Keyon head on and saw the harrowing damage on the street. Cars were overturned. Trucks were on fire. Taxis were lying in pits six feet deep. He could even see the subway system. The street was still caving in, and Louis could do nothing about it. It seemed this was way more damage than what was being created by the dimensional imbalance.

Crims were still racing toward him, but Keyon had vanished. Louis couldn't look for him now. That would take too much time.

He swerved the car around. He had to get to — *Where is Galonious?* With this thought, one of the Alonis's screens popped on, and Louis could see Galonious. The menace was interviewing the audience in between introducing videos.

"Now, what is your name and where are you from?" Galonious asked a teenage girl in the audience.

"I'm Tami, from New Jerz," she said.

"Tami. What is the deal, girl? Jersey in the house," Galonious said.

The crowd cheered, and Galonious smiled. He loved the warm reception. But it was nearly ruined by the fact that he had to constantly deal with and hide the tug that he felt on his body. It was getting stronger and stronger as Louis got closer.

Galonious was not going to let this stop his fun. He directed his attention back to his new friend Tami.

"Tami, now that I am here, things are going to be different. I want you to think about what you really want to do. Something that you couldn't do before, but wanted to. Tell the people out there and here in the studio. We want to know," Galonious said, pumping the crowd.

"Well," Tami said, pausing . . .

"I want to smoke weed in the house. . . .

"My dad got a new Benz. A S-Class! I want to just take it whenever I feel like it. . . .

"I want my best friend's boyfriend. . . .

"I want to smack one of my teachers across the face. . . .

"My mom has crazy funds, but she's stingy. I want to just go in her purse and snatch a few hundred.

"Oh, and this is at the top of my list. I want to go to an Ivy League school, but my parents say I shouldn't get my hopes up and told me to only apply to 'safety' schools. I was going to, but forget that! My grades are phenomenal, and I have tons of extracurricular activities! My parents just don't want to pay if I get in. Like I said, stingy! I want to apply everywhere—I want to go to Harvard! Is that too much to ask?"

She sounded as if everything was a bit lighter.

"Of course, of course. I would not say that was too much. Those are reasonable requests. Why have you not done any of that?" Galonious prompted.

"Yeah, why haven't you?" cried out dozens of voices.

"I don't know. I can't remember. When I get home, I'm doing all of those things. Why didn't I before? It makes no sense," Tami said.

"See, people? There you have it. We at *TRL* are concerned that you guys out there have not been living up to your potential. You should do whatever you need to do to be happy—it's that simple. What more can I say?" Galonious said as the regular *TRL* host stood by his side, nodding in agreement. The teenage audience roared with approval.

"I couldn't say it any better. So you guys work on that, and up next we have a video by—"

Louis turned off the monitor, knowing that everywhere this broadcast was seen, people were shedding their inhibitions. Louis was surprised by Tami's desire to apply to Ivy League schools. That was a really good desire. He had no idea that Galonious's presence could inspire such a thing. But with that one good desire came five bad ones. Everyone was entitled to a little selfish behavior now and then, but the deviant behavior Galonious was invoking would have no boundaries. Louis had to put a stop to it even if a bit of good would be forsaken.

Gridlock. The troops had reached the city only to get blocked in traffic. Getting to Louis in time to help him seemed out of the question.

"What'll we do? We can't just sit here," Lacey said.

No one responded.

The kids knew they had run out of time, so they got off the buses and unloaded the bikes. There were not enough bikes.

"If we run there, we'll be too tired to do anything. I don't know much about the subway, and I don't think we have time for that. I don't even know if it—," Brandon said before he was interrupted.

Overhead the kids saw a sleek, high-tech white-and-blue luxury—but battle-ready—JetiCopter. The JetiCopter looked like an oversize helicopter, but it had jets burning brilliant blue flames. It moved with the speed of a rocket and had the maneuverability of both a fighter jet and a helicopter. It bore an emblem underneath: MPG—The Magnificent ProliFnGlitch. Prolif and Glitch had been monitoring everything from their lab and finally decided to show up. No way were they going to let these brave kids travel into harm's way without proper equipment.

From the JetiCopter fell little glowing boxes—not enough for each kid, but enough. Those who got one found that the box contained a fully powered, sleek two-wheeled vehicle which scaled to the proper size for the kid who rode it. Before the box disappeared, a

flashlight device and helmet popped out. Like everything created by Prolif and Glitch, it had their emblem
on it. The devices looked harmless, but they were
fiercely powerful mechanisms. The kids had no idea of
the strength of the weapons bestowed on them.

One thing was left for the kids. It was a simple message that Glitch projected in front of them.

> "Galonious will help you to pursue what
> you really want. Make sure you are guided
> by what you really want as you venture
> forward."

They didn't know what it meant, but nonetheless
most of them locked it in their memories and thought
about what they really wanted to accomplish by being
here. Hopefully they would be able to glide easily
through traffic on these vehicles and assault the bad
guys with the mysterious devices. Those who did not
get boxes used the bikes they'd brought with them.
They had more than forty blocks to cover. Lacey and
Brandon knew Prolif and Glitch were watching and
gave them the thumbs-up. When everyone was mobi-
lized, the JetiCopter led the way toward Louis.

They had to make it there in time.

CHAPTER TWENTY-SEVEN

It had been brewing, but now it was truly on. The city was going majorly insane. The closer Louis got to Galonious, the wilder the weather became. The sky was almost overtaken by the crimson streaks. Bright sunshine turned to black rain. A cool, fresh breeze turned into a horrible stench of decayed death. That was soon replaced by hot gusts of wind that carried the smell of lemons and toothpaste. Parking meters uprooted themselves, sprouted legs, and walked the streets, overflowing with endless cash. Sidewalk slabs flipped themselves and swapped locations in a playful manner. Unbelievable craziness.

Inside, adults and children were meeting Galonious intermittently between music videos on MTV. He was a phenomenon, and word quickly spread that he had to be seen. That was okay, because the greatest city on Earth was meeting Louis Proof.

Louis was still rushing to Times Square. Never before had New York witnessed anything like Louis, the Alonis, or the wild events that were taking place. People took pictures, and those with video cameras got the action on tape. This war would be fought in front of the world. No covert operations.

In the distance Louis could see the Viacom building and the glass windows that allowed passersby to look at the *TRL* studio. Racing through the streets. He would soon be there.

Then the world stopped.

Nothing moved and nothing was in focus except for one person—a teenage girl. She was a few years older than Louis. She was Horribly Marvelously Beautiful, but this was not what drew Louis to her, as she was drawn to him. This was nothing like the experience he'd had when he first saw Glitch—in fact it was quite the opposite. That was inviting. This was disharmonious.

She was . . .
Carrying two bags, walking with a boy her age.
She was . . .
Getting into an expensive-looking car.
She was . . .
The girl Galonious had spoken to earlier.
She was . . .
Cyndi Victoria Chase.

Yes, Cyndi Victoria Chase. She was right there in the flesh, but Louis could not stop.

Louis had to purge her from his mind. The world came back. Times Square was his destination, and he had no time to focus on her. The Alonis once again sped up, burning the Broadway asphalt. Louis could now see

Galonious and the *TRL* host through the second-story window. People on the street were holding up signs that could be seen during the broadcast.

Louis had to get up there instantly. He had no time to argue with or overcome security guards. He knew what to do: surprise attack! The car ejected him, thrusting him toward one entity—Galonious. Flying through the air, nearing the huge window. He could see Galonious turn to face him, and their eyes met. Make contact with the window. *Crash!* Broken glass everywhere. The audience scattered. What was he thinking? He could have hurt those people. He'd been possessed by emotion, oblivious to the effects of his action.

Even before the glass had settled, Louis struck Galonious with a crushing blow to his face. Galonious had no time to react, as Louis immediately punched him in the stomach, sending him tumbling.

"That's what's up! No treaties, no peace talks! You're out of here!" Louis yelled, as he stood firm on the stage Galonious had once occupied. Galonious felt an immense dimensional pull on his body since Louis was so close. They could not both be here at once, and Galonious was being forced back. He had to destroy Louis or entrap him in the thought dimension if he was going to stay. He cursed Midlandia and the iLone for complicating the situation and disrupting his plans.

The pull on Galonious's body was now nearly unbearable. It caused him no pain, but it was as if he were moving with an elephant-size weight on his body. He was CE, and he would just have to deal with it. He would not let that child send him back to the thought dimension.

While he was down, Crims came to his defense, jumping at Louis from every angle. All of this was on live TV. The Crims came in serious numbers, and Louis had to struggle to send them flying. Galonious stood up. The crowd and their Crims were now enjoying the excitement. They'd seen sports and reality TV, but this was better than anything. They had a free front-row seat to the father of all battles. They rushed to the sides of the studio for their own preservation, but they were intent on watching. Besides, they had to cheer on their new friend Galonious.

"So violent. So angry. I am tired of this fighting—" Galonious had to pause to struggle against the dimensional pull.

"You iLone always want to fight to stop us. It produces nothing, because we will never stop. No one can truly win on Midlandia. It is like being caught on an endless train ride. That is why we left. You iLone can have Midlandia in its entirety. All we desire is the freedom to seek out our own goals. Are we not entitled to that? Is that not what you all want? We tried to escape our 'perfect' home and leave it for the iLone, and you still fight to stop us. Fight! Fight! Fight! But what else would you do? If this is how you want it—pain, destruction, loss of your precious lives—you can have it," Galonious said, unharmed but fighting the dimensional pull.

The iLone and the eNoli. The eNoli and the iLone. Hand-to-hand battle. Galonious rushed toward Louis with a speed that could have accelerated the Earth's rotation. He was at half strength because of the dimensional pull. Louis was outmatched and outnumbered. Galonious had help, but Louis had none in sight. Now he wished he'd listened to his friends and not rushed into the battle. Luckily, he was able to hold his ground—not through skill, but by sheer power.

Fists. Punches. Feet. Kicks. Martial arts. Boxing. Street fighting. All styles. All of it still on TV. They fought viciously until Louis got lucky and knocked Galonious out the window, sending him crashing to the street below. Everyone hurried to look at the superior being that lay in the street nodding his head from side to side in disbelief.

What a great guy Galonious was to fight for your freedom!

"Teens these days. No respect for their elders," Galonious said.

Before Louis went after Galonious, he took the microphone from the host and looked into the camera.

"Hi. My name is Louis Proof, and I am going to try my best to get everything back to normal. I know it's hard, but please don't do any of that crazy stuff you want to do right now. Mom, I'll be home as soon as I'm done. I left a note. Hi, Dad."

Louis stood in the broken studio window. He looked at the chaos that was now New York City. The sky was totally torn with violent crimson streaks. Bright fingers of lightning rushed across the streaks and made sounds similar to heavy machinery tearing and beating metal. There was no breeze at all; the air was eerily still. No, wait. Wind soon came in gusts with huge, circular, rippling pulses that originated from some far-off center. Everything caught in the pulses' path was changed. The buildings rippled and distorted. They became translucent, like solid three-dimensional blueprints, then glasslike, and then as they once were. The clothes that people wore changed from ancient to futuristic and everything in between. The pictures on forty-foot billboards became more and more alive with each passing pulse, until they looked about ready to leap to the street.

Oh, boy! This was all crazy, and Louis could only think of one remedy for it—breaking Galonious apart. He jumped out of the window . . . sneak attack!

Louis would not reach the ground to beat on Galonious. He was hit from the side as if he were an underweight quarterback sacked by a Godzilla of a linebacker pumped up on Celestial steroids. Totally caught off guard! Keyon had returned to protect Galonious. Louis and Keyon tore a rugged forty-foot-long crater in the ground upon their impact. Infuriated, Louis stood up and so did the general.

"Had some business to take care of. You're over now, Proof."

"I'm over?" Louis said sarcastically.

Louis could see Galonious walking toward them with a smile on his face. One thing Louis still did not want to do was fight them both at the same time. Louis looked at the general and made the decision that somehow he would take him down now. He had to.

Just as it had in the thought dimension when he'd fought the Crims to defend Lacey, Louis's fist began to furiously glow blue. This startled the general.

As Galonious drew closer, Louis advanced swiftly toward Keyon. Louis was CLE, and the general was neither that nor a full CE. General Keyon knew he was in trouble.

Louis pulled his fist back to strike, but he did not punch. He hesitated in order to read Keyon's moves. The general tried to attack, but Louis dodged the punch and rose up to place his open palms on the general. Louis forced a jolt of energy to vibrate Keyon's body. The impact sent the general flying into the sky out of sight. Louis could not believe he had done so much damage.

"Yeah!" he shouted. He was sure Galonious would be no problem after that. He didn't even realize that his fist had stopped glowing.

Galonious immediately knew Louis was getting stronger, and he now regretted not making that general a bit more formidable. Oh well, next time. At least Keyon had given Galonious some time to gather himself.

Galonious called out Louis's name, and the fight was on once again. They fought through the streets, block by block. They threw each other into buildings. They crashed through glass. They launched each other into billboards. They fought for nearly twenty minutes among the crazy effects of the pulses until they reached Twenty-third Street and Broadway. The streets were flooded with people eager to watch. That is what they wanted to do and they did. Nothing could tear them away. News vans and helicopters were everywhere, catching every second of the battle on TV. Neither Galonious nor Louis had suffered a scratch.

"See. We are getting nowhere. This is why I left. What good is this?" Galonious said to Louis.

Louis had no answer. He was just dead set on fighting until there was nothing left of Galonious. He had no idea how he could make that happen, but as long as he was alive, he would fight.

"Louis, you know there is a difference between when I was on Midlandia and now. Here I can win. Here the 'hero' is you, and you are not even my equal as a CE," Galonious said. Galonious's chest turned into natural CE form. It was infinite black with streaks of energy. Galonious reached inside of himself to pull out his sword. With his other hand he pulled out the vial of Louis's blood. He opened it, smeared some over his sword, then closed it and tucked it away. Galonious returned to his earthen form.

Louis should have become terrified or at the least extremely cautious, but he was too angry, unaware, and overconfident after beating Keyon.

"That weapon can destroy you. Run, Louis, get out of here!" a familiar voice cried. It was Timothy Collins—Timioosiyon, iLone CE.

Hearing his own name startled Louis. He turned to look at his friend. In that instant Galonious charged.

Louis Proof didn't realize that he could indeed be harmed, even killed. Trife had obtained the blood when Louis was in his coma. It would now serve as the one thing that could inflict a mortal wound upon him, if it was used properly.

Galonious took a mighty swing at Louis with the sword. Louis rushed in without thinking. It didn't matter that the Alonis was automatically activated to protect him. Galonious struck through it and disrupted its energy flow. It sparked and became worn and riddled with jagged holes. It tried to reconstruct itself, but failed and quickly faded away. Galonious would not stop his assault as the sword repeatedly made contact with Louis and violently tore through his physical shell.

Galonious quickly grabbed Louis's neck, then yelled

at Timothy. "You! How dare you! You miserable iLone dog! I owe you something, do I not?" With those words Galonious motioned as if he were about to attack Louis again. Timothy rushed forward. He did not think about himself as he moved, and he was wide open to get hit by the energy blast that fired from Galonious's fist. It sent Timothy flying far out of sight, beaten, broken, and disorientated.

"Well, it seems your iLone brethren just dropped by to say hello. Sorry, but I have no time to entertain anyone but you, Louis." Louis had no response and Galonious did not mind. Not in the least.

Horrible. Unimaginable. Unbearable. Galonious had struck a child with the goal of killing him. He had done a Horribly Marvelous job of carving Louis up. Louis was in shock. He could see the electriclike substance he had glimpsed only once before—when he'd pulled the metal pin from his arm after waking up. Louis gasped for air and panicked.

Galonious stood back, knowing that he had struck a series of blows that would end the life of Young Mr. Louis Proof. He had never truly feared the child. He'd always known that if he became a real problem, he could end his perfect life this easily.

Galonious sneered and took another swing, cutting Louis once again across his chest. The dark substance sparked and flowed. Louis's blood kept it from recon-structing his body. Louis fell to the ground. Timothy was nearly motionless. Galonious looked down on Louis as he lay in horrific agony.

"Your kind—no, your *side*, the iLone—did not want us to leave, but we did. Your side wanted to continue a useless war that no one would win. You fight on the side of steadfast idiots. We offered them the entire universe. We offered them peace everywhere but on this tiny planet, and they fought us. They should be annihilated. I will start with you."

As Louis lay on the ground in pain and disbelief, Galonious kicked him in the face, sending him flying into the air to land many yards away in a mangled heap. He lay still on the cracked New York City street. Louis was not dead, but close to it. He could barely think. He could not figure any equation he could solve for winning. None of his perfect thoughts of friends, family, and great experiences could do anything for him now except ease his mind as he slipped away. As Louis got weaker and weaker, so did the dimensional pull against Galonious. He could barely feel it now. The city was almost normal again, and the cracks in the sky were fading fast.

Galonious walked effortlessly over to Louis Proof. His minions surrounded him, cheering and celebrating the easy victory. No one watching this would dare interfere. Why would they? They all seemed to be on Galonious's side.

Galonious needed to deliver one last blow that would

sever Louis's head from his body. But he wanted to savor the moment.

"How does that feel? Can you even still feel pain, or has your body gone into shock? Dumb question. Look at your face. It tells me everything. You are a child. A joke. No more games. You hear me? Your ears still work? You die this moment," Galonious bellowed for all to hear.

He raised his sword, painted with Louis's blood, and it glimmered in the sunlight. How could the instrument that would bring about the fall of humanity appear so beautiful? Louis could do nothing, but he would not believe that it was over. Yet it was. No one would help.

Was it seconds? Minutes? Hours? Louis had no concept of time, only pain.

Galonious held the sword ready to separate Louis's head from his body, making it a free agent. Then a sound was heard. It wasn't a whisper. It wasn't a crash. It wasn't an explosion. It was the sound of yelling children. They had arrived. They had hope.

"Louis! L. Proof!" they called.

"Louis! Hey, you! Back off from him!" shouted Louis's friends in his defense.

"What? You have got to be kidding me! You would even consider stopping this? Do you not know what it means for me to kill Louis Proof? He is not your savior — I am!" Galonious said. Galonious was so self-absorbed at this point that he actually forgot about Louis.

The kids paused for a second and took in the words and sight of Galonious.

What would they do?

Brandon and Lacey led the charge. They jumped off the vehicles and bikes and ran at the Crims, swinging baseball bats. The Crims seemed to be everywhere among the people in the street.

Surprisingly, they were aided by Galonious's presence. Because of him they felt no fear of law, pain, consequence, or anything else. Right now and right here what most of them really wanted to do was get dirty and wreak havoc to defend Louis. Some would be distracted by a desire to explore NYC or by whatever in their hearts seemed more important than helping Louis. But most were focused.

Wanting to cause pain and destruction to aid a friend is okay, right?
Right!

As the Crims jumped at them, the kids pointed the devices at them and pressed flashing red buttons. High-speed projectiles flew out, expanding into glowing nets, which rotated and reached for their targets. It was like they were alive, with tentacles made of unbreakable mesh. The nets would not miss their targets. They were guided by a sophisticated targeting system. The

Magnificent ProliFnGlitcH attacked Crims from the JetiCopter and made sure no kid got into a situation they could not handle. They had to keep their distance to monitor everything.

These nets were not meant to trap Crims. In fact, they were not nets at all. Once the "net" made contact with a Crim, it effortlessly sliced it into many even bloodless square pieces, which quickly disintegrated. The Crims could be utterly fierce when they wanted to be, but they were no match for these weapons.

With each Crim's demise, a parent was pulled out of the thought dimension whether or not he or she wanted to be. Not all the parents would return. They were pulled out where they stood now, so they were scattered all over the place but mostly still in New Jersey. Neither the kids nor Louis would have any knowledge of their return.

Louis's friends soon overwhelmed the Crims and wanted to continue with their goal of helping Louis. Naturally Galonious was the next target. The kids had no fear as they rushed in his and Louis's direction. They were nearly ravenous with a desire to rip him apart, because they knew he was the cause of Louis's horrid condition. Seeing Louis like that made them want to inflict the same amount of damage on Galonious. That was just crazy. They may have been able to handle Crims, but if provoked Galonious could end them all. Prolif and Glitch had to protect them from Galonious and themselves. From the JetiCopter they emitted a force field that stopped the kids from getting too close to Galonious. This infuriated the kids to no end, and they banged on the force field and would not stop trying to get past it.

The return! Timothy had regrouped and made his way back to the battle. He had suffered a surprising setback, but it had worked to his advantage. Galonious was unaware of his presence. Although Timothy could not fight for Louis, there was something he could do. He had to call upon a massive amount of energy. This battle was exactly the distraction that Timothy had needed, and finally he was ready. Now he would show why he had been chosen to assist Louis. Louis was composed primarily of energy. Although energy cannot be created or destroyed, it can disperse. If this happens, it has to be recollected. Timothy had to combine with the Alonis to revive Louis.

If he did not act immediately, Louis's energy would escape completely, and his current form would die. Concentrate. Timothy called to the Alonis and spoke words known only in Midlandia. The Alonis's energy rose above Louis's body while still connected to him.

Timothy spoke more words, and the Alonis rose even higher. Timothy was no longer in a solid human form. His true form could now be seen. He was pure Dark Matter and Dark Energy. The Alonis flew into Timothy while still attached to Louis. Light flooded everywhere, and the newly combined Timothy and Alonis flew into Louis.

Louis took a deep breath and opened his eyes. He was wounded, but he could feel that he was no longer near death. His body began to glow and emit sparks. The light that was once Timothy and the Alonis flowed all around Louis's body. The cuts across his chest began to close until they were completely healed. The only hints that they'd ever been there were Louis's mangled shirt and the cuts in his brother's precious leather jacket. Soon even those would be restored to store-bought condition. Louis could now stand. Timothy flew out of the Alonis to watch the reborn Louis Proof take a second chance at his destiny.

This new Louis could remember everything that had happened when he was in the "coma":

Louis remembered that the key to all that had passed and was to come was his time on Midlandia.

Louis remembered that he knew exactly who Arminion was and what he was trying to do.

Louis remembered everything about his CLE twin, Cyndi Victoria Chase. She was just as significant and powerful as he. She was going to . . . He had to stop her or maybe even help her . . .

Louis remembered how to fight! A battle with only one eNoli CE? Even with the Crims, how lucky was he to face only one CE? The man he'd bumped into on the street, Mister Orenci, on the day he'd first returned to school was not CE. However, he'd trained Louis and he would be so disappointed that Louis was having trouble. Although Louis had been far from alone, he'd had to face hordes of eNoli CE while on Midlandia.

Most important, Louis remembered what it meant to be one of Olivion's Favorites and that under no circumstances, barring the definite destruction of not just the majority but all existence, was he to . . .

"Louis is getting up! He looks like hell, but he might be okay!" one of the kids from behind the force field yelled.

Louis called out to Galonious. He was still not fully recovered, but he was going to end this struggle now.

As Louis regained his strength, the dimensional balance was thrown off once again, and this time it nearly got Galonious. Dogs were walking upright. The sun and moon were out. Fire hydrants and water mains exploded. Mini tornadoes swept though the streets, flipping cars into the air; some were thrown into buildings. The wind blew at sporadic speeds. Rubber ducks and cranberries fell from the sky. Spiders crawled out of the sewers. None of this affected Louis. This would end now.

Glow! Devastate! Divine radiation. L. Proof, the Last Dragon. Louis was nearly at full power and ready to bring it to Galonious. He was a spectacle of supreme light. The energy that had once left Louis's body formed a protective force field around him.

Galonious couldn't believe any of this. He was so dumbfounded and frustrated that the kids weren't on his side that he barely noticed the dimensional barrier strengthening. But now, as he turned toward Louis, it nearly overtook him. He was surprised by something he'd never expected to see. The battle was far from over. It was just about to begin.

Galonious summoned his Crims, and they came in hordes to attack Louis. Louis spun the Alonis twice around his neck, and just as Vivionya had done, he called upon a Crystal Soldier. It was a moving form of brilliant, flexible, and energized crystal. It refracted light as it skillfully fought the henchmen, leaving Louis to deal with Galonious.

"So, you did come to play," Galonious scoffed.

"I told you I won't lose. Galonious, I want to show you something . . ." Louis took his stance. Short Moon Rising.

"Yeah, Louis," Lacey yelled from the crowd.

> The Alonis Medallion!
> Marvelous
> Louis Proof's Fist Glow!
> Marvelous
> Louis Proof is about to set it off!

Marvelous, Megadramatic, Remarkably Marvelous! Yes!

Galonious launched devastating blows, and Louis parried each one flawlessly. Then he answered back with his own. Louis and Galonious were well matched, and Louis would stand down to think.

There was a wealth of Midlandian knowledge at Louis's fingertips. He was nearly a master of Midlandian battle tactics. He removed the Alonis Medallion from around his neck and held it in his hand. He let the medallion go while he held on to the chain. It would not fall from his body. They were inseparable unless Louis decided to release it. With a quick motion he swung the Alonis Medallion toward Galonious; the chain lengthened, and the Alonis Medallion smacked Galonious in the face, disrupting his energy flow and leaving his face disfigured.

"Excellent! So you remember a few things. Now we have a real fight! But what difference does it make? I can't lose," Galonious threatened while he focused his energy to reconstruct his face. "Louis, Louis, Louis. Why is that you want to fight? You are as guilty as I!" Galonious hollered.

"Let me guess," said Louis. "This is the part when you ask me to join your side, right?"

"No. Better yet, hell no. You see, you are already on my side," Galonious said.

Louis, not wanting to hear any more, darted at Galonious, showering a storm of fury upon his enemy. His motions caused his chain and medallion to swing and switch from hand to hand, slicing at Galonious as a weapon. Galonious had a hard time fending off Louis's punches but was mostly successful with hyperfast dodges and steadfast blocks.

Louis paused.
Galonious yielded.
The Alonis rested.

So many skills at Louis's disposal. What would he do? Yeah, that would be cool. Engage the target once again. Louis grabbed the Alonis and charged toward Galonious. Galonious put his guard up but would have no defense for this. Louis quickly pressed the Alonis on five parts of Galonious's body. Right shoulder. Left shoulder. Right lower torso. Left lower torso. Chest. Each spot began to burn with a vivid blue light. *This is some real nonsense,* Galonious thought. Louis then punched each spot in the same order. The last hit at the chest created a mini supernova inside of Galonious that sent him flying back.

Galonious landed in the street and broke it apart. He stayed there without getting up, but he laughed to try to hide the fact that he was in serious trouble and had to really struggle not to be sliced apart and ripped out of this dimension. He took some comfort in the knowledge that he had one trump card left.

"Yes, you are on my side," Galonious said, chuckling. "I came here because I belong here. Do you not all know me well? How is it that I just got here, but you know me and my minions as if we are your closest friends? We have always been here. Not in this form, but our influence has always been here!" Galonious exclaimed. "Louis, you are the one who is supposed to send me back? You want to stop me? What gives you the right? How come you are not starting with the people I am freeing? I am not influencing them to do anything they did not want to do, good or bad. They are only seeking out what is truly in their hearts without the fear of failure or consequence. What is a life without all of its passions fulfilled? The seeds are within them to be much more than what they are, but so many hindrances get in the way. How dare you deny them this freedom that you have come to enjoy yourself?"

"Enjoy myself? I don't know this fake freedom you are trying to spread," Louis replied.

"Oh, no? Fake freedom? Look in the mirror, Louis! Do you ever think about what you are doing? You control a sampling of the purest form of energy in the universe. You could have done anything with it. You could have purified every drop of water on the planet. You could have made every crop on Earth grow and flourish. But what was the natural thing for you to turn it into? A weapon. You are fighting me with it without even considering some other more peaceful alternative. You even used it to race the cops in the streets and drive up the sides of buildings. I suppose that is model behavior? So yes, you are enjoying this new freedom. With it you brought destruction. You brought this violence, not me. Look at this city—among the greatest in the world, and you are destroying it. This is all of your own accord! I have no influence over you! You and the iLone are a grand hypocrisy!" Galonious sneered.

Louis couldn't help considering Galonious's words. He looked at the condition of the city:

Buildings were damaged.
The streets were torn up.

Louis had done everything Galonious had said he had.
Was Galonious right?
All of this was for a greater good, right?
The iLone were correct and the eNoli were wrong, right?
Right?

Louis had not thought about his actual role in all of this. Galonious now had his opening. With split-second quickness he pulled out the knives that matched his sword. He hurled them toward the young CLE. They would do nothing. The Crystal Soldier shielded Louis, and this time the child would not be harmed. Galonious expected as much. That was only a distraction.

"Trife!" cried Galonious, and instantly a portal from the thought dimension opened behind Louis. Trife hurled a blood-coated knife at him. It would surely meet its target as it sailed unseen toward Louis.

Fwoomph! The knife was disintegrated by a net from Brandon's MPG device. Brandon did not need super-powers to watch his friend's back.

"Well, at least I tried!" Trife shouted before disappearing behind the closed portal.

Louis stepped calmly toward Galonious. He looked into Galonious's eyes and knew what he had to do. He pulled his fist back and the Crystal Soldier focused itself onto it, infusing it with a blinding light. Every color imaginable sparkled in its brilliance. Perfect sweeping motion. This could be the blow that would end, or maybe start, it all.

"Go ahead. I care nothing of this. You can never defeat me!" Galonious yelled as Louis's fist swept toward him.

The entire city went white for just a second, and then Galonious disappeared. No one—not even Timothy or Louis—had any idea where he had gone. But gone he was. Vanished. The sky was clear, and the city seemed to be back to normal again.

It had been such a wild ride. Everything had been beyond belief, and Louis, for the first time since he woke up from the coma, was able to breathe. Not in the sense of just taking air in and out, but as in taking a moment to himself that was totally his. Yes, there was much to do. He had to resolve the issue of the missing parents, deal with the individuals who had been "freed" by Galonious, and prepare for the inevitable actions of Cyndi Victoria and most importantly the actions of Arminion. In fact this battle had been nothing compared to what was in store or what had happened on Midlandia. Louis had even come to realize that this fight would have been much different if Galonious had not had to deal with the dimensional pull on his body. But none of that was on his mind. He freed himself from it all for a moment.

The moment could only be that—a moment— because there was something that he had to deal with right now.

"You've got to help them return to themselves, like you did with Brandon," said Timothy, who as usual had appeared out of nowhere.

His friends were still behind the force field, about to do who knows what. Galonious had affected them all, and now that he and the Crims were no longer in sight, they were dead set on making their most pertinent desires come true. Louis looked to the Magnificent ProliFnGlitcH, and they turned off the force field.

Louis did not know what was in his friends' hearts. They were all good kids, but what about the darkness that was in everyone? What about that darkness not having any limits? Louis was in many ways living a life without limitations. He was good, right? Minus the destruction of New York City he'd kept it all in check, right? Was it proper to deny others the same thing?

What is the truth of who and what each and every one of us is? Who is right and who is wrong in all of this? He'd thought he knew, but now he honestly knew he didn't.

Louis then remembered what he had encountered in the thought dimension. The demons, the homicidal grandmother, and above all else the heinous images he'd seen within the glass cases. He could not let any of that roam free for the sake of the good that would be the opposite of it. He was an iLone CLE, and his responsibility was clear. He would believe in that, for now, anyway.

"Look at me!" Louis commanded his friends and countless onlookers.

Louis spoke no further words. Just as he had done with Brandon, Louis created a quick flash of light that traveled through the crowd. Everyone calmed down and returned to their normal pre-Galonious states.

All those who had stood up for Louis ran to their friend with apologies for the way they had treated him. They thanked him for being the friend he had been. Louis accepted their apologies and thanked them in return, knowing that without their help, he would have lost not only the fight but also his life. The way his friends made him feel was beyond words.

"Gee, Proof. You're the wrong guy to mess with. I'm sure glad we won't be fighting anymore," said Ali Brocli as he shook Louis's hand.

Others went about their normal lives while reporters and camera crews representing almost every news channel, domestic and foreign, ran up to Louis. Although Louis was victorious, he was in no condition to deal with them. Brandon, being the friend that he was, stepped in for Louis. He grabbed one of the microphones with Lacey at his side.

"His name is L. Proof. Short for Louis Proof. And he just shut the game down! It's a wrap!" Brandon yelled, looking straight into the cameras.

That was all that needed to be said, and Brandon had said it brilliantly.

The kids sheltered Louis from onlookers and reporters. They gathered their vehicles and bikes. The Magnificent ProliFnGlitcH aircraft picked up a few, including Brandon and Lacey, then hovered overhead. Everyone was behind Louis, waiting for his directions.

Louis looked back, smiled, faced forward once again, and then began to run. The Alonis came out to play. The kids followed Louis as he headed home.

⇒ EPILOGUE ⇐

A black electric cloud floated freely over the thought dimension. Parents and other adults, some quite happy to be there and others desperately trying to get back home, marveled at it. It was a unique spectacle—even in that dimension—and would touch ground when the time was right.

Floating. Thriving. Infinitely existing. It would be drawn to a pack of ravenously wretched demonic entities that it had never encountered during all of its time here. They would surely make great comrades. Although it did not know them, they knew it and greeted it cordially. Yes, it would come down and take on its chosen form. Galonious stood, calm and collected, and the demonic entities crowded around him. Great comrades indeed.

Back to business. *Build me an empire.* With magnificent ideas Galonious built a greater, grander empire to replace the one destroyed by Louis Proof. The commotion alerted the Crims to the return of the Imperial Evil, and thousands of them rushed to meet him. Trife witnessed all of this on one of his screens, thought up a vehicle, and made his way to Galonious. He had a few ideas as to what they should do next.

Things were not that bad. Galonious looked at his "defeat" as inevitable. It was not his destiny to face Louis in battle—that was a task that lay on Arminion's path. More or less, Galonious had done what he was supposed to. The generals would soon be in place, many people had experienced true freedom, and he had sent the eNoli CLE on her way.

With another thought Galonious conjured up Arminion on one of the screens that Trife loved to stare into.

"Arminion, excellent news! The iLone have also violated the treaty, and I have found the first Earthbound eNoli CLE. She is Cyndi Victoria Chase. She is well on her way and will be able to grant safe passage to all eNoli," Galonious said.

Arminion looked at Galonious with approval. Arminion would soon be here, and Galonious was sure that somehow Galonious would be permanently and properly released from this dimension.

Trife reached the new empire just as Galonious took his throne. They were surrounded by what would prove to be a new and old army. Galonious would have to thank Louis for his new minions the next time he saw him. It was always in Louis Proof's nature to help . . .

The eNoli were winning.
Everything was falling into place.